J. E Mayer

The Humour and Pathos of Anglo-Indian Life

Extracts From his Brother's Notebook

J. E Mayer

The Humour and Pathos of Anglo-Indian Life
Extracts From his Brother's Notebook

ISBN/EAN: 9783337142230

Printed in Europe, USA, Canada, Australia, Japan

Cover: Foto ©Andreas Hilbeck / pixelio.de

More available books at **www.hansebooks.com**

THE HUMOUR AND PATHOS OF
ANGLO-INDIAN LIFE

THE HUMOUR AND PATHOS

OF

ANGLO - INDIAN LIFE.

Extracts from his Brother's Note=book,

MADE BY

DR. TICKLEMORE.

EDITED BY

J. E. MAYER, M.D.

LONDON:
ELLIOT STOCK, 62, PATERNOSTER ROW, E.C.
1895.

CONTENTS

No. I.

INTRODUCTORY.—THE 'ELEPHANTA': CAPTAIN TREVANION AND MR. MARSTON.

IF the reader could call back the flight of time some twenty years, and with an Ariel's wing transport him or her self on board the homeward-bound P. and O. steamer *Elephanta*, he or she would, on a certain evening between the hours of 7 and 8 p.m., or rather on most evenings at that time, have seen assembled in the saloon, near the piano, some twenty persons, ladies and gentlemen, standing, sitting, or lounging about. In the centre of the group stood Captain James Ward, the commander of the vessel, a tall, thin, wiry man, with handsome, but weather-beaten, features, who had been for many years in her Majesty's Navy, and retained in all respects the manner and bearing of a gentleman.

On the Captain's right hand sat Lady Jervois, the young widow of old General Sir Thomas Jervois, K.C.B., and a very pretty sample of widowhood the Lady Sarah was. Her mourning became her wonderfully, and showed the graceful outlines of her figure to perfection—a figure so beautifully proportioned that the most rigid censor could find nothing to object to, unless it might be a slight tendency to *embonpoint*, which many regarded as an additional charm. Generally Lady Jervois bore her recent loss with beautiful resignation ; sometimes, indeed, the piquancy of her observations or replies

1

showed that her vivacity, if subdued or scotched by affliction, was not altogether killed ; and as the world at large, and especially small worlds like those on board ship, will ever build on slight foundations, the universal opinion seemed to be that she would not long remain a widow.

The two ladies next in place to the Lady Sarah were Mrs. Smythe and Mrs. Forbes ; the former of these ladies sat on the Captain's left hand, and the latter next to Mrs. Smythe ; both possessed pleasing features, and were good-looking persons, and both estimated the value of their respective positions to a hair's breadth.   Both of them were wives of civilians in the Indian Service of about equal standing : the first a commissioner, the second a collector.   In manners and appearance both these ladies had much in common ; both exhibited certain points of difference, which attracted the attention of the *oi polloi* on board, and probably caused them some amusement.   Mrs. Smythe was shocked, and felt immediately called on to correct the transgressor, if anyone was thoughtless or un-mannerly enough to call her Mrs. Smith ; and Mrs. Forbes, whose sister kept a milliner's shop in Ayr, lost no opportunity of calling attention to the pedigree of her husband. She possessed several books on heraldry, and was in some degree acquainted with the shields, cognizances, and crests of most of the titled families in Scotland.   She was absolutely perfect in those with whom her husband's family had intermarried, or were entitled to claim kindred.   Whenever an heraldic séance had taken place (as Mrs. Smythe used to term the researches and expositions of Mrs. Forbes), the former lady would compassionately remark, as soon as her friend was out of hearing, ' Poor thing ! her little weakness in this respect serves to amuse her and occupy her mind ; her own family were nobodies, that we all know, and she has no children, therefore we must make' excuses for her.'

Good-nature, perhaps, was not one of Mrs. Smythe's strongest points, and she was a little over-sensitive regarding the pronunciation of her own name, but, nevertheless, her talents as a musician won universal, well-merited admiration. A good voice had been greatly improved by good training, and the results were very charming. She was also a very superior performer on the piano, and was consequently regarded as a great acquisition to the whole party on board the *Elephanta*.

Two other ladies only (although the number of lady passengers was nearly forty) appear to have attached themselves to the Captain's party. They were both spinsters, Miss Perkins and Miss Wiseman. These two girls were certainly to be commiserated, inasmuch as they had gone out to friends or relatives in India in the hope of exchanging their maiden names for some others, and had not succeeded in effecting this much-coveted exchange. Their temporary protectors having been removed by death, sickness, war, or other unhappy causes, nothing remained for them but to return to the land from whence they came. Under such circumstances it is not wonderful that an air of disappointment hung over them, and that they sometimes gave utterance to remarks that betrayed the feeling which it would have been wiser to have concealed. How it happened that these young ladies failed to achieve their object I am quite unable to explain; they each of them possessed an average share of good looks and feminine attractions, nor were they destitute of most of those accomplishments in which young ladies strive to shine. They played and sang *a little :* they were grand at croquet, first rate at converting a glass or delft jug into a china vase; did card and shell marks; understood the language of flowers; could talk with their fingers; danced round dances with a constancy and resolution that defied fatigue, exhaustion, or even daylight; and, to crown all, they were proficients in the science of flirtation ; they had, in fact, become graduates, by adopting the surest road to perfection ; they had gained experience by a most extensive practice, which commenced before they were thirteen years old, and which since then they had never intermitted.   With such winning cards in their hand, their failure does seem surprising, and might almost lead us to question the value of the last-mentioned accomplishment, and to ask whether, independent of the case-hardening of all young, fresh, and genuine feeling, it may not lead those who resort to it to become on all occasions more or less deceitful ; and whether it may not sometimes recoil on the practitioner by teaching the opposite party to practise equal deceit.   I leave these questions to be debated and considered by those whom it most concerns.   I would only protest against any argument being deduced from the wide adoption of the practice.

I am not writing an essay on ' manners ' or ' morals ;' I will therefore content myself with submitting to the candour and judgment of those most likely to be affected by the issue, whether the practice of demonstrating special interest and liking for any person, where no such feeling exists, may not as often lose a husband as it gains one.   I think I have seen several instances of such a result.   I will not affirm that the two young ladies who gave occasion to these remarks were examples in point ; it is not at all unlikely that they may have been, and that the mortification they were then suffering arose from the proficiency alluded to.   Be this as it may, these two young people, smarting under disappointment, were objects for sympathy, as it seemed to me, but the society on board entertained, I believe, little of this feeling.   ' As they have made their beds, so they must lie,' if I mistake not, spoke the general opinion regarding them. And the judgment of the passengers on board the *Elephanta* will, I fear, be that of the world at large. Let me here urge on those who make the pleasure of the moment their guiding star, to lay this truth to heart, that in the battle of life those who do not succeed must ever expect, rightly or wrongly, to have the cause of failure set down to some fault or failing of their own. With this note of warning we leave the ladies, and turn to the gentlemen composing the party we are speaking of.'

On board our steamer there were several officers of higher military rank than Captain Trevanion, but as some of them were distinguished more by their epaulettes and cocked hats than by any special qualities, and as others did not belong to our party, they call for no special notice.

The reasons that induce us to give the young Captain of Artillery the first place in this sketch will appear immediately. His reputation as a gallant and accomplished soldier was attested, not only by the medals he sometimes wore, and by the general orders which recorded his services, but by the unanimous voice of those he commanded. The bursting of a shell, which he had caught up and carried to a distance in order to save his men, was the cause of his having been sent home ; just as he flung it away it had burst, shattering his left fore-arm. At first he suffered much from the injury (which obliged him to wear the arm in a sling), but he rejoiced in it. He knew he had saved his battery, his men knew it, and his Queen, who had sent him the Victoria Cross on that account, knew it also. Since he had been at sea, so great an improvement had taken place that he was beginning to use his fingers again, and was able to join in the dance, or in almost any amusement proposed. He possessed, moreover, a good voice and a quick ear, which gifts, with a little drilling from Mrs. Smythe, soon enabled him to join her in part-songs and duets. In addition to his fame as a soldier, and good gifts as a vocalist, the Captain was a most unassuming person, always good humoured and obliging, for all which reasons, to say nothing of a commanding figure and polished address, he was the most popular man on board.

The young gentleman who stood next to Captain Trevanion in general estimation was Mr. John Marston, a young civilian, who during the fearful scenes so recently enacted in India, by his remarkable foresight, decision, and courage, and by the aid solely of his strong sense and keen perceptions, read the signs of the times with such accuracy, that before any acts of mutiny or rebellion had occurred in his district he had taken possession of an old mud fort, disused for years past, had it thoroughly cleaned out and repaired, that it might be ready, as he said, for use as a granary.   He next had the well thoroughly cleaned and put in order; he then sent in supplies of every description. Having made these preparations, he gradually called in every European and Eurasian within his range.   By personal application to the headquarters of the division, backed by an official request in writing, signed by the collector, he obtained a supply of arms and ammunition. Finally, by running up mud walls, cajan roofs, pandals, bamboo mats, etc., and tents of every size and description, he actually found accommodation for one hundred families, besides those of the collector and some immediate friends, so that when the impending storm burst on the locality in question, and was raging all around, the party in the old mud fort were, at least for a time, in safety. Within the area of the old mud walls, which were luckily very thick, and about thirty feet high, there were located a garrison, amounting to 120 men, counting both Europeans and Eurasians.   Besides these, there were some twenty native servants, mostly ayahs; the men, all of whom, I think, were kitmunghars, or dressing-boys, did not amount to half a dozen. No native was suffered to go in or out of the place, and none were trusted with arms of any kind, for reasons that are obvious.

By means of the mats, punkahs, connats, pandals, etc., noticed above, the place was rendered habitable; but still, when all had been done that could be done, the ladies with their families had much to endure : they did it nobly, with a patient resignation and fortitude that had seldom been equalled, never surpassed. As time wore on the surging tide of treachery, blood, and cruelty made its way to the district in question, and at last the yelling, screaming, hooting crowd of butchers, threatening destruction in every shape and form, appeared before the fort, gradually spreading themselves on every side. The number of these ruffians might at this time amount to about 6,000. The nucleus of this swarm of armed natives was composed of the bulk of two regiments of Bengal Sepoys, amounting to about 1,000 men ; the rest was made up of liberated gaol-birds, gang robbers, thieves, and the idle riff-raff to be found everywhere. At each angle of the fort small projecting turrets had been built, which, by means of some repairs and sandbags, were rendered tolerably secure. In each of these turrets four of the best shots amongst the defenders were placed, so that every face of the building was, to a certain extent, commanded. Sandbags between the embrasures were further employed all along the walls, thus affording additional protection to the defenders.

After the yelling and howling, accompanied by the beating of gongs and tomtoms, and by noises of all kinds, had continued for some time, the fire of small arms and gingals was resorted to, and kept up for two days and nights, with little intermission, varied by occasionally throwing fireballs into the place. These, however, except the burning of the

cajans, or thatch, of some of the extemporized huts, did
little or no harm.   The continued discharge of gingals and
musketry had inflicted no damage whatever.   Seeing this,
and that the siege made no progress, the leaders ordered
scaling-ladders to be constructed, which was accordingly
done, and two attempts at escalade were made ; both were
repelled, and considerable loss inflicted on the besiegers.
In fact, the garrison had so well employed their guns, rifles,
and muskets, that more than one hundred of their adver-
saries had been slain, and many more wounded.   The besiegers had, in consequence, retreated beyond the reach of
small arms, resolving, it seemed, to trust rather to the effect
of starvation than to that of storm.

The siege had now lasted six days, and no damage had
been sustained by the garrison, except the burning of some
thatch already noticed, and the loss of one young man who
had rashly exposed himself—he was shot dead—and a poor
little girl, going to get water at the well, was killed by the
rebounding of a gingal-ball.   Some few others had been
wounded, but not severely, and this was all.   The great
danger to be apprehended was that, as large bands of the
rebel Sepoys were marching in every direction, the besiegers
might be powerfully reinforced by numbers of men thoroughly
well trained and disciplined, and that these last would effect
by escalade what less numerous and less trained soldiers
had failed to accomplish.   The very thing so much feared
did actually occur two days afterwards ; several thousand
of the trained traitors joined the besiegers, bringing with
them a battery of field-pieces, luckily only nine-pounders.

Animated by the possession of artillery, and the presence
of so large a force of regular soldiers, two desperate attempts
to storm the place were made on two successive nights,
the fire of the guns on each occasion having been kept up
for many hours without intermission before the parties

bearing the ladders moved forward; then the fire ceased, and the stormers, making a rush, succeeded in planting several ladders, up which the men swarmed with the greatest hardihood; but few reached the tops of the ladders, and fewer still reached the top of the rampart, or lived long enough to raise a cheer or shout to encourage their comrades. All were shot, or hurled over the walls; and most of the ladders were overturned before anyone could reach the upper steps.

The fire from the walls and turrets during these proceedings was so hot, that more than 200 men were slain outright, and many more wounded. The besiegers, in consequence, again drew off their forces beyond the range of rifle and musket. At this time, the number of foemen surrounding the fort could not be less than 9,000 or 10,000; they had completely encompassed it on every side. They had pitched tents and erected huts in every direction, seeming determined not to move from their position till they had effected by starvation what they had failed to compass by bolder and more rapid means. Provisions were beginning to fail the garrison; all felt they could not war against famine. They had defended themselves fifteen days, one against hundreds; but now their doom seemed approaching. All were oppressed with the most gloomy anticipations.

In this extremity Mr. Marston called a committee of all who could be spared from the walls. When about seventy of the brave defenders had assembled, he explained to them the state of matters unreservedly, but urged them not to despair, as it was clear, after counting the mouths and carefully reviewing the supplies remaining, that by giving out half-rations they could still hold out a week or ten days longer, and that in this interval there was every hope of relief, if any one of the officers commanding a loyal column of sufficient strength could be apprised of their situation. Several voices cried out that no one could pass through the numerous and watchful lines of the enemy, and that it would be certain death to attempt it. Mr. Marston smiled, answering that it would be certain death to all not to attempt it. 'I have taken measures,' he continued, 'relative to the course of action advisable, which I shall communicate when the fitting time arrives. Meanwhile, let every man hope for the best, and do his duty as he has hitherto done it.'

All, after hearing their young leader's words, and observing his cheerful countenance, felt their hopes and courage revive, and all determined to hold out to the utmost. Mr. Marston, having arranged for the serving out of the reduced rations, called aside two friends—Mr. Stewart, a civilian, junior to himself, but one on whose courage and determination he knew he could rely, and Assistant-Surgeon Manners, attached to the Collectorate, whose cool indifference under fire and whose fame as a daring and successful tiger-shot were well known. To them, and to Sergeant-Major White, whose services and experience had been invaluable during the siege, and who, though old and wanting one leg, retained still the courage of a lion unsubdued by years or wounds, he spoke as follows :

'My friends, in our present position I see there is but one thing to be done. I will myself attempt to penetrate through these thick-set lines. Should I succeed, I will, if human effort can effect it, bring you relief ; if I fail, and fall into the hands of these butchers, you will know I did all I could, and died in doing my duty.' 'Marston, you shall not go !' exclaimed Manners. 'Your life is more valuable, your headpiece twice as good as mine. Send me : I am quite ready, and will do all I can.' 'No, no,' said Stewart ; 'I am the youngest, and can best be spared.

Manners, as the only medical man, cannot leave. Send me, my dear Marston; I will shrink from no peril, and will go at once.' 'Dear friends,' replied Marston, taking a hand of each, while the tremulous motion of his lips told how truly he felt their devoted friendship, 'this is not a time for words. I shall therefore only say, I feel your kindness deeply, but cannot accept of it. I am resolved to make the assay myself, and do not think me vain if I add that, from habits of study and observation, I think I shall run less risk than either of you would encounter in such an undertaking.'

The two young men continued to press arguments and entreaties on their friend, till he cut Manners short by saying: 'You must, as the only medical man, remain here.' And to Stewart he added, with a peculiar expression of interest : 'How could you think for a moment, Charlie, that I would run the chance of making Clara's bright eyes tearful for a lost brother, when I could have saved him! Fie, man! think better of your friend. And now for business. You must, all of you, in the first place, solemnly pledge your faith to say no word to any soul respecting my intention before I go, and afterwards to conceal my departure for as many days as may be possible. My only chance of safety depends on your silence, and your knowing this will, I am confident, ensure it.'

During the time of siege an aged peon, who had for thirty years been in attendance on the Collector, died. His belt, shield, tulwar, and dagger were brought into Mr. Marston's tent ; then, under the plea of sunstroke, his head was shaved, and he was kept in bed till the browning of his face, hands, and body with coffee-berries was sufficiently strong ; his moustaches were then dyed black. After these preparations, he equipped himself in every respect like a Collector's peon, and his disguise was so perfect when he

stood before his friends that even those who had watched
the various steps by which the metamorphosis was accomplished could scarcely believe that John Marston the
civilian and the turbaned and belted peon before them
were one and the same person. But, however well calculated for deception the brown skin, shaven head, and equip-
ments may have been, Mr. Marston's fitness for the part he
had to enact did not stop here ; his knowledge of the
Oordu, Bengali, and other dialects of Hindustani, was so
remarkable, and so locally idiomatic, that he had no difficulty in personating any Moosulman character. He felt
this, and therefore conceived that he was best qualified to
face the perils to be encountered in carrying into effect the
enterprise contemplated.

As soon as the night was sufficiently dark, the newly-
manufactured peon stood on the parapet, ready, by means
of a basket, rope, and pulley, to be let down, on that side
of the fort completely in shadow, by his two friends and
the old sergeant, who muttered : 'Had I but the other leg,
I would gladly go instead of him ; but I'm a useless old
stump.' 'No, no, my good old friend,' said Marston,
shaking him cordially by the hand ; 'you are best where
you are, and instead of being useless, will be invaluable to
Stewart, who will find himself strong in your experience.'

The peon now seated himself in the basket, holding on
to the rope. No words were spoken, except that 'God
bless you,' was reiterated as his friends, with moistened
eyes, lowered the basket. It soon reached the ground ;
the peon stepped out, and moving cautiously, always in the
shade, was soon lost to sight. His friends watched him as
long as he was visible, putting up silent prayers for his
safety ; but no one ever expected to see him again.

It would be too tedious to describe the numberless perils
and trials encountered and surmounted by our wise young

peon, through his perfect knowledge of the manners and customs of the Moslem race, his imperturbable coolness and presence of mind. It is enough to say that, after journeying three days and nights, he on the fourth day fell in with General Neill's column, who, with his undeviating kindness and humanity, as soon as he understood the imminent danger to which the party left in the old mud fort were exposed, marched to their relief without an hour's delay. During the march the General's only fear seemed to be that he might not arrive in time. His constant mutterings as he rode at the head of his men, with a wet cloth under his pith helmet, took something of this form : 'The bloody, dastardly, treacherous scoundrels ! May God save the poor women and children, the poor defenceless creatures !' 'Keep up, my lads ! keep up, for Heaven's sake ! It's hot work, I know ; but remember what you're striving for.' 'I pray God to grant us His help, to give us strength to get up before the butchers begin their work, and then ' -his fiery spirit showing itself in his flashing eyes and firmly-set teeth—'then, if we don't let them know what cold steel means, may I never see the blessed sun again.'

The noble fellow did live to see the blessed sun again, but not before he had inflicted a crushing punishment on those leagued around the old mud fort, which he entered amidst the tears, blessings, and convulsive sobs of those he had rescued from torture and death. The General's eyes, as he looked around, were filled with moisture. 'Dear friends, I haven't a hundred hands. I wish I had ; but God bless you all ! He has granted my prayer ; He has sent me in time ; but had He not long since inspired my young friend here with indomitable courage, extraordinary knowledge, decision, and foresight, you would never have been placed in a position to be defended, nor have had the supplies to enable you to hold out, nor should I have had the opportunity, the blessed opportunity, of rescuing you.'

Here we bid good-bye to the noble, true-hearted General Neill, who, like almost all the men who are good and great, was vilified by the pitiful wooden-headed worshippers of red tape. He despised it and them, devoting his whole soul to saving the lives of his countrymen, with those of their wives and families. He died at the taking of Lucknow, comparatively young in years, though old in renown —died as he had lived, in the service of his country ; but his name still lives in the hearts of Britain's sons, enshrined by that halo which undaunted courage, guided by strong sense and a pure unpretending love of country, alone can give.

The poor people whom he had rescued with one voice poured out their hearts in blessings, and with tears in their eyes joined in the prayers and shouted the names of Neill and Marston. At first they could scarcely realize to themselves that they were safe ; after nearly a month of daily and nightly dread and danger they could scarcely believe that their sufferings were over. To describe scenes like these accurately is scarcely possible ; such description must be referred to those endowed with the highest powers of expression and the most grateful hearts, since they alone may imagine, or can picture to themselves or others, what they would have felt had they been placed in such a situation, and this is all that we can do to make it understood.

In so far lifting up the veil from Mr. Marston's antecedents, more than enough has been done, we trust, to explain why, young as he was, his reputation stood so high. We feel that the amplitude of the narration amounts almost to a digression, yet if the details interest the reader half as much as they did the writer when first made acquainted with them, their want of brevity may perhaps be forgiven.

The young civilian, wise beyond his years, and the soul of all that had been done to shelter and defend his helpless friends, was throughout specially cautious that everything required should be done in the name of his chief, although the poor old Collector was so overwhelmed with the novelty and unexpected horror of the position, that his utmost contribution to the measures adopted amounted to no more than a ' Yes,' or ' By all means,' or a nod of his head : but by this caution Mr. Marston prevented any slur or blame from being thrown on his senior, who, though unable to act in such an emergency, was fully capable of appreciating the high feeling and delicacy evinced by his junior ; and he loved and respected him for it, as did every member of his family.

When his friends had been placed in safety Mr. Marston was actively employed till the taking of Delhi, which put an end to this horrible war. Fatigue, exposure, and constant headwork, added to what he had previously undergone, at last broke down the young man's strength, and he became so ill that he was advised to return to Europe. The truth was that, the excitement being over, there was nothing to sustain him against the inroads of disease, and we consequently find him among the passengers on board our steamer. Youth, sea air, and buoyant spirits soon enabled him to rally, and he became one of the most light-hearted, joyous men of the homeward-bound party. He unpacked his cornet (on which he played really well) and in a short time almost rivalled the popularity of the Captain of Artillery.

There were many officers amongst the passengers who, in very trying situations, had nobly upheld their country's fame and honour, and several of these were not less worthy as men than agreeable as companions, but as they did not possess qualities or accomplishments that rendered them conspicuous, we do not notice them individually. The exceptions

to be made to this somewhat sweeping assertion or statement refer to those gentlemen who sometimes described
what they had seen on the line of march, or gave some account of the various engagements, or affairs of less importance, in which they had been personally concerned ; or to
those who sometimes favoured the company with sporting
narratives, or finally to the doctor of the ship, Dr. Tobias
Ticklemore, who was a man of observation, had read a good
deal, and was withal a very good-natured fellow, so that
while some smoked and others sipped brandy pawney, he
could remember or invent some tale for their amusement.
He therefore occupied a prominent place amongst those
who belonged to the section of story-tellers, or, as our neighbours would term them, *raconteurs.* This partial sketch
of the party assembled round the piano in the saloon of our
noble steamer will, it is hoped, invest their conversation
and remarks with some interest, which otherwise could
hardly have attached to them.   The ladies and gentlemen
referred to shall now speak for themselves.

Captain Trevanion and Mrs. Smythe had just finished
that charming duet between Don Giovanni and Zerlina, ' La
ci darem,' to the general delight of the audience, and perhaps to their own, if we might guess so much from the
obvious pleasure with which they received the thanks and
applause of those around them.   After a judicious interval,
Captain Ward's voice was heard entreating someone to
follow the good example that had been set.   ' Come, ladies,
come, gentlemen, do not let me beg in vain : we have had a
sweet duet, sweetly sung, and previously we had Mr. Marston's cornet rendering of " Ah che la morte," which made us
long more than ever to get home, that we may hear it once
again from Mario the unapproachable.   But we are losing
time : will no one help us to charm the fleeting hours, yet
make them seem too short ?'   ' Really,' said Lady Jervois,

'the Captain grows so poetical that we shall begin to suspect, when he tells us he is looking at the sun, that he is
communing with Apollo.' 'No, dear Lady Jervois, I only
seek to find the angle at which the sun's ray strikes my
sextant, when my chronometer tells me it is twelve o'clock.
I angle for nothing else.' 'Well,' returned the lady, laughing, 'if we accept that statement for fact, I fear you must
stand convicted by your own admission of great disrespect
to the god of day.' 'How so, lady fair?' 'Why, do you
not admit that you seek, in an indirect way, to obtain certain information by your angling? And is that not equivalent to putting fishing questions to the day god, which is
very disrespectful? So take care and rein in your wit.'
'How can I do that, Lady Jervois, when there is nothing to
rein in?' 'What, angling again?' returned the lively lady;
'but you will catch no fish this time, I won't see the line.'
'Upon my word,' whispered Miss Perkins to Miss Wiseman,
'this is, I dare say, very witty, and I suppose classical, but I
don't know anything about heathen gods and goddesses;
nevertheless, it seems to me not a bad attempt on the part
of my lady widow to get up a flirtation.' 'Not at all unlikely, I dare say,' replied Miss Wiseman. 'I didn't hear
all; there seemed to be a good deal of laughing, though.'

Captain Ward's voice was again audible, begging that someone would sing a song. Then, after a silence, 'If that is too
great a favour to expect, will no one give us an anecdote,
or tell us a story? Surely, among so many gentlemen who
have been in the field, and who are almost all of them
sportsmen, there must be much to speak of? Come, gentlemen, a tiger hunt, a quarrel, a sample of Afghan clemency,
a specimen of red-tape, a bit of pipeclay, anything, re-
miniscences, experiences, *quelquechose pour passer le temps.*'
After a time, 'Is it really so, all silent? Then we must ask
the Doctor; he has, I know, an inexhaustible stock; he is

in this respect the double of the " Pasha of many tails."
Come, Doctor, you are our sole resource.'   'I really can't
see that,' returned the Doctor ; ' upon my soul I can't !
How can I be your sole resource so long as you affirm that
I am the double of some other gentleman, which, if I really
am, makes me singularly double ; which, again, everyone
must admit is doubly singular ?'   ' Oh, Doctor, Doctor ! how
can you go on so ?' said the two young ladies, tittering.
'And after all your promises of reformation and amend-
ment,' said Mrs. Smythe.   'Never mind, Dr. Ticklemore,'
interposed Lady Jervois, ' your quips and quillets make us all
laugh, whether we will or no.'   ' Don't take his part, Lady
Jervois,' said Captain Trevanion, 'he's incorrigible, and it
was the same from the commencement of our acquaintance.
The first inquiry I made on reaching the deck of the *Ele-*
phanta was for the Doctor (the then state of my arm making
me rather anxious to see him) ; a little sprat of a middy,
who seemed to be the only person on board in the shape of
an officer, answered my inquiry by informing me that the
Doctor had taken a run on shore, but was to be on deck
again before eight bells.   These adverse conditions being
beyond my power to control, I had nothing for it but to
wait, and to amuse myself as best I could.   Some tea and
dry toast, which the steward sent me, and the last number
of the *Cornhill Magazine,* enabled me to effect this pretty
fairly, and by-and-by the looked-for son of Esculapius arrived, but in such a pickle that——'

' I say, Trevanion,' exclaimed the Doctor, ' fair play, no
tales out of school ; that would be taking a dirty advantage
of a man's misfortunes, and be altogether unfair.'   ' Well,'
returned the Captain, ' there's no need to take any dirty
advantage ; the *statu quo* was dirty enough in all conscience.'
, Oh, let us hear,' exclaimed the ladies, ' pray let us hear,

Captain Trevanion !' 'Come, Trevanion, don't be so shabby,' said the Doctor ; 'if the incident is to be told, at all events let me tell it myself.' 'On one condition,' replied the artilleryman, ' *i.e.*, that the narrative is to be recounted *bonâ fide*, without alteration or subtraction ; and you'll not make any addition to it, I'm quite sure.'

'But,' said Lady Jervois, 'in enforcing a confession of past misfortunes from poor Dr. Ticklemore you seem to me, Captain Trevanion, to be wholly oblivious of the charge you brought against him as incorrigible. You were about to adduce something in support of this charge, if I mistake not ? Pray afford us the opportunity of judging of the value of this support, and we can hear Dr. Ticklemore's confession afterwards. We, who form the jury in this case, are not willing that the accused should be borne down by clamour or many words, as I have been told sometimes happens in other places.'

'You see, Lady Jervois,' returned Trevanion, 'I was interrupted in my narrative by the accused himself, who claimed to be his own reporter in this matter, which in courtesy I think we must allow him to be ; therefore I will only say, judging from his crushed hat and sandy, muddy coat, that there had been a fall, and a closer connection with Mother Earth than gentlemen generally like to indulge in when attired for a ride on the Madras beach. Of how this came about, as he promises to inform all present truly, I say nothing, but at the time, seeing him under the influence of a little excitement, I did all I could to calm and soothe him ; I advised his taking a glass of brandy and soda-water, which he did. I listened to his statement with a gravity which, considering the details, was truly marvellous, even to myself, and allowed him in silence to recover his equanimity by giving free scope to all and sundry of his pious little wishes for the benefit of more than one individual, but specially for that of a certain Mr. Jack Horseyman ; whom, it would seem, though an old schoolfellow, the Doctor devoted for a long time to come to quarters which have so often been described with such precision and minuteness as almost to induce suspicion of personal acquaintance on the part of those who furnished the interesting details. But, be this as it may, this *embarras des richesse* entirely relieves me from the necessity of description. I will merely indicate the locality by remarking that I believe they don't want any coals there. Having shown my sympathy by my silence, by the gravity of my countenance, and by my attention as a listener, I endeavoured still further to soothe the Doctor's feelings by telling him some of my own mishaps in the hunting-field, and in particular, on the last occasion of my putting in an appearance there, the narrow escape that myself and my horse had, when both of us, in consequence of coming suddenly on a sloping rock, the face of which (from the severe weather) was a sheet of ice, slid down near a dozen yards, the horse, as it were, sitting on his haunches and actually scraping his hocks. " Oh," observed the Doctor, " that was nothing ; merely a freak of Mr. Jack Frost, by which he converted you both into a pair of slippers." Now I appeal to you, after this, if his is not an inveterate form of a disease which, continually indulged in, becomes highly criminal, and if he is not justly condemned to suffer all the pains and penalties laid down in the statute provided for duly restraining and intimidating such stubborn offenders ?'

'Why, truly,' said Lady Jervois, laughing merrily, 'you have brought forward strong evidence, I confess ; but you know one swallow does not make a summer.'

' Oh, that argument can scarcely be admitted,' said Mr. Marston ; 'I agree entirely with Trevanion, Ticklemore is really a dreadful character. It was but the other day I remonstrated with him on account of these evil proclivities of his. In reply, he asked me, in the gravest manner, if I did not know that he was a surgeon? "What's that to do with it," said I, "except that it's all the more reason that you should conduct yourself with greater sobriety?" "That's all you know about it," retorted he, "but you ought to remember that the study of the 'humerus' is a part of my profession. Ha!" continued he, "have I caught you on the funny-bone?" and then he went off chuckling. "Confound you, you catch one at every turn," I muttered, though I could not help laughing. You see, he's incorrigible.'

'I suspect,' replied the lady, 'there are more incorrigibles than one; but let us hear the Doctor; I see he is about to speak.'

After a pause, Dr. Ticklemore stood up, and with a solemn air spoke as follows: 'I thought till now that at least my fair friends would have granted me a fair hearing, but instead of that I have not even been allowed to state the reasons that make it impossible for me to comply with Captain Ward's request. I have been interrupted by false friends—I might say covert and insidious enemies' ('Hear, hear,' from Captain Trevanion and Mr. Marston)—'for no other purpose than to harrow my feelings, and exhibit their own malicious enjoyment of another's woe by trumpeting forth little matters not worth repeating, each discharging an envenomed arrow because of the trivial passing confidences which my guileless disposition and trusting nature had induced me to make. "Friendship's but a name," the poet says, and I, alas! have found it so.' (Loud laughter from the gentlemen, with 'Bravo, Doctor; you have made a capital defence,' the ladies joining in the laughter, allowed that the Doctor had come off with flying colours.) 'But,' said Lady Jervois, 'what about the crushed hat and muddy coat? I should like to hear something about these little matters.' (Cries of 'Explain, explain! listen to the Doctor's explanation.') 'Lady Jervois, and ladies and gentlemen all,' returned Dr. Ticklemore, 'I have promised that I would explain these mysteries, and I will do so; but, like men in more exalted places, when certain explanations are called for I do not find the present time convenient, or the public welfare will not permit me at present to be more explicit, so I would rather, if you will graciously concede so much to me, finish the argument referring to Captain Ward's request.' 'Oh!' said the lady, 'it is impossible to deny a solicitation urged in a manner so complimentary; pray proceed, Doctor, with your argument.' ('Go on,' from all sides.) 'You see,' said Dr. Ticklemore, 'I had not said half I intended to say when I was interrupted; but now that the sequence of the propositions has been broken, I am required to go on. It will not be so easy for me to show their logical dependence one on the other as it would have been. The fact is,' continued the Doctor, 'you were most of you in such a hurry to condemn me, that you would not let me speak when I was ready to do so, and now I must rearrange my ideas.' 'We admit you have been very ill used,' said Lady Jervois, 'but pray go on. We are all sure that there will be no difficulty about your ideas if you don't make any. Once more we pray of you to proceed.' 'Pray go on,' said Captain Ward; 'you may be sure, after this alarming preface, he has more crackers to let off.' ('Go on, Doctor; go on,' from all sides.) 'Well,' said the Doctor, 'to stop me in the middle of my speech, as you have done, is rather an Irish mode of getting me to go on, isn't it? But I suppose it's like the remark about the crackers, to be taken by contraries; you say, go on, but I apprehend you mean, go off!'

More tittering and laughter, but this time the Doctor would not be stopped.

He continued thus: 'You, Captain Ward, have gravely affirmed that I am someone's double, which is neither more nor less than stating that I am a ghost, an immaterial airy nothing; but let me tell you that it is not immaterial to me to be made nothing of; it is not treating me with the respect due to a man of my weight. Besides, although you are so ready to deny my gravity, and to accuse me of lightness in many respects, even in my behaviour, you will find that the force which pulls all things over the surface of the globe towards its centre requires upwards of twelve stone to counterbalance my corporeal entity, which, I take it, is a very good material proof that if I am a ghost, or, as you term it, a double, I am also an individual of some weight. Now if I am myself and also a double, I must be something besides myself; for such a one to attempt to comply with Captain Ward's request would not only prove him to be an insane double, but doubly insane; therefore you see——'

'Hear the fellow!' cried Captain Ward. 'Never did a thimble-rigging Political double as he is doing. I'll tell you what, Dr. Tobias Ticklemore, if you don't stop your atrocities, which are ten times worse than those of the Bulgarians,* for yours are not manufactured in nineteen cases out of twenty by the Russians, but are actually perpetrated before our very faces, and in the presence of those whose nerves ought to have been spared such terrible trials, I see, we shall be obliged to order a drumhead. court-

* The author is quite aware of the anachronism, but hopes it may be pardoned for the sake of its applicability.

martial, and we'll call in Judge Lynch to act as provost-marshal, who always convicts, and not only convicts, but carries sentence into execution with such wonderful rapidity that the offender is suspended almost before he can look round; so be wise in time, Toby Tickle, or you'll get a tickler for Toby, that you may rely upon.'

'Oh,' replied the Doctor, 'if you really have the cruelty, the inhumanity, the barbarity, to threaten me with *sus. per col.*; I fancy I must not hang fire lest I hang myself! Nevertheless, I think it due to myself to protest against the whole proceeding as illegal; there is a manifest flaw in the indictment. Your orthography is all wrong; I have neither three tails, nor many tails.'

'That's being hypocritical as well as hypercritical, Doctor, if not contumacious; spell it another way, and you have not three tales, but as many as you please.'

'Oh, oh!' said the Doctor, 'is that the plan you would adopt to get innocent people into trouble? but you won't take anything by your motion, for I shall presently show that, spell the words as you will, tails and tales are in truth equivalents. "T" is common to both words, and therefore goes for nothing, being equal to itself; and ales, at least in India and all tropical climates, is represented by ails; therefore, whichever way you spell the word, you gain nothing. For the second part of the word has been shown to be equivalent to the second part of the second word; and the first part of the first word having been found equal to the first part of the second word, the two wholes are found to be equal, Q. E. D.'

'Gentlemen,' said Captain Ward, 'what do you say to this—is it not intolerable? Is it not trifling, barefaced trifling, with authority? After the atrocities of which this man has been convicted, on the most unanswerable evidence, that of our own senses, for him to begin again in the same strain is clearly an aggravation of the original offence ; to me it seems a case of unexampled audacity, deliberate and premeditated, with his logic, his mathematics, and his Q.E.D. I declare, I think there is nothing for it but to confirm the sentence reserved for consideration, and on account of the aggravation to order that the suspension be carried out in chains.'

'Oh, horrible ! most horrible !' cried the Doctor ; 'then I must bend to fate. No one likes suspense, to say nothing of the chains, and I in this am no exception to the world at large. True, I have seen men hung in chains who seemed to be proud of them, and wore them ostentatiously, but——'

'But, sir,' said Captain Ward, 'you are keeping us in suspense, thereby incurring heavier penalties. Remember, alacrity in the performance of duty is the only way to obtain mitigation, or the sentence will have to be carried out in chains.'

'Chains,' said the Doctor, 'are horrible—chains of all kinds, except silken ones, of which I have no knowledge save by hearsay.'

'Oh, oh !' cried Miss Perkins, 'who do you think will credit that statement, Dr. Ticklemore?'

'And why do you wear that gold locket that you never show to anyone?' said Miss Wiseman.

'I fear, ladies,' observed Captain Ward, 'that this Doctor is a gay and faithless character, and an old offender against a certain little deity that it is not necessary to describe more particularly just now ; he has for other offences been convicted as an incorrigible, and is at this very time under sentence of *sus. per col.*, unless he saves himself by ready obedience to the order of the Court ; therefore it may be as well to postpone the consideration of this additional charge relative to the locket till we see how he conducts himself: if truculent and refractory he knows his doom, if, on the contrary, he exhibits a proper and decent penitence for his manifold offences, and incontinently addresses himself to his task——'

'Incontinently!' exclaimed the Doctor. 'Surely, Captain Ward, you would not recommend anything bordering on that in the present company.'

'You abominable misinterpreter of words! you know very well that I used the expression in the sense of quickly, immediately.'

'Oh,' said the Doctor, with as much simplicity as he could throw into his countenance, 'I am greatly relieved; but, in truth, Captain Ward, knowing my highly delicate and sensitive moral organization, you should be more considerate.'

While this colloquy was going on, a shade of more than usual gravity was visible on the features of the fair auditors, and the laughter of the gentlemen was immoderate. Captain Ward's only remark was: 'Really, the cool temperature of that fellow is without parallel; it is a pity he's not an Irishman. He ought assuredly to have been born one, for he certainly is what they term "a broth of a boy"; but come, let us have an end of this "bald, disjointed chat." Pray make yourself a little agreeable, Doctor; give us something to amuse us, and for a time forget your quibbles, your "pribbles and prabbles," as good Sir Hugh has it.'

'Well, as you ask so pretty, as our juvenile friends say, and will promise not to abuse me any more, I'll try what I can do; but it must be something very short. It will soon be eight bells, and then we break up for the evening.'

'Don't waste any more time, then,' said Lady Jervois, 'and instead of abusing we'll all combine to praise you.'

We have no record of Dr. Ticklemore's short tale. All we know of it is that it amused the ladies very much ; and of course, being approved by the fairer half of the creation, the gentlemen were in a manner compelled to applaud too. The next morning the Captain appeared to be specially occupied with his maps and charts, and two of the boats, each in charge of a junior officer, were sent out to take soundings, while the *Elephanta* scarcely moved on her way. The Captain suspected that an under-current had carried the vessel several points to leeward, and, if this were not seen to in time, we should not make Suez so nicely as he wished. Leaving the Captain, who was not only a thorough seaman, but a most careful officer, to attend to these matters, the party on board occupied themselves according to their inclinations : the ladies brought up their work, as there was a fair breeze, which under the awning was pleasant enough ; and the gentlemen either wrote, or read, or chatted, or made arrangements for the evening with the ladies who sang or played. 'I wish I was a vocalist,' said Lady Jervois. 'Do you ?' said Captain Trevanion : 'tell me why.' 'Oh, everyone wishes to be accomplished as a musician, and I can do nothing in that way but play over the lessons I learned at school.' 'Suppose it be so, it is not too late to learn. When at home you will find numberless ladies capable and willing to help you to cultivate music.' 'Ah, Captain Trevanion, they can't give me a voice.' 'But how do you know that you have no voice ?' 'Oh, they told me so at school, and I feel I have no voice.' 'You must not set things down against yourself ; don't give up till you have had the opinion of a first-rate master, and, if I may advise, I should say, go about and hear as much good music and singing as you can.' 'I think I'll take your advice; it is at all events very agreeable, should it not eventually help me.' 'Ah, but I think it will!' said Marston, who had been standing by during the whole colloquy. 'And now, Lady Jervois, if you will go with us to the piano, and do us the honour to listen to our practice for the evening, you will, as it were, be taking the first step in your projected course of study, only under amateur musicians instead of masters. Mrs. Smythe will, I am sure, feel highly complimented by your attention to the practice. Here she comes.' 'Dear Mrs. Smythe,' said Lady J., 'will you permit an untaught ignorant creature like myself the pleasure and advantage of hearing your practice?' 'Dear Lady Jervois,' returned Mrs. Smythe, 'your presence at the practice will give us all sincere pleasure, and be esteemed a great compliment, too.'

Thus Lady J. became a regular attendant on the morning practice of the musical party, and of course became more intimate with them than she had been before. When the practice was over the party dispersed—some to chess, some to read, and some to play at the old game of 'Crambo' (in which they all eventually joined); and though they might not manage so well as Queen Elizabeth and Sir W. Raleigh did, still it caused some amusement.

When the din of tongues, and the mutual raillery and the laughing consequent on the game at 'Crambo' had subsided, Captain Ward and Trevanion sat down to a game at chess. They selected for their opening move that subtle one known as the Evans Gambit. They had scarcely begun when Lady J. came to the table, and seated herself near enough to watch the game. She said, 'Don't mind me; I promise not to speak a word; but though a very indifferent player, I am fond of the game.' After a tough battle it ended in a draw.

'I did not know you were a chess-player, Lady J., or I should long since have asked for a game.' 'I fear you are laughing at me; I am not at all strong enough to contend with you.' 'But you will give proof, I hope, as I am one of those stiff-necked people who take nothing on trust.' 'Oh, you may take my word for that—on trust.' 'But will you not give me proof?' 'Certainly, to-morrow morning, if you like. It is too late to-day to begin a game.' 'But it is not too late, if you do not know it, to show you Philidor's legacy.' 'I do not; yet I should like to know it.' 'It arose in this way. It is admitted that you cannot give checkmate with *two* knights.' 'I think I have heard so.' 'In one of the cafés of Paris, and in Philidor's presence, this was strongly insisted on. He heard all that was said, and then asserted that he would give checkmate with one knight, and without any other piece or pawn to assist it. One of the speakers said in reply, "I'll bet you £1,000 you don't." "Very well, I take your bet," said Philidor. "Mind, you are not to have any piece or pawn to help you." "'The checkmate shall be perfect and complete by the move of one knight alone," returned Philidor.' 'And, pray, how was it accomplished?' inquired Lady J. 'That I shall now have the pleasure of showing you,' said Trevanion. And to the lady's no small delight he showed how the checkmate with one knight was brought about. (I see since this was written that the final position in Philidor's legacy is published in one of the periodicals of the day as a problem, but without giving the credit to the famous old master, whose ingenuity and skill in playing the game so as to arrive at the position in question seems almost beyond human power to conceive.)

Lady J. had not attended the morning practice longer than a fortnight, when the benefit derived from it was perceptible, not only to herself, but to others.   In order to gain courage and to strengthen her voice, she sang at first in unison with Mrs. Smythe a number of sweet and admired airs : ' Oh ! come to me when daylight sets'; ' You shall walk in silk attire'; ' Oft in the stilly night,' and a great many simple melodies.   Finding that she could remember these airs and sing them to herself gave great pleasure to Lady J. and to her friends too ; she found that her voice was gaining power, and Mrs. Smythe declared that her ear was true, and that if the voyage had lasted another month she would have been able to take part in glees and duets.   ' I fear you are flattering me too much,' returned Lady J. ; ' but I certainly shall persevere.'   ' I told you long ago that you were wrong to set the thing down against yourself, did I not ?' said Trevanion.   ' And I threw in my little help, did I not ?' said Marston.   ' You both did, and so encouraged me, that I am now hopeful of myself.'   ' When we get home, and you meet with a good teacher, I'll bet a dozen pairs of gloves that in less than six months you take part in any of the duets or glees we are practising now.'   ' I will not venture on a bet, but really, I do feel infinitely more hopeful than I was !'

The *Elephanta* was now at Suez, and as usual the weather was so dreadfully hot that no pastimes nor amusements could be thought of; to exist was a difficulty, and it was the same all through the Red Sea, and so it continued till the party reached Alexandria.   Then came the bustle and trouble of transhipment to the steamer for England, and the delightful change of the Mediterranean breeze and cool climate for the dreadful heat of the Red Sea.   All the passengers enjoyed the change immensely ; the walking the deck was so enjoyable that it superseded all other modes of passing time. Trevanion and Lady J. were indefatigable in taking this exercise. This attracted the notice of Miss Perkins and her friend Miss Wiseman ; the former observed that she perceived that the widow was a great general. ' She first flirted with Captain Ward, but finding that was of no use, she took up the singing line, and that seems to have answered much better. Trevanion is evidently spoony.' ' I thought so too, when I saw them walking the deck morning and evening.' ' The truth is, my dear, that there is no being up to a widow—no, they come over a man when he's not thinking of anything.' ' That's just it, they take him alto-gether unawares. Now, to think of that cunning creature pretending to want to learn to sing, merely to get on terms of intimacy with that spoon Trevanion, and he so dull and so besotted with his music that he does not see it.' Much more in the same strain was said, which it is not worth while to put down.

The new steamer, the *Bucephalus*, tore along at a great rate, and passed some of the most interesting and storied scenes the world has to show. As the Pillars of Hercules were passed, and the noble vessel pointed towards old England, the anxiety to get the first glimpse of the dear land was so great that some of the passengers sat up all night. At last the ship came in sight of the blessed shore, and shortly afterwards anchored off Southampton. When the ladies were safely landed, and with their luggage installed in the Grand Hotel, the gentlemen, after seeing that their own goods and chattels were all right, adjourned with the whole party to the breakfast-room.

The breakfast was scarcely finished, when two strangers appeared to take charge of Mrs. Smythe and Mrs. Forbes ; one of them a brother of the first-named lady, the other first-cousin of the latter. These gentlemen, anxious not to lose the train for Scotland, scarcely allowed the two ladies time to say good-bye to their friends who had been their late ship-mates. This was, however, at last accomplished, with promises of corresponding, the gentlemen vociferating, 'Come, or you will lose the train !' and they were off to the land of cakes. Shortly after breakfast was over, down came Lady J. dressed for travelling. 'You go, I think,' said Trevanion, 'to your aunt, Lady Drummond, in Eaton Square ?' 'Yes,' replied Lady J. ; 'and you go to the Army and Navy Club ?' 'Yes,' said Trevanion. 'And I,' said Marston, 'am bound for the Selwyns' in Devonshire.' 'I think I have heard a whisper that there are certain bright eyes in Devon that are irresistible on this occasion.' 'Ah, Trevanion,' said Marston, looking a little red and conscious, 'you have been a traitor ! I see how L. J. has become possessed of my secret.' 'I really could not help it,' said Trevanion, laughing. 'Let me say,' said Lady J., 'though I have never seen the fair young creature, that with all my heart I wish you every success, Mr. Marston, and every future happiness.' 'Hearty and sincere thanks,' returned the young gentleman, blushing deeply, in spite of himself; 'and may I shortly be in a position to congratulate you, Lady Jervois ?' It was now the lady's turn to look down to her feet, as a blush mantled over her beautiful features. 'Well, Marston,' said Trevanion, coming to the lady's assistance, 'when shall we see you in town again ? But, perhaps that is not a fair question, as it will probably depend on another's will.' 'Come, come, you shut up ! It's a comfort to think that there are a pair of us. Now let me shake hands, and bid good-bye to Lady Jervois.'

When Marston was gone, only Miss Perkins and Miss Wiseman, beside themselves, were left of all the party which had landed that morning. Lady J., with her usual kindness, asked them if they were bound for London ; they said they were. Then said Lady J., 'You had better come with us ; Trevanion and I have secured a first-class carriage to London, therefore your doing so will put us to no expense, and no inconvenience.' ' How can you say so !' whispered Trevanion. ' I reckoned on the privacy of our ride to say a great many things that I could not so well say before. But you, you wicked creature, have entirely spoilt my plan.' 'And did you not deserve it, sir, for planning anything so deliberately wicked ?' And as she said this her eyes sparkled and danced with sportive malice, and Trevanion was more hopelessly in love than ever.

In the meantime the two young ladies were profuse in their acknowledgments of Lady J.'s kindness and generosity. And so the party managed to get to London, where the young ladies made their adieux ; and then Trevanion, having ordered a close carriage to take them to Eaton Square, looked exultingly at Lady J. ; but she was peremptory, and then an open carriage was ordered. I am quite at a loss to guess why she was so determined as to these arrangements, but, nevertheless, the ride was very delightful. Trevanion held Lady J.'s hand in his all the way, and this rewarded him for everything ! There was a sweet long pressure of hands ere the two parted, and the look of tenderness that stole from Lady J.'s eyes overcame Trevanion so entirely that he hardly knew what he was doing or saying. Lady Drummond sent out the most kindly invitation to Trevanion, which he did not accept, begging to be excused till the next day ; he then bade adieu to Lady J., and as he did so felt more depressed than he had ever felt in his life, and as if all around was gloom ; he felt truly that the sun of his life was gone.

The next day, about two p.m., Trevanion called in

Eaton Square, and to his great mortification found that the ladies had gone out ; he left a card for each of them, and tried to console himself as best he could.   He then went to look at a horse that Colonel Brisbane, who was about to return to India, wished to dispose of: a very handsome creature, warranted to be sound in wind and limb, for which eighty guineas was to be paid.   'Well,' said Trevanion, ' I'll try him in the " Row " this evening, and if he suits me, I'll buy him.'   The horse went beautifully, and seemed to feel at once that he had a rider on his back, and the rider was so pleased with him, that he made up his mind to take him ; and after he had been round the Row, he was enjoying an easy canter, when he was obliged to rein up by a stylish pony phaeton, drawn by a pair of silver grays not quite fourteen hands high, but very lovely.   Two ladies sat in the front, and the younger one was driving ; a groom sat behind.   The recognition between Trevanion and the younger lady was instantaneous, and immediately after the introduction to Lady Drummond had taken place, she said that she regretted she was out when he called, but they did not think he would have chosen so early an hour, and thought that they should be at home in time to see him.

' Ah !' said Trevanion, ' all this arises from those vile Indian customs I have got used to, but I shall become more civilized by-and-by.'   'No, no,' said the lively old lady ; ' it arises from your formality and stiffness in refusing my invitation yesterday.'   'You are exceedingly kind to say so,' returned Trevanion.   'I suppose you'll adhere to it now by refusing my invitation for this evening ?' ' No, Lady Drummond, I accept it with great pleasure, but as I have no groom with me, I must ride back with the horse to Colonel Brisbane's stables, and return for the evening ; he won't be mine till the Colonel has got his

price.' Both the ladies were loud in their praises of the
horse, and were glad that he was to become Trevanion's
property. 'And now,' said the gentleman, ' I must go and
dress, and I have no time to spare.' ' Now, mind you are
there in time—eight p.m. precisely.' ' I will be punctual,
depend upon it, Lady Drummond.' ' Well, I do in some sort
depend upon it, for reasons I don't think it necessary to
mention just now,' and away went the ladies, and away went
Trevanion, after the bows and *au revoirs* had been duly paid.

As he anticipated, he spent a most pleasant evening.
He found Lady Drummond a very agreeable, sensible, and
frank old lady, and consequently found himself at home at
once. The presence of Lady J., a real personification of
grace and beauty, whose quiet happiness beamed in every
glance, insensibly enhanced the enjoyment and pleasure of
all three, the two ladies and their visitor. Trevanion, in
fact, reckoned this evening as one of the white periods of
his life.

It will be neither amusing nor instructive to trace the
progress of a courtship where everything was in favour of
the lovers. The consent of friends, mutual inclination, and
ample means, made everything smooth. The one cloud
was the necessity of going to India for some years. At this
time cards from Mr. and Mrs. Marston reached our friends,
with letters in which M. declared that he would stay at
home to the last possible day, his Clara not liking the
thought of India, though the darling was willing to go anywhere with him. Trevanion wrote back to say that his
marriage was finally arranged, and would shortly come off,
which it did on the 10th of the following month, when Captain
Trevanion and Lady Jervois were made one. They spent
their honeymoon at a pretty old ivy-covered place called the
Priory, which was lent to them for the occasion by a friend

of Lady Drummond's. When the honeymoon was over, they went to Italy, where they spent some time. They visited Juliet's reputed tomb in Verona; then they passed on to Venice and read Shakespeare and Otway with redoubled zest, 'swam in gondolas' daily while there, then returned on their footsteps, stayed a few days at Fiorenza, and did not forget to see and admire 'the statue that enchants the world.' They then determined on a short stay at Rome, where the wonders of the Vatican delighted them greatly. The exquisitely expressed agony of the Laocoon, the matchless, manly beauty of the Apollo, the resolute endurance and suffering of the Dying Gladiator, indelibly impressed themselves on their remembrance. To use their own words, these marvels spoke in stone. Nor were the masterpieces of Michael Angelo, Raphael, and others overlooked, but the bare enumeration of them would take up too much of our space and time.

They returned home saturated with admiration and enthusiasm for Italian sculpture and painting. Nor did they come home altogether empty-handed. They brought with them some lovely specimens of Italian work as presents for friends and relatives. These were too many to be separately noticed, but a Hercules destroying two centaurs was particularly admired, and was much prized by Lady Drummond, to whom it was given; and a Theseus delivering Ariadne from the sea monster, which was sent to Mrs. Marston, was so much thought of by that lady and her friends, that she declared it to be the most beautiful specimen of sculpture she had ever seen, and she wrote such a charming letter to Lady Trevanion on the subject, that it gave rise to a kind and affectionate correspondence between the two ladies, though they had never seen each other. However, in the spring Mrs. Marston, with her little boy, arrived in town, and there the ladies became almost inseparable. The last we heard of them was, that they were the two special attractions at a grand ball given by Lady D. just before Captain and Lady Trevanion sailed for India. Mr. and Mrs. Marston remained at home another year, then reluctantly embarked for the land of the East.

CAPTAIN WHISTLER, AND LIFE IN CANTONMENT AT SECUNDERABAD.

IN the year 18—, the —— Regiment, Madras N.I., marched for the cantonment of Secunderabad. The march was accomplished in the average number of days without any more serious mishap or sickness than was usual in those days, owing to the wise precautions taken by the officer in command, in communication with the doctor of the regiment. The length of each march being known, the hour of rising and commencing it was so fixed as to enable the men to reach the ground appointed before the sun was powerful; this, on an average, fell out between six and seven a.m. No encamping ground whereon any large party of human beings, or any other regiment, had halted was ever made use of for their purpose, experience having shown that the poison of cholera dwells in such places long after the people have departed from them, and in some cases even when (as reported) the former sojourners had not been afflicted with this terrible disease. The débris which they leave, and other foul matters, appear to generate the plague when fresh men occupy the ground, if such incautious reoccupation occurs within the period of twenty or thirty days. The camp was always pitched as far from the villages as convenience would permit, and placed, wherever possible, on high open ground. The reward of these precautions was that the regiment reached Secunderabad without losing a man.

We had escaped the cholera, but as we approached the Kistnah we became unpleasantly acquainted with another of the pests of India. It is true that tigers are found more or less frequently all over the country, but wherever there is much low jungle, high grass, reeds and rushes, these monstrous striped cats are very numerous. The complete cover afforded by this kind of vegetation encourages their increase greatly, and then they become so formidable that no one dares singly, or, indeed, without a strong escort, to pass or repass through such places. They will even, if they are hungry, attack a whole regiment, which, with the families of the Sepoys and followers, will scarcely number less than 4,000 or 5,000 souls—men, women, and children ; accompanied by some hundreds of animals—horses, dogs, donkeys, and bullocks, and sometimes also by elephants and camels. The noise and hubbub of such a camp, the lights and fires at night, would, it might be imagined, be sufficient to keep these beasts at a distance, but it is not always so. Even before eight p.m., when silence is (in well-regulated camps) imposed on all, as all are supposed to retire to rest at this hour in order to rise for the early march, the tiger will spring into the midst of men and animals, tents, etc., seize an unfortunate tatoo, or donkey, or man, and bound with his prey over all impediments. But more commonly he defers his attack till all is quiet, and most of the lights and fires are extinguished or reduced to a few glowing embers here and there, and when nothing is heard but the sentry's ' All's well !' Then is the time when this ferocious animal is most to be feared, especially if the moon is up, as it affords him light enough to select his victim, but does not give the latter time or opportunity to provide against it, neither can others follow in pursuit, the robber being generally lost to sight in a few seconds ; but even in this case the rule is not absolutely without exception, as I shall shortly show.

The loss sustained from these feline thieves during our march was first that of a draught bullock, which was taken out of the midst of the camp, or out of that part of it occupied by the camp followers. There was a great noise of men and dogs, and some Shikaries, who were with the camp, sent a few shots after the thief, but he was so soon lost to sight that they may have been fired less from sight than from guess. The second capture occurred on the night following that on which the bullock was carried off : it was of an unfortunate tatoo (pony) belonging to a Jemadar, who could ill afford to lose it, as he was an old man not well able to march. He had not long, however, to overtax his strength by marching, as the officers of his company subscribed twenty rupees to enable him to buy another pony, which he soon did, rejoicing that the tiger had taken his former one away, as, by the generosity of the officers, he had secured a much younger and better one.

The next march brought the regiment to the banks of the Kistnah, one of the large rivers of India ; there the officers and men had an opportunity of seeing those round boats which we read of in Herodotus, and which we are told were used in the days of Semiramis. They certainly answered the purposes for which they were used exceedingly well. They are made of pieces of split bamboo and bamboo mats, and externally they are covered with bullock hides sewed together and stretched whilst moist over the bamboo frame-work, to which they are securely fastened. It is astonishing what weights these round boats will carry when they are new and well made. Guns, with their carriages, every kind of cart, besides men and animals, go safely across deep and broad rivers. This, however, we did not practically know till the next morning, when, in obedience to orders, the regiment crossed the Kistnah on these primitive machines, and without difficulty or accident.

On the day before the crossing was effected, a man was taken out of the very midst of the camp shortly before eight a.m., and that although everyone was on the alert and watchful, knowing that they were in near vicinity to high grass and jungles abounding with tigers, and bearing in mind, besides, the warnings which they had received on the two preceding nights. In consequence of this state of watchfulness, scarcely two minutes elapsed before a strong party of men and officers were in hot pursuit of the man-eater, aided by several dogs. The beast was, as heretofore, almost immediately lost to sight, but the dogs showed the track the tiger had taken, so the men were able to continue the chase. The sagacity of the dogs in following up was very remarkable, either instructed by the experience of the two preceding nights or by their natural intelligence. Though following the scent continually, they were very careful not to go farther than a few yards in advance of their masters. seeming to be quite aware that they would be wholly unable to cope with the enemy they were in pursuit of. This prudence on their part was noticed by the men and the officers, and was encouraged by them.

Suddenly the dogs halted, barked, and uttered a plaintive cry ; the officers brought their rifles forward, but, not perceiving the tiger, they carefully walked forward, ready to fire on the instant. At this moment a Shikari called out that there was something on the road, and the next instant that it was the man who had been carried off. All then hastened up to him, and found him weltering in a pool of blood, which, on interrogating him, they found was not his own ; it was almost entirely that of the tiger. The poor fellow had been so shaken and exhausted that at first he could scarcely explain himself; however, a small dose of brandy, the sense of safety, and the encouragement he received from all round him, soon restored him sufficiently to enable him to explain how he had effected his marvellous escape. It further appeared, both by his own statement and that of the surgeon (who was one of those who had gone in pursuit), that though his side was torn and lacerated by the teeth of the beast, he had sustained no broken bones, nor, indeed, any actual injury.

His story was this: at first he was so stunned by the shock of the tiger's spring that he was hardly conscious of the grip that fastened on him, or of the spring which carried him out of the camp; his first feeling of consciousness informed him of his position, and that he was being rapidly carried along to be devoured at leisure. The prospect was so unpleasant that he bethought him whether there was any possible mode of extrication. He had his bayonet with him, having, when seized, just come off guard. This 'Koodah-ki-fuzzul sey,' as he said, put it into his head to attempt to get free. The skin and flesh of his left side was in the tiger's mouth, and his right hand and arm were free. With his hand he felt for the heart of the tiger, then slowly drawing his bayonet out, he placed the point of it between the animal's ribs, just opposite the beat. Having thus prepared matters, he drove in the point with his whole strength, and with such effect that the tiger, making a spring and a cry at the same time, let his prey fall, and after limping a step or two fell down, himself bleeding copiously. He, however, rallied so far as to be able to crawl on farther, but, added the little hero (a Sepoy, five feet one inch in height), 'I am certain he cannot go far.'

On hearing this, the pursuit was immediately resumed; the doctor, greatly to his annoyance, was ordered to remain by the side of the sepoy, who, as soon as a dhooly could be got, was carried in a sort of cradle back to the camp. His story was so wonderful, and his escape so extraordinary, that had not the doctor's orders been peremptory, the poor little fellow would have had no sleep all the night ; such numbers were anxious to see him, and to hear him repeat the narrative of his defeat of the ' burrah bhague.' Indeed, it is said that for a week after he was out of hospital he was still called on occasionally to tell the story.

The party who went after the wounded beast, by the aid of dogs, lanterns, flambeaus, and the stain of blood, soon tracked the foe (it was a female tigress) to a cave near at hand, where they found her dying, and three splendid little cubs about two months old, which they lost no time in taking possession of. They were very desirous of making acquaintance with the proprietor of the cave, but this gentleman, it would seem, was absent from home. His anxious friends spent an hour in searching for him, but without success. This probably was fortunate for them, as it was a very imprudent thing to search for such a customer by torchlight. The officer commanding, indeed, positively forbade any repetition of that kind of search, for which he properly thought the daylight was essential. One of the party, before they left the cave, gave the tigress a bullet, which put an end to her lingering struggles.

So far is simply Lieutenant B.'s story just as it was told to me ; but the sequel I can positively affirm to be true, from my own knowledge. When I landed at Madras in 18 – , the little hero of the tiger incident was on guard at the entrance of the Adjutant-General's Office in the fort, and was really the best show of the place. The little Sepoy who had come off victorious after being in the jaws of the tiger was the lion of the fort, and it was customary for every new-comer, to whom he was presented, to give him a rupee. Thus the little man reaped, independent of his pension, a revenue which, to him, was very considerable, and the Government was exempted, or conceived itself to be exempted, from making any special provision for him. What finally became of this wonderful small man I do not know. I suppose, in the language of a great conqueror of another race, *ivit ad plures*. 'The paths of glory lead but to the grave,' so sings the poet and the moralist; and probably poor little Ram Sing was no exception to the rule.

But we are digressing, and it is necessary to resume Lieutenant B.'s account of the *march*. The very word 'march,' while sitting by a comfortable fire in a nicely-carpeted room, is fearful. The getting up at one or two a.m.; those dreadful taps (striking the tent pegs), and the tents falling about one's ears—the whole is appalling—*horresco referens*—and yet, instead of the gout and other infirmities of age, how gladly would I face it over again, with the untold privations, fatigue, and sun superadded, could I but feel again the elasticity, the glow of health, youthful energy, courage, and confidence in my own strength and endurance, which I once possessed; but *nunquam retrorsum* is the banner of existence, and all must submit to it. I return, therefore, to Lieutenant B.'s account of the march of his regiment to the cantonment of Secunderabad. The only incident deserving of any notice during progress through this part of the Deccan was, on more than one occasion, a difficulty about supplies. Who was to blame no one could clearly make out, opposing statements being freely made use of; it was an old disputed responsibility, but there could be no dispute that the Sepoys suffered. They were reduced to short commons several times. On one occasion there were absolutely *no* supplies to be had when the men arrived on the encamping-ground. The poor fellows had already marched fourteen miles, and had done it well, reaching the ground before seven a.m. They had started at half-past two a.m., and were just congratulating themselves at having got over the march before the sun was very powerful. Their congratulation was, however, short-lived, as they soon learned from the quartermaster that they must go on to the next village, *i.e.*, another fourteen miles, to obtain food. The sun was then quite hot enough in all conscience, and to proceed another fourteen miles under progressively increasing heat was appalling ; but there was no help for it, the peril must be faced.

The officers at that time wore those horrid little forage-caps covered on line of march with black oilskin. To ride fourteen miles with such a covering to the head, under a burning sun, was infinitely worse than being exposed to the hottest fire. My informant, the doctor, assured me that if he had not devised a special defence he must have fallen from his horse from sunstoke. His plan was this : he arranged with the regimental puckally (that is, the man who attends with a bullock carrying two mushues, or bullock-hides, filled with water) to be always close at hand during the march. Nothing but this could have saved him. He utilized the mushues in this way : before starting on the second march he had taken out two towels, which the puckally kept constantly soaked with water. One, well-soaked, was placed under the forage-cap, and as soon as it got heated it was replaced by the other. All the officers resorted to the use of wet cloths, but no one carried out the plan so systematically as the doctor did, and he escaped as well as any of them, though he had previously suffered from sunstroke.

At last the second march was accomplished, but the men were so tired and exhausted that they had taken five hours and a half to do it, though they had performed the first fourteen miles in little more than four hours. Both men and officers were so dead-beat that, on reaching the ground, everyone wanted to throw himself down where he stood ; but necessary duties had to be attended to. Luckily some Bamans, Bunganies, as they were called, had halted at this stage, and readily supplied the men with the various grains they wanted ; and large mango-tops afforded shelter from the sun, and gradually food and rest were obtained. By-and-by palanquins, tents, and carts arrived, and the officers got better shelter and their usual food ; and as there was a halt for the next day, all things gradually fell into working order. On the morning after the halt, the march was re-sumed, and in a week the regiment reached the cantonment of Secunderabad.

To give a full account of the European mode of life in cantonment, even at the largest station, would scarcely repay any reader. The reveille, the parade, or sham-fight, the general's concluding remarks to the men and officers, the march home, the conversation on reaching the barracks, the disencumbrance of the war-paint, the chatty bath, break-fast, and the edifying chat respecting dogs, horses, guns, or billiards ; he must indeed be fond of pipe-clay who can be entertained by such things. And when the coffee and tea and toast, the eggs, the grilled moorgey (a sudden death, and accordingly as tough as need be), with the curry, chutnee, etc., have been discussed—as well as Ensign A.'s wonderful leap, or Captain B.'s splendid shot, or Major C.'s grand dis-play at the billiard match, have all been served up, and duly commented on ; or arrangements made for a shikar-party—nothing is left but to adjourn to the billiard-room. All this is the very embodiment of Shakespeare's twice-told tale, 'stale, flat, and unprofitable.' It is repeated at every station year after year, and it has besides been given in detail so well and so often in works of fiction relating to India,

that it would be no less foolish than impertinent to reproduce it here. The same may be said of the occupations of
the fairer half of the creation : wherever it may be, it is the
same thing—the morning exercise on horseback, the ball,
the breakfast, the toilet, the staying at home to receive
visitors, or going out to pay visits, the remarks on the last
party, or the one that is expected ; Mrs. W.'s dress, and Miss
L.'s good looks, Miss M.'s engagement, and a thousand
other topics of equally overpowering importance. These,
and the all-imperative duty of leaving cards for everyone,
which, if neglected, or even postponed, is an offence that
nothing can expiate, an offence never forgiven, and one
that has probably, in this land of the sun, produced
more quarrels, more heart-burning, and more bad feeling
than any other cause that can be named. Mrs. General
D. goes in her carriage to pay Mrs. Ensign Smith a visit,
and never omits to leave her card. Mrs. Captain G. goes
in her palanquin-coach to pay a visit to whom you please,
and scrupulously leaves her card. Mrs. Quartermaster
goes in her bullock-coach to visit the ladies of the regiment,
and never fails to leave cards wherever she stops. The
system is indeed so universal, and so well understood,
that even the bullocks themselves have adopted it, as all
those who know the habits of these animals can testify.
It is indeed a positive fact that, whenever the owner of
the coach stops at anyone's door, the polite creatures never
fail to leave a S.P.C.—strange, no doubt, but nevertheless
true.

The monotony of cantonment life is not unfrequently
varied, I regret to say, by scandals, and stories circulated to
the detriment of this or that lady. They may be true, or
they may be false, but as a rule there is generally some imprudence or want of due circumspection on the part of the
lady pointed at; and if her fault is of the most venial

nature, her female friends are sure to attribute the worst to her ; their own virtue is so pure and perfect that they cannot bear the remotest suspicion of the reverse in any of their friends. A curious and instructive instance of this noble, amiable, and highly moral disposition occurred at the house of Mrs. O'N. Lady G. entered just as a lady who had paid her a visit got up to leave. Mrs. O'N. offered Lady G. the seat her former visitor had vacated, which was refused in this way : ' Was not the person who left the room Mrs. S.?' 'Yes,' said the hostess. ' Then,' returned Lady G., ' pray give me any other chair.' Her wish was complied with, and she paid her visit without suffering the contamination she dreaded. When Lady G. departed Mrs. O'N. indulged in a hearty laugh, which she explained to another visitor by telling her of Lady G.'s horror at the thought of sitting on a chair that had been occupied by a questionable character. ' She was herself so chaste, my dear,' said Mrs. O'N., ' that she couldn't bear the idea of anything of that kind.'

Scandal runs riot in all small societies, and therefore perhaps the scandals in Indian cantonments are, to a certain extent, merely *en règle*. But at the same time it must not be forgotten that after breakfast, for several hours, both sexes have nothing to do. The ladies dress and receive visitors as often as not when their husbands are away on shikar parties, or are amusing themselves at the billiard-table. These morning visits are sanctioned by custom. But in India they are not altogether without danger. First, both sexes, when they mingle in society, have nothing to occupy or amuse them but philandering, *i.e.*, paying compliments or listening to them ; and this, though innocent enough, it may be, in the beginning, is by no means so when often repeated by the same individuals. ' What a nice little creature Mrs. So-and-so is ; I wonder how Captain B. can occupy himself so much away from home ; he is always away on some shikar party, or at the billiard-room, or at the racquet-court, or on duty, or attending court-martial duty. I know if she was my wife I wouldn't leave her to herself or to others as —— does.' By-and-by something of this oozes out, and then there is a laugh, the young gentleman is roasted by his male friends in a gentle, or even an encouraging way. Something perhaps like the following will occur :

'What, Jack, are you getting spoony about Mrs. B.? She is an enticing creature, I must confess; but take care of B.: if he finds out that you're too sweet with his wife, he'll have you out as sure as fate.' 'Oh! I don't fear B.'s turning rusty; he knows very well I often make morning calls, and he often invites me to dinner.' 'The more fool he, especially as he leaves the lady at home so much.' 'I'll tell you what it is,' says another of these young philanderers, 'if a fellow won't stay at home to look after his own property, he must expect that other fellows will try and supply his absence. I know I should be dooced glad if the chance was mine.' And really you can't blame the petticoat much if she shows that she likes the attentions of one who gives her to understand, in every way he can, how he adores her and worships her, etc. ; and though he may be only leading her into what is called a 'fools' paradise,' she doesn't know that until it is too late and she has disgraced herself, thrown away her good name, and made a serious scandal; or she is sent home and a divorce is obtained, or the husband calls out the Lothario and shoots him, or gets shot himself.

I have in my experience known a young gentleman pray heartily that the injured man would call him out, as then, being a good shot, he should certainly hit him, and in all probability put him out of the way, which would make all things smooth for him and Emma. These and unnumbered other results, more or less serious, arise from the want of occupation and the system of calling.

It is a saying as old as the hills, that a very prying inquisitive old gentleman always finds work for idle hands, and certainly Indian experience does not discredit the truth of it. The kind of morality that obtains in these matters amongst young men in general is not very exalted, whatever vocation or profession they follow, and amongst army men it is proverbially not very strict. I might put it the other way, but let it pass ; they have a great deal more idle time than most other young men, therefore, according to the postulate above given, they are more likely to do wrong. Well, an idle young fellow pays a young married lady a morning visit ; she may be very attractive both in manner and in person ; she may possess a pretty face, may possess much intelligence, and may be an accomplished musician, may ride and dance well ; and if she possesses these various attractions, or some of them, is it natural that an inconsiderate young fellow, who may also be clever, good-looking, gentleman-like, and withal a finely-figured man, one who may also be a vocalist, and a good dancer—is it natural, I say, that these two young people should spend an hour together without being more or less prepossessed in each other's favour ? This result is inevitable ; the gentleman soon repeats his visit, he admires the lady more than before, and does not fail to let her see it ; she, on the other hand, begins to think that Lieutenant —— is really a very pleasant and agreeable young man. So much being admitted, the frequent repetition of these morning calls, and perhaps some invitations to tiffin, or dinner, or to spend the evening, from the husband, who, all unsuspicious of mischief and danger, instead of being displeased, is rather proud that other men admire his wife, lead up to a footing of great intimacy. This, again, leads to morning rides, to engage-

ments for partnership at dances, and to every kind of em-
ployment or pastime wherein the parties can be coupled
together. This stage in the affair naturally excites the observation of the bystanders, the lookers-on, and they not
only take note of the intimacy between Mrs. —— and Mr. So-
and-so, but without more ado set down Mrs. So-and-so not
as guilty of imprudence, and the indulgence of a little
vanity, but of an improper and disgraceful intimacy, which
up to this time has perhaps never been thought of, at all
events has not been yielded to. Thus the lady, being at
this time innocent, is rendered indignant, violent, and to
some extent reckless, at being falsely accused, and she, in
consequence of this state of feeling, unwisely and perversely
argues thus : 'Oh ! if society chooses to accuse and condemn me for nothing, what does its opinion signify ?   I
am sure I am not going to give up my friends to please
society.   I have done nothing wrong, and I am not going
to do anything wrong.'   And perhaps she means what
she says, and really thinks she has done nothing wrong,
and perhaps truly means that she does not intend to do
wrong ; which, being expressed in plain English, means that
she does not intend to commit adultery ; and she may
honestly mean to keep her word.   Her really doing so is
quite a different thing.   After she has overstepped all the
barriers, or almost all, that society, etiquette, and high moral
feeling have established to restrain the intimacy between
the opposite sexes, it is very questionable whether a lady
has it in her power to say to herself : 'Thus far shalt thou
go and no further.'   From the hour that she admitted any
exceptional degree of intimacy, from that hour she has
placed herself on an inclined plane, and the further she de-
scends on it the greater is the difficulty for her to draw back.
In the very large majority of such cases, the truth of the
French axiom is made painfully manifest : *C'est le premier*

pas qui coute, and in those few cases where shame does not succeed to such intimacies, the escape is due to accidental causes.   These appear to me to be simply the teachings of experience; but it would be altogether one-sided not to add that men, who, from unbounded reliance on the virtue of their wives, permit any continued attentions (however harmless) from any other man, are in a great measure responsible for the consequences.   Nor should they leave their wives too much to themselves; if they do, other men will endeavour to step into their places, and it is a husband's duty to protect his wife against such endeavours.   There are, no doubt, cases which of necessity involve long and continued absence.   Military and naval men are specially exposed to these risks when on active service.   In these cases the lady's honour, principle, and sense of religion should be her defence.   In cases in which, from duty, office-work, or business, the husband is absent during the day, the lady should be able, if she is honest and true, to defend herself.

But these exceptions give no just warrant for a married man to go alone for weeks or months on tours of pleasure, of sport in distant lands, or fishing in distant seas, and, for such reasons, to leave a young wife without protection; nor are unhappy cases wanting to show the bitter fruits of such neglect.

Details of any intimacies such as those referred to here will scarcely prove interesting to the majority of readers, and if they were, my pen would feel too much disgust and sorrow to become the means of chronicling such unhappy doings.   Neither do I think that the ordinary humdrum details of Indian life in cantonment would repay perusal. I therefore say nothing of the sensation created in the cantonment of Secunderabad by the arrival of Mrs. ——'s new dress, made in the latest mode by the French milliner at Madras, nor of the new carriage that reached its destination but last week from Simpson's for the Colonel's wife, nor of the pretty Arab that Captain S. sent down from Bombay for his wife. All, no doubt, tremendously important and absorbing events to those concerned, but not quite so much so to the general reader.

The only event that I will chronicle is Captain W.'s persevering and ultimately successful search for a man-eating tiger. All those who have been at Secunderabad know that there is a clump or collection of the ordinary gneiss rocks about a mile and a half from the cantonment, and on the opposite side to that on which the Hussain Sanger Tank is situated. These rocks have, time out of mind, been famed and feared by the natives as the abode of tigers; and sporting men, when stationed here, have, at different times, made raids, or shikar parties, with the view of destroying or driving away these deadly tenants of the rock-built towers and caves that Nature had made ready for them. The effects of these efforts, however successful for the time, have never been very long continued. Occasionally a royal beast has been killed by some lucky or well aimed bullet, and sometimes some of the beaters have been carried off in spite of numbers, guns, and determined foe-men, and sometimes the beast and his family relinquished for a time their chosen lair; but ordinarily, unless some sporting men were at hand, a sort of compact or sufferance on the part of the natives existed, much after this fashion. At one time a native riot, or cultivator, lost a bullock, or a sheep, or a donkey; another time some other person lost one of such animals, or tatoos, and on a third occasion some other individual was the sufferer, and so on. As the injury was, as it were, distributed with something like equality, and as they did not, generally speaking, suffer in their own persons, they began to look on the infliction as a sort of necessary evil; it was their fate, their 'hickmut,' 'ickbal,' etc., and they bore it patiently, and with resignation. Indeed, so long as they were not themselves devoured, they rarely made any exertion to rid themselves of their enemy.

This passive state of affairs, however, only lasted so long as the striped gentleman kept his paws off human victims. If by dint of hunger or failure of other prey, he chanced to get the taste of human flesh, the fastidious beast would never, if he could get it, feed on any other. At first the villagers round about were struck with terror and grief. After the first man had been taken, not many days passed before another was carried off, and so on till fourteen had been seized and made away with. The poor people were in great dismay; they had made two attempts, by setting baits, and watching at night, to slay the marauder, but without avail. The baits were taken, but the wounds inflicted by the men were not, so it appeared, much thought of by the tiger, for he bounded off with his prey in spite of them. The villagers were in despair; they did not dare to go into the fields, or scarcely to appear outside their doors. All sorts of sacrifices were made to Muniah, and donations to the Fakeers and Brahmins, but nothing availed.

At last reports of the distress of the villagers reached the ears of the men of the M.N.I., and these mentioned them to their officers. The very next day a strong party of sportsmen and beaters set out for the rocks before mentioned. Besides Captain W., there were four crack ball-shots amongst the sportsmen, so that it was thought the fate of Mr. Burrah Bhague was tolerably certain, but in spite of the most careful and indefatigable search no tiger could be found.

A couple of hours had been spent in the search, and it was burning hot, so it was agreed that the whole party should adjourn for a couple of hours to the mess-tent, which had been pitched in the Maidan a few hundred yards off, to rest and refresh themselves. The effects of cold water, soda-water, dashed, I must admit, with some fire-water, along with sundry cheroots, together with the shade and shelter from the terrific sun, soon restored the eyes and steadied the hands of the hunters, and as the man-eating gentleman seemed to have left his accustomed haunts, it was agreed to proceed some three miles farther, where there was another aggregation of rocks. The ghorrey wallehs were then called for, and soon led the various tatoos to their several masters, who, on reaching the second pile of rocks, at once dismounted, and after looking at their caps, proceeded to make the necessary arrangements for inspecting the new pile of rocks with care and caution.

Without troubling the reader with these details, it will be enough to say that every precaution which skill and experience could dictate was employed, but still without finding any beast. More than three hours had been spent in this second search ; everyone was now greatly fatigued, and beaten by the sun, therefore at last they agreed to relinquish the search for that day, vexed and disappointed though they were. In remounting their ponies, a sullen silence weighed on the spirits and the tongue of everyone. How different to the volatile chatter and chaff that everyone indulged in at starting ! The cheerful jest and saucy jibe of the morning, the uproarious and hearty laugh, were all hushed, and but a few gruff words were heard now and then. The only business of the entire party seemed to be to smoke and to meditate.

As they again approached the rocks first examined, Captain W. proposed that they should try again by making another examination, but he got no one to second his proposition ; they were all so sunned and so tired, that all declined to do anything more that day. 'So be it,' said W

' You're lazy fellows ; go home, and I'll go by myself, and have another look for our shy friend. I'm certain he's there, though where I can't imagine. There's one peak that I didn't climb up, because I couldn't conceive that it led to anything; but it may, and 1 shall certainly examine it before I go home.' ' Oh, don't, Godfrey !' exclaimed his friends ; ' for God's sake, don't ! We're all so done up that we're fit for nothing.' ' My eyes are so dazed by the glare,' said B., ' that I couldn't see the beast, I verily believe, if he was standing a few yards before me.' ' Well, Master Frank, if you are in the happy condition you describe, whose fault is it ? If you will empty your own flask, and then borrow mine, which I perceive is now empty also, how can you expect to see ?' This smart rally from W. raised the laugh against B., who, though a most ready-witted fellow, had drunk so much that he couldn't say anything in reply. ' Don't go, Godfrey,' said poor Bob M., ' don't go. We're all so tired, that we really should be of little use.' ' Oh,' returned W., ' you're quite right ; much better stay away. How do I know with that inflamed visage of yours that you would not take me for the tiger ? No, no, Bobby ; you've been too deeply associated with B., and have paid too much attention to his flask and your own to permit me to trust you.' Bob replied : ' Nonsense ! I can see very well. Don't go. Upon my life, in such a place as that, to go alone is simply to throw your life away. I say again, for God's sake, don't go ! We're none of us in a fit state to give proper help, and we can't let you go by yourself. Besides, it's unkind and unfriendly of you to undertake the thing single-handed, and thus to leave us out of it. Don't think of it, Godfrey, for to-day; we'll all be at your command to-morrow, or any other day you please.'

The other sportsmen, S. and C., said the same. C., who was a very experienced and successful tiger-shot, again pointed out the great and needless risk W. would run if, under such extraordinary disadvantages, he would alone go amongst the rocks, wherefrom, on any side, above or below, the beast might spring on him before a glimpse had been seen of it. All was to no purpose. W. was convinced that the animal was concealed somewhere in the rocks before them, and that in the morning he had omitted to search that particular peak he had spoken of, so nothing would content him till he had made a fresh search. Almost with the objurgations of his friends he went solus up the rocks again. His friends, though at that time not game, or rather too done up, to follow him, could not bear to leave him in a situation of such difficulty and danger. They halted under the shade of a few tamarind-trees near at hand, waiting in great anxiety for W.'s return, or for some signal from him. Some sat on their ponies, others dismounted, and made their boys spread mats for them with camblies, or anything that might serve for an extempore pillow. But, however they disposed of themselves, their tongues were not idle, and all were agreed that W.'s going up the rocks by himself was egregious folly, and that he was as determined and obstinate as he was foolhardy in doing it. W. was such a favourite that the great risk he was needlessly running made some very angry; some were in great fear and excitement, and some had called for water, and were bathing their heads, washing their eyes, etc., in order to go after him, being unable to endure any longer the painful suspense they were suffering.

M., C. and S. were just beginning to move towards the rocks when their footsteps were arrested by the sharp crack of a rifle, instantly followed by the roar of a tiger. 'My God! it's all over with poor Godfrey!' exclaimed M. 'I feared it would be so,' said S. 'Let's get forward,' said C. ; 'we may not be too late to help. It was up this rock he went.' All were scrambling up, keeping their guns ready for instant use, when bang went another rifle-shot. 'That sounds healthy,' said M. 'Oh, it's grand!' said C.; 'you may depend on it he has found and killed.' 'On my honour,' said S., 'it's almost too good, too glorious, to be true.' Then arose shouts for Godfrey, and 'Where are you; how can we get at you?'

By this time some of the natives had found out where W. was, and then confused cries of 'Saib Ateha hi, hither owe! is turrup sey, hither owe! hither owe! Bhague murgia, koodah ki fuzzul sey, Saib my mana,' and many other cries and utterances and exclamations crowded on the ears of those who had lately been in such painful anxiety that they could bear it no longer. By-and-by W. was seen descending by a path so difficult and dangerous that it was hard to say whether the tiger or the pathway were the more so. At last he achieved his descent without broken bones, and could converse with his friends, who at once overwhelmed him with questions and inquiries. He was not hurt? No; he had not got a scratch! 'How was it? How did you find the beast?' 'It was just as I suspected. That rock which we neglected to examine this morning led to the beast's fortress. When I had climbed to the top of it, I found that there was a vast chasm between the rock on which I stood and all the surrounding rocks. I also observed that there was a ledge jutting out some two and a half feet from the body of the rock about twelve feet below me. This ledge ran along the face of the rock for some thirty yards, and then gradually descended on the left side from where I stood. From the sight of some half-gnawed bones that lay on the ledge nearly in a perpendicular line below me, I suspected that my friend's dwelling could not be far off, but how to let myself down puzzled me for a time. The precipice went down from the ledge probably near a hundred feet. I did not, therefore, like to risk a jump, lest I should lose my balance after landing on the ledge. I could let down my gun by means of my shot-belt and some twine I had about me, but I did not see how to let myself down so that I could be sure of keeping my balance. I walked from one end of the top of the ridge to the other, and thus found that at one part of it I could get down nearer to the ledge by two feet, and that by hanging from that part of the ridge I should only have two feet to drop. Having made these observations, I gently let down my gun, so that it rested on the ledge upright against the ridge. I then got down as far as possible, and afterwards dropped on to the ledge as gently as I could. On reaching the ledge I instantly seized and disembarrassed my gun. Two paces to the right brought me in front of a large and deep cave, formed in the body of the main rock, at the bottom of which I saw two balls of fire. I aimed just between them and fired. My shot was a very lucky one, as it hit the beast so hard that on attempting to spring he fell down almost at my feet. Could he have sprung, I must have been dashed to pieces by being knocked down the precipice. Finding that the animal was not quite dead, I gave him the other barrel, which was the second shot you heard.'

As soon as he had finished his explanation, he was so overwhelmed with laudation and congratulation of all kinds that he said : 'Come, let us think of getting home, and to do that we must get hold of the carcase of the cat, and we must take his measure before we take off his coat.' 'What a queer customer he is !' said B., who had from excitement and the persevering use of chatties of cold water in some degree recovered himself. 'Most fellows have their coats off before they begin to fight; this chap waits till the fight is over.' 'What! you've found your tongue, have you,

Frank?' said W. 'I thought you were too far gone to have eyes or ears for anything.' 'Not a bit of it,' returned B.; 'I must have been dead drunk, indeed, if I had not heard the row that poor beggar up yonder kicked up when your messenger made him give tongue. But, by Jove! here he comes! What fellows these natives are! They have not taken ten minutes to sling the beast on bamboos, to get him out of his dark mansion, and to bring him down here.' This explained the tom-toms and songs and music, as well as the crowd of Sepoys and beaters and villagers that was now advancing from the rocks, bearing in triumph, and in a sort of procession, the enemy that had lately been so dreaded far and near. The tiger, an immense creature, was borne along slung by all fours to a bamboo carried at least by twenty men, for every villager tried hard, if only for a yard or two, to have a hand in carrying his enemy, not only to ensure future good luck, but to triumph over him. With all the sounds of rejoicing described the crowd brought the tiger, and laid him at W.'s feet. 'Ram Sing' (the naigue of his company), said W., 'how did you manage to get the beast here so quickly?' 'Oh, sir, we were all ready; we had bamboos, and ropes, and ladders all prepared, and plenty of willing hands anxious to do anything I told them.' 'Oh, that was it, was it?' said W. 'Well, my men have been wonderfully speedy. I'll reward them by-and-by; but now we must take the dimensions of our quondam friend.' 'But, sir, the villagers want leave to speak, if you will allow them.' 'Well, let them say their say, if they will promise not to make it long.'

Accordingly, the head men of the several villages which had lost inhabitants from the man-eater came forward, accompanied by the surviving relatives of those who had been carried off. These poor people, many of them with tears in their eyes, came and threw themselves at W.'s feet anxious to touch his garments or kiss his shoes. In their untaught and simple way they made poojah to him, *i.e.*, they literally worshipped him as a superior being, and implored their deities to shower blessings on the brave Ingrasy Sahib who had rescued them and theirs from the fangs of the devourer. 'Well, that's enough,' said W. ; 'you had better get up, now.' ' But,' replied the head men, ' we have not yet done what we came to do—we have a bag of 500 Rs. that we beg the Captain Sahib will take from us ; it is contributed jointly by all the villages that have suffered.' W. knew well the general poverty of the villages, and being wholly unprepared for any such unusual demonstration from the natives, was for a moment thrown off his equanimity. He walked away a few yards, and it was observed that his eyes were moist, but he soon recovered his ordinary quiet and unmoved demeanour. Then, turning to the people kneeling and prostrate about him, he said, speaking Hindustani fluently : ' My good friends, for what I have done I am amply repaid in the consciousness of having delivered you from your enemy ; besides, the search for large game is to a British officer and a sportsman a very great pleasure, and he would feel himself dishonoured if he accepted money or presents for anything he might do as a sportsman. Do not, my friends, suppose that it is from pride that I do not accept your bag of rupees ; I feel grateful to you for the kindness shown in the offer, and to show my sense of it will accept from each of the villages that have suffered a pair of doves or quails. But as to money, that is out of the question. On the other hand, I am debtor to you all for the assistance and information you rendered me in the beginning in tracking and beating, and now in bringing down, the dead beast. I have ordered my head boy to pay to each of the villages 15 Rs. All I want you now to do is to lay the carcase straight, that we may

measure the exact length from the nose to the tip of the
tail' (which was found to be nine feet and nine inches—a
grand specimen).   And when this had been done, he said :
' Now all I have to ask is that you will help Ram Sing to
take off the skin.   Ram Sing knows all about that.'

When W. had finished speaking, the natives one and all
again broke out into pæans of praise in behalf of their
deliverer, so extravagant, indeed, judged by our notions,
that W. was scandalized, or, if not, he feared ridicule ; so he
gave orders to his head boy to take them away, and to his
friends he said, ' Come, let's get home ; I am not a little
hungry, and trust they've kept something at the mess for
us, which I shall attack, as soon as I've had a bath, with
as much ferocity as ever our dead friend his choice food.'
' We all say ditto to that, and God help the mess butler if
he doesn't show to-day in good form, for he'll find us on
this occasion all tigers.'

W., in his extreme modesty, had sought to avoid the
triumphal parade of bringing the tiger into the cantonment,
and had therefore given the orders already mentioned.
But his intended curtailment of the public triumph did not
at all suit Ram Sing, or any of the natives, Sepoys, beaters,
or villagers, in any way connected with the deed.   They
could not comprehend the doing a noble and daring action
with the wish to say and make as little as possible of it.
They therefore determined, whether W. liked it or not, that
he should have a public ovation ; and, accordingly, they
entered the cantonment in grand procession, with lights
and torches and drums, tom-toms, horns, trumpets, and
all sorts of heterogeneous instruments, making a most
infernal row and outrageous discords, in the centre of an
immense concourse of people, bearing along the tiger, singing songs, setting forth Burrah Bhague's evil deeds, describing his conqueror as nothing less than Rustum, giving the

attributes of a demigod to him, and describing his skill and
courage as invincible and irresistible ; these hymns of praise
they assisted with all the noises they could bring together,
not forgetting squibs, crackers, rockets, and all the fireworks
they could procure. In this way they paraded through the
whole cantonment, partly back again, till they reached the
compound of the mess-house of the regiment. There, to
W.'s intense disgust, they would have recommenced their
tom-toms and their music, with fireworks and songs, but W.
ordered them at once out of the cantonment. 'Confound
the rascals !' said W. 'I shouldn't wonder if they set fire
to the lines with their d——d folly.' W.'s indignation
amused his friends amazingly. They exclaimed against his
severity in this way : 'You, the hero of the day, the Roastum,
ought to sympathize with the poor devils, and not be so
irate with them for doing you honour in their own way.'
'The deuce take them ! I wish they'd keep their honour
and their d——d noise to themselves ! If I had allowed
them to remain in the cantonment, I shouldn't have had a
wink of sleep all night long, besides the shame of having
my name connected with their absurd proceedings. I declare I am sorry I told Saul Jaker to give them any money ;
perhaps he'll give them more than he ought to-night, and
then the great majority of them will drink too much rack.'
'Well,' said B., 'if they do once in a way, it's a poor heart
that never rejoices.' 'Quite true,' said W. ; 'but sometimes the hearts that are not poor rejoice so much that they
are not able to help their friends, however great the need
of help may be.' 'Oh, Godfrey, that's a shame, to cast a
fellow's misdeeds up to him in that way !' 'Why, then, do
you take the part of such a noisy set of rascals as those
yonder ? Thank God, I can scarcely hear them now, so
I'll go to bed, and wish you all good-night.'

Many years after, W. arrived at the French Rock, and

was staying there for a day or two as a guest of the mess, being *en route* to Bangalore. There was at the same time a young lad, whom I shall call Gascoigne, who had but lately arrived from England. He had brought a letter of introduction to W. from some of his friends at home. The young gentleman, a studious and quiet lad, was, in consequence, putting up with W., who, as hospitable and kindly disposed as any man in the world, welcomed the youth cordially, and was, by shikar parties, and every other means in his power, trying to entertain him. On W.'s account, everyone in the regiment did the same. Young G. had besides, as a pretty horseman, and an excellently good shot for so young a man, won the hearts of most of the young men of the regiment. He came from one of the Midland counties famous for hunting and sporting, and was therefore quite at home.

After dinner one unfortunate evening, when all the men of the regiment and the two guests mentioned were sitting outside in front of the mess-house, with their teapoys, their cheroots, and their eternal brandy-pawny, the conversation turned on the different styles of horsemanship. The young stranger spoke rather in ridicule of the cavalry seat and the long stirrups it enjoins, and he wondered how anyone could possibly ride across country with them. His remarks produced some sharp replies from B., the cavalry man present. 'Well, G.,' said W. to his friend, 'although you and I prefer the short stirrup and the usual cross-country seat, others ride well and strongly with the long stirrup. Our friend B. here rides with a long stirrup, and few men ride better than he does.'

By such kind and judicious observations W. threw oil on the troubled waters, and for the time stopped any further unpleasant remarks; but he could not, on the part at least of B., do away with the irritation that had been caused by young G.'s observations, and the remembrance of them rankled in this officer's mind. However, W. turned the attention of the party to other matters, and all seemed smooth. After a time he said, 'Come, let's have an all-round rupee shot at that weathercock on the top of the school-room; the first man that hits it carries the pool, and we'll draw lots for the order of firing.' 'Agreed, agreed!' said all present. 'I'll hold the stakes,' said Colonel D., 'as I don't intend to compete.'

Accordingly the firing commenced, and great was the laughing and the chatter as the whole party one after the other missed the weathercock. 'I should have hit the confounded thing,' said B., 'but just as I fired the wind swirled it round, so that I lost my chance.' 'Well, never mind, you haven't lost your stake, and you can try again,' said the Colonel.

Accordingly a second stake was placed in the Colonel's hands, and the competitors fired all round a second time. Young G. claimed a hit, but almost at the instant he fired B. followed, and he said, 'Come, make me a bow, youngster, for wiping your eye.' 'I would with the greatest pleasure,' replied G., 'if you had done it; but my shot was a hit before you fired.' 'I deny it,' said B., 'and I claim the pool.' 'This cannot be determined by individual opinions,' said W. 'What does the Colonel say?' 'I really cannot say whose shot the hit was, as at the moment I had taken a pinch of snuff and was using my handkerchief.' 'This is unfortunate,' said W.; 'we must take the votes of all present.'

B. made some grumbling remark that was not audible, but he said nothing in direct opposition to W.'s proposition. The votes were then taken, and it appeared that the party were not agreed as to whose the winning shot was. Some were not watching, and of those who were, three

5

were on B.'s side, and four on G.'s. There was a great
deal of talking, and as the talking increased the excitement
increased. W., who seemed to have a presentiment of the
evil that was coming, exerted himself to the utmost to prevent mischief, by making proposition after proposition in
order to put an end to the dispute, but without avail. He
believed that his young friend had made the hit, and gave
his vote accordingly, which, strictly speaking, should have
decided the question, as it gave G. a majority ; but this W.
declined to insist upon. He wished that the two claimants
should divide the pool, but this neither would consent to.
Thus all his efforts to put out the fire were unavailing, and
accordingly, as one word drew on another, it burst out in
this way :

'Do you assert,' said Captain B. to G., 'that the shot
which struck the weathercock was yours?' 'Yes, I do,' said
the youngster, 'because I believe it was mine.' 'Then,'
replied B., 'you lie !' Before G. could speak, W. said to
B., 'If you say that the shot was *yours*, it is you that lie !'
Instantly B. got up and rushed at W., who remained calmly
seated. He warded off the blow aimed at his head by B.,
and said, 'That will do, B. ; I understand you, and I will
not disappoint you.' At gun-fire the next morning these
two men stood opposite to each other at twelve paces. At
the first exchange of shots W.'s cap was shot through, and
the buckle of B.'s waist-belt was cut away, but neither party
sustained any personal injury. The second shots were both
misses, neither party being touched. The third exchange
of fire were both hits, but still only coats and buttons
suffered. Both men were desirous to have another exchange of fire, but their seconds refused to allow the matter
to proceed ; they added, that unless their principals chose
to go into the jungle by themselves, they would not permit
another shot to be fired.

The two men still remained on the ground dissatisfied, nor did they move until Colonel D. made his appearance. He had been made cognizant of what had been done, and all he said as he rode on to the ground was this : 'Gentlemen, any attempt to carry this further places both of you in arrest. Both of you know me ; good-morning. Adjutant, you will see my orders strictly carried out, and tell Captain B. that he has my orders to proceed on his road within an hour.'

Young G., who was a plucky young fellow, though, as W. knew, wholly unacquainted with the use of the pistol, had been almost in a state of frenzy throughout the business. He swore he would follow B. and have him out wherever he could find him, till W. got him to calm down, and Colonel D. explained to him that he must place him in arrest and report him to the General commanding the division, if he did not give him his word of honour not to stir further in the matter. At first the young lad refused to pledge himself as required, but his refusal was as respectful as it was manly. His words were : ' How can I do that, sir? I have been called a liar publicly ; surely no one who has the honour to bear her Majesty's commission can put up with that ! and besides, the life of a valued and respected friend has, from his chivalrous generosity, been placed in danger to shield me, which, though I am deeply grateful for it, makes me blush, and places me in rather a humiliating position. It's no use for you, Godfrey, to shake your head and deny it. I know perfectly well why you anticipated me.'

He had in the few days he had been with W. learned to regard him as an elder brother, and, by his own request, to address him as the others did. W. and the Colonel looked at one another as young Gascoigne spoke, and when he had finished the Colonel said : ' The words you have spoken and the sentiments they convey do you credit, Mr. G., but you mistake if you suppose that either I or your friend Godfrey wish you to put up tamely with the gross insult that has been offered to you. I will obtain for you from Captain B. a proper apology, and at the same time I will take care that it is publicly known that I only obtained your promise to proceed no further in this matter on this assurance.' 'Well, sir, as you take so kind an interest in my good name, and will undertake to let it be known that there was the strongest wish on my part to right myself in the way that is usual amongst gentlemen, I will give you my word to do nothing more, especially as I see that Godfrey wishes me to do so.' 'That's a sensible lad,' said the Colonel ; and Godfrey added, 'Yes, I do wish it ; and you may rest assured that I should not do so were I not sure that your good name is perfectly safe in Colonel D.'s hands, who has acted on this occasion as he always acts.' 'Godfrey ! Godfrey !' said Colonel D., ' I shall have to arrest your body, to arrest your tongue !' 'Well, that is hard,' returned W., laughing. 'This is the second time in one morning that I have been threatened with arrest by you.' 'All your own fault,' returned the Colonel, smiling. ' I must do my duty and obey the orders of the service, though other people choose to set a bad example and do otherwise.' 'There,' said W., 'you see, G., what military service is : you are liable to get it on both sides of the face before you can turn round.' 'Well,' said G., 'if this is getting it on both sides of the face, I trust that my commandant will be like Colonel D. ; but that's too much good luck to expect.' Colonel D. again laughed, and said, 'You've got too much talk, young man,' though he was evidently pleased with the compliment. 'You've been in Ireland, I fancy.' 'No, I haven't, Colonel,' replied young G. ; 'but I should like very much to go there, for a time at least.' 'I don't think,' said Colonel D., turning to W., 'that your young friend has any great need to go there to learn one of the accomplishments said to be in fashion there.'

So the three adjourned in high good humour with all the world to the parade ground, where a coursing match was to come off between two famous dogs. I will spare the reader a description of the beautiful form of these two canine heroes; it is enough to say that they were marvellously fine greyhounds, and that they killed in the most approved fashion, in spite of all the efforts and doubles of the poor hares. I must further confess that I was much more interested for these harmless creatures than I was for the dogs, though I dare say their performance was matchless in its way; so, at least, it was on all hands pronounced to be. I sank many degrees in the estimation of my regimental friends, I believe, for expressing unreservedly this opinion. The young lads could not understand how any man, even a doctor, could feel no interest in the performance of two such magnificent dogs as Juno and Jupiter. I admitted the merits and beauties of their canine friends— indeed, no one could admire them more than I did. Still, I could not enter into their feelings, nor share in their delight at seeing the hares writhing in agony in the fangs of Jupiter or Juno.

'You don't like fishing, you say, and we see you don't like coursing. What do you like?' 'To hunt the fox, or the jackal, or the wolf, I should think glorious sport.' 'Then,' said M., 'why don't you go out with us in the morning? Whenever we can get a chance we go after jackals. Foxes are rare, and wolves never let us get within rifle distance.' 'Besides,' said S., 'we can't afford to knock our horses off their legs, which we should do if we tried to run down those brutes so as to get within shot.' 'You know,' returned I, 'that in the morning I am not my own master. I have my hospital to attend, my patients to visit and prescribe for, to enter all cases in the journal and case-book, as well as to see that all other hospital books are kept up to date. Perhaps my superintending surgeon might not be altogether pleased if he heard (and these things do travel in an extraordinary way) that I postponed my visit to the hospital till after I had had my run with the dogs ; and perhaps the Colonel might not altogether approve of my setting at naught the standing orders of the service, and before his face too.' 'You are quite right,' said W., 'you may rest assured that the Colonel would not approve of any such thing ; indeed, he could not.' 'What's that, W., that the Colonel wouldn't and couldn't do ?' said Colonel D., who, as he came up, had overheard the last part of W.'s remarks. These were explained to him, and what led to them. His comment was, ' Boys will be boys. The Doctor has acted perfectly right ; he could not ride with us in the morning, as the standing orders lay it down precisely that he shall visit his hospital at certain hours, and these would, if we found anything, be just the hours when we should be at the best of the chase ; and if he wished ever so much to join us I should not allow him to do so, and W. is quite correct in what he said.' This settled the question, and took away any distant hope I might indulge that the Colonel might now and then take no notice of any infraction of the standing orders as to the time of visiting the hospital. I departed, sorrowing that fate had destined me to be medical instead of military purely.

The subject of sport was, with my young friends especially, a never-ending one, constantly renewed, and still beginning. On my return from Bangalore, to which place I was called under circumstances so peculiar that I think the recital will repay perusal, although they necessitate a digression, and have nothing to do with sport, which is at present my legitimate theme, the possibility of my joining in the sporting was again introduced.

On account of the marriage of her brother's wife's sister, Miss S., my wife had gone to Bangalore and was to return to the F. Rocks in a few days. I was, in fact, anxiously looking for a letter to say on what day I might expect her. Instead of this. I received from her brother a communication stating that it was his and the Garrison-surgeon's opinion that if I wanted to see her again alive, I must start with the least possible delay for Bangalore. With tears in my eyes, and this letter in my hand, I went at once to Colonel D., who in the kindest way took on himself the responsibility of giving me permission to go. At the time, very luckily, there were no sick of any importance—some slight cases of fever, and some chronic cases there were in hospital which the dresser could treat. No officers sick, no children—I mean European children—sick or well, in the cantonment, and no lady, except Mrs. G., who had but lately been married, and was in perfect health. But the F. Rocks was a single station, and if any accident occurred, or sudden sickness broke out, no medical officer was to be had nearer than Bangalore. For at this time there was no Durbar surgeon at Mysore, fifteen miles off, and the dwelling-place of the Rajah. These circumstances being considered, to let me leave the cantonment was really taking on himself a serious responsibility which the General himself declined to incur. Bangalore was 87 miles from the F. Rocks, and the question was how to get there in the shortest time. Here was seen the brotherly feeling cherished in this regiment. I had no sooner made known my difficulty than almost every man of those present offered me his horses. I had two of my own, which I sent on, so that the one was to halt twenty miles from the station, the second forty; of the borrowed horses, one was to go with me the first twenty miles. With this help I started a little before gun-fire, and reached Bangalore about 4 p.m., and found that there was no need for anxiety; my wife had suffered from a severe hysterical attack, and was well enough to ride out that very evening. I was too much delighted at the condition in which I found her to find fault with a mistake which had in the end given me so much pleasure. The next morning I waited on the General, and the dialogue that took place was so peculiar that I shall endeavour to present it to my readers in its integrity, so far as my memory will allow me.

'Good-morning, General. I trust you will be kind enough to excuse the absence of the proper costume, as I had no time to put in any change of dress, I came off in such a hurry, General.' 'And where have you come from, sir?' 'From the F. Rocks, General G.' 'From the F. Rocks? Who gave you leave?' 'Colonel D., my commandant, General.' 'He gave you leave, did he? He has no power to do so.' 'I am here, General, to explain the circumstances.' 'Oh, you are here to explain the circumstances,' observed the General. 'Well, you'll be clever if you can explain how Colonel D. is authorized to take upon himself my duties. Let me hear, sir; but are you not the Assistant-Surgeon in medical charge of the regiment?' (The old gentleman had by this time recalled my features.) 'Yes, General.' 'How, then, did you presume to quit your charge without any provision having been made for the carrying on of the duties devolving on you?' 'Have the goodness to read that letter, General G.' 'It seems rather a long one; can't you give me the contents?' 'Certainly, General. It states, on the authority of the Garrison-Surgeon and Dr. L., that if I want to see my wife alive again I must lose not an hour in proceeding here. I showed this letter to Colonel D., and he very kindly allowed me to proceed hither. I rode in yesterday in twelve hours, but happily there was no occasion for me to have done so, as my wife is quite well; the attack was hysterical only, though it looked so serious. And now, having reported myself, and the un-usual reasons for my being here, I beg that you will be kind enough to give me one day's leave to post back my horses.' ' The best thing I can do for you is not to know that you are here.' Then turning his chair round, he said, ' I don't see you ; I don't know that you are here.' ' But, General, pray give me one day's leave, or I shall not be able to post my horses so as to divide the distances on the road.' ' I don't hear you, nor know that you are here ; if I knew who you were, and that you had left your charge without any proper leave, it would be my duty to place you under arrest ; but as I don't know who you are, or where you come from, or indeed anything about you, you see I can't do it.' ' But, General, I——' ' Don't say anything ; I might find out who you are, and might be compelled to act on that know-ledge. Now, I haven't seen you, and know not who you are, or where you come from, or anything else.' ' Once more let me entreat of you, General G.——' ' How many times must I repeat that I neither see, nor hear, nor know, that anyone is here ? If I did, it could only be unpleasant for us both. I not only don't see or hear, but I am deter-mined not to see or hear, or to know anything about you ; so whoever you may be, return at once to the place from whence you came, and let me have no communication on the subject, of which, indeed, I am wholly ignorant and un-informed.' ' Permit me to wish you good-morning, General ?' ' No, I can't permit anything to a stranger, and one I know nothing about. But as a courtesy one might offer to a stranger, I wish you good-morning.'

I rode home meditating on the mysteries of red-tape, but without being able to fathom them. Why should it be more orthodox to pretend to be ignorant of that which was perfectly well known, than it would be to admit the know-ledge, and to say, ' Well, I am glad to learn that there is now no reason for anxiety ; get back as fast as possible, and I will take no notice of the irregularity '? The need for enacting a palpable farce sorely puzzled me, and I went back to my brother-in-law's house to report the ill-success of my application. Then it was settled that I should lie *perdu* for the day, during which time I could post back the horses, and could start at gun-fire, or a little earlier, on my return to the F. Rocks. It was hard to leave my young wife, whom I idolized, after being with her only one day ; but I had taken the shilling, and therefore it was a case of 'no compulsion, only you must.' So, after many kisses and moist eyes, I started just as the gun fired, and I rode into the mess compound at the F. Rocks just as the second bugle was sounding. There was a shout of welcome, and eager inquiries from all present after the state of my wife's health. Everyone heartily congratulated me on the letter being merely a false alarm. Then the dinner came, and I did great honour to it, being not a little hungry after my return ride, on which I received many compliments ; the riding nearly 180 miles in two days with but one between was regarded as something of an equestrian achievement, and my pluck was commended accordingly.

This led to a renewal of the invitation, on the part of the younger men, to join them in their cheetah and tiger expeditions, which at first, being no ball shot, I was not anxious to do. No one likes to exhibit his want of skill in any exercise or pastime, and therefore I declined. My young friends, either out of playful malice, or out of an unacknowledged unwritten belief that medical men, not being combatant officers, are not equal to them in courage, overwhelmed me with banter and chaff (as the phrase now is) of all kinds. I cannot remember a tithe of it, but it was in the main something of this kind : ' Don't say any more, Bob ; the Doctor is a clever fellow ; he knows as well how to take care of himself as to whip off a fellow's leg, don't you, Doctor?' and before I could reply to this jibe B. said, ' Don't forget, all of you, what an important personage the Doctor is. If he was chawed up, what should we do? But if half a dozen of us poor devils came to grief that way it wouldn't much signify. We are paid for being shot, or for being ready to be disposed of; we are, in the customary phrase, " only food for powder and shot," and you see that's not the case with the Doctor.' Turning from one to the other as they discharged their little shafts, I was silly enough to get very angry, and my indignation broke out thus : ' Confound you, what has led you to make this dead set at me? If you fancy that I value my life one bit more than any one of you, you make a very great mistake, and you will compel me to give one of you an unpleasant proof of it if I'm to be subject to more of this kind of conversation.'

No one said anything, but the Colonel wore a broad grin on his face, and W. laughed immoderately. I was now in a towering passion. I got up, saying, ' I haven't often been your guest at mess, gentlemen, and I can't say I think my welcome on this occasion such as to induce me to intrude on your hospitality again.' W. started up and caught hold of my arm, saying, ' Surely you are not so silly as to take offence at a little harmless chaff? not one of us would intentionally say or do anything to hurt or annoy you. I really thought there was more manly stability in you than to fly off in this way.' ' And, pray,' said I, ' what have I said or done to give cause for your fit of laughter?' ' It was your getting so angry that amused me, but as you have taken it so much amiss, I am really sorry for it,' at the same time, with an open frank smile, offering his hand. Who could resist W.? I heartily shook his hand, and said, ' W., you make me ashamed of having shown such want of temper, but these young good-for-nothing scamps here, with their jibes one after the other, threw me off my balance for the moment.'

J., one of the three men who had been chief jokers, then said, 'But, Doctor, you ought to have known that if we had really suspected that there was anything of the white feather connected with your not joining us in our expeditions, we shouldn't have thought you worth poking fun at, and should never have cared whether you went out with us or not.' 'Pray say no more; I am convinced that I was hasty, and in the wrong to get so angry!' 'Now,' said the Colonel, 'after what the Doctor has admitted, let's say no more on the subject.' 'One word more, if you please, Colonel; I wish to prove to all my friends here that they did not judge me wrongly. The very next time you go after cheetah or tiger, I will go with you' (a shout of approval). 'Well said, Doctor!' 'I will lend you a rifle,' said W. 'Or I, or I,' said M. and S. 'And I, if I had one to lend,' said B., 'but as I haven't, all I can offer is a pith-hat with a brim as large as an umbrella, and if that doesn't of itself frighten the tiger, he must be a peculiarly un-apprehensive beast; and I'll venture a trifle that the Doctor does more execution with the hat than he would with the gun, although he is such a peppery gentleman.' 'The pepper is all out of me now, B., and you may say whatever you like; and I would accept your redoubtable pith-hat, had I not one of my own. Besides that, I couldn't think of depriving you of such a powerful weapon, so if you mount your hat and have your rifle in your hand, you will be doubly armed, and will no doubt do double execution.' 'By Jove!' said B., 'the pepper isn't all out of you yet.' 'But you will take my rifle?' said W.; 'if you bring the double-sights in a line with the object, you can't miss him.' 'Best thanks, W., but as I am altogether unpractised, I shall go out without a gun or weapon of any kind, not even my friend B.'s pith-hat.' 'On my word, Doctor,' said the Colonel, 'that's the wisest resolution you could come to ; it will be better for you to become a little familiar with the rifle before you go after tigers or cheetahs.' 'Besides,' said B., 'who knows but the Doctor might take a sly pot at one of us, and wing the unlucky individual for the sake of a little surgical practice ; he's had none since he's been with us.' 'Well, B., that blow might have been effective if it had not been somewhat below the belt : at all events, it was not so bad as your shot at the pariah-dog that you missed this morning, and that M. rolled over immediately after.' There was a general laugh at B.'s expense. 'And, pray, how did you know that?' said B. 'I only saw it, that's all !' 'Why, you rode past three or four minutes before we fired ; you must have had eyes behind to see that.' 'Oh, B., if that's the style (stile), I shall leave you to get over it as you can ; the present attempt is rather lame, and I wish you a steadier hand when you come to make close acquaintance with the striped or spotted coats, unless you've got M. behind you to wipe your eye.' Another laugh at poor B. 'Come, B., whip and spur,' said W. ; 'don't let the Doctor walk over the ground.' 'Oh,' replied B., 'no one can fight against a fellow who has got eyes behind.'

Poor B. ! that was his last speech and dying confession. Amidst the general laughing and chaffing going on, the Colonel said to B. :

'Better take more shots with the rifle, and fewer shots out of the flask, Mr. B., and then you won't miss your mark as it seems you did this morning.' B. said nothing, but walked off somewhat crestfallen. One after the other left, till at last only W. and myself were left with the Colonel. He then said : 'I'm truly sorry for B. ; he's a frank, open-hearted young fellow, but I fear he's going too fast by a great deal ; he was until recently a capital shot. It was just the same with poor Tom Manners, whom I knew intimately in Bengal. The first indication we got of his breaking up was his missing his aim ; he had been the crack shot of us all, but sangaree (we used to drink sangaree in those days) and brandy was too much for him ; he died of delirium tremens, a raving lunatic, after having tried to kill himself and two other persons. Now, I have stayed behind the others to say that I think it would be well done of both of you if you would take an opportunity of talking seriously with this unhappy lad. You, W., have great influence, and you can speak as a senior and an old friend ; and you, Doctor, can speak as a professional man, and the medical officer of the regiment ; choose your opportunity well, and the young fellow will then see that you mean kindly. Good-night to you both.' W.: ' Before you go, Colonel, I think it right to tell you, that I have more than once spoken seriously to B., but I regret to say hitherto without effect. I will, however, do so again.' 'And I, Colonel, will certainly do my best ; but if W.'s advice has been of none effect, I fear mine will avail little. Once the pernicious habit has got hold of a man, it is such a besotting and besetting vice, that nothing seems able to cure it except placing the man under restraint for two or more years, and rigidly keeping all alcoholic stimulants away from him.' 'Well, try your best. Good-night again.' 'Good-night, Colonel.'

W. volunteered to walk home with me, the bungalow being but a few hundred yards off. As we leisurely strolled along, W. said, ' D. is really the most excellent commandant I ever knew. Without being over-strict, he knows well how to hold his own, and to enforce obedience ; at the same time, what could be kinder, I might say more parental, than what he said just now ? And what could be better than his taking on himself to let you leave the cantonment ?

Not one commandant in a hundred would have done it!'
'So I found out,' returned I. The singular scene that
passed between myself and the General of Division was
then told to him. He was greatly amused. 'You must
let D. have the story, it is really too good to be lost; it
only shows what a life of routine makes of a man, unless he
has a mind powerful enough to raise him above such influences. I agree entirely in the view D. takes of B.'s
condition; indeed, I have feared it for some time; the
misfortune is, that I don't see what can be done to save
him. Would it be possible to send him home on sick
leave?' 'The case is this,' said I, 'the authorities and
the medical board take what I regard as a narrow view of
what is best to be done. They argue that it is encouraging
drunkenness to send a man home on that account, and they
would rather keep him in this country to die, or be dismissed
the service, than they would sanction his being sent home for
the effects of alcoholism. The only alternative is, that the
doctor must make up a false case, at the risk of losing his
commission, or the man must hang on till he gets his
furlough. It has, I know, been placed before several boards
officially, that many a man's life might be saved, and the
evil habit subdued, if he were allowed to go home in time,
and have the sea voyage, the European climate, and the
home influences; but these representations have elicited
nothing but anger and reproof. Such being the views
adopted at headquarters, nothing is left to the executive
officer but to act on them.' 'I am quite aware,' returned
W., 'that what you say is correct. You have, in fact,
scarcely gone far enough, for they add, that it is more for
the advantage of the State to let in fresh blood, in the shape
of fresh men, than to keep on the list men who have broken
down from their own vicious habits by sending them home,
and thus prolonging their lives. Such patched-up men,

they say, can never go through fatigues, and wear and tear, that a sound man could and would go through. And to say the truth between ourselves, I think they are right. Compassion and friendship make one feel that the regulations are hard when they are applied to one of our own friends and intimates ; but, looking to the advantage of the service only, I cannot say that they are ill-judged.' 'To some extent I agree with you, but everything is in degree, and a margin should be allowed. As you put it, to send a man home merely to prolong his life, I think, carries with it the condemnation of the whole system ; had he been sent home in time, he would, in all probability, have been saved from any serious injury, but if the poor creature is to be kept here till he is at death's door before the medical officer dare recommend his being sent home, then likely enough it is as you put it, and he comes out injured in physique and in efficiency.'

W. would not enter my bungalow, but after good-night slowly walked to his own. As I looked after him, recalling his generosity, and his unequalled bravery, as well as his superior wisdom, his powers of foresight and reflection, and contrasted all these high qualities with his singular and imperturbable calmness and self-possession when anything dangerous or unpleasant occurred, I could not but feel that he was a remarkably constituted man, or that he had suffered in his earlier years some bitter life-killing disappointment that had rendered him careless of, and indifferent to, every danger and risk. Too lofty a character to yield outwardly to despair, or to shorten the term of existence appointed for him, he seemed to dwell in an atmosphere of his own, that he suffered no one to share with him or even to approach. Some quiet sarcasm, always good-humoured, and the rare indulgence of the risible faculty, were the only indications I ever observed in him of any passing emotion strong enough to ruffle the glassy placidity of his existence. I could not help whispering to myself, 'a wrecked heart,' so deeply was I impressed with his gentle, kindly manner, and his utter recklessness of life, yet I knew nothing whatever of his early history; it was merely fancy's web woven without my knowledge or consent. Nevertheless, it impressed me with a feeling of sadness that I could not for the time banish, and I went to bed to dream of a tiger with an angel's face gnawing W.'s heart.

Not many days after my return to the F. Rocks, some of the villagers near at hand, or one of the Shikaries employed to look for game, brought in word that there was a cheetah to be had near at hand. As soon as possible after breakfast all the sporting men present were on horseback, or, rather, pony-back, to proceed to the spotted gentleman's lair. I accompanied them as a spectator, attended by beaters and villagers. Altogether, besides natives, there were fourteen of us. As we approached the jungle we dismounted, leaving the tatoos to the care of the ghorey wallahs. The primary rule impressed on all was to endeavour to preserve a line; but in a jungle where people could see but a very short distance on any side, this proved to be impracticable, and the consequence was that after the beast was disturbed by the beaters, and one or other of the guns caught sight of him, there was firing on all sides, or, rather, bursts of firing, cross firing, so that every now and then the singing and hissing of balls, and the cracking of branches, was heard on every side. During the whole time the firing lasted, I only caught sight of the cheetah once as he bounded from one thicket to another; but from the whistling and cracking going on all round, any one of us might have been shot a dozen times over.

Before the cheetah was disposed of he had been hit

6

thirteen times, but in no mortal part; the last ball had, however, struck him in the loins, which prevented any more of his rapid springs and bounds. The next ball laid him at M.'s feet. He was a beautiful fellow, though not a large one; and he had made a gallant defence against a dozen guns. Though he had hurt no one seriously—his foes were so close and so many and such practised men, that he had no time to maul or mumble anybody, though it was evident that his intentions were good—he had knocked over two men, a Shikary and a beater; but in the first case a ball from S., who was close beside the Shikary, had sent him off with a broken forearm, and in the second case a ball from W. had driven him off with a wound in the side and two broken ribs, by which the ball, which otherwise would have been fatal, was turned aside. Both his springs were so strong that after knocking over the men he rolled over himself, once in the first instance, and twice in the second, before he could pick himself up, which gave W. the chance of giving a mortal blow; but, as I have said, the ribs turned the ball—all which particulars were learned when the beast was skinned, and the course of the balls traced. It was most extraordinary good-fortune that no one was shot on this occasion; but the folly and absurdity of the method adopted, as well as the greatly increased and unnecessary risk incurred by it, were obvious to everyone, and it was agreed *nem. con.* that no such large parties should ever go out again.

Some weeks elapsed before any fresh game and its whereabouts were discovered; but as soon as this was clearly made out, another shikar party was decided on. Four guns, and myself as guest or spectator, composed it. The sportsmen drew lots as to who the four should be, and the lots fell on W., M., B., and the Colonel. Not to weary the reader with repetition, it is sufficient to say that the beast, said to be a tiger, turned out to be a most superb cheetah, so large that he resembled a tiger in size; but this magnificent fellow was killed with the second shot. When disturbed by the beaters and by their noise and tom-toms, he looked at them for a moment, then, as if confident in his strength, in the most contemptuous way turned on his posteriors and began to walk slowly away. One of the guns—I think the Colonel fired—wounded the grand beast, who, with a terrible roar, turned at once and prepared to spring. Before he could do so, two shots lodged in his brain, and he fell at once and died almost immediately. Thus this huge cat made scarcely any fight, while the smaller one rolled over two men and took fourteen shots to dispose of him. W. and M. had fired at the same instant, and apparently both shots were mortal. They tossed up for the 'spolia opima.' M. won. The skin when taken off, stretched and dried was the finest I ever saw; in beauty it far exceeded W.'s tiger skin, and in size fell little short of it.

Had I been placed permanently in medical charge of the regiment, and it had remained in a sporting country, I should certainly have learned to use the rifle; but not many weeks after this I was relieved by Dr. B., the man for whom I had been acting. I did not consider it as a relief, I must admit. I had become attached to the men of the regiment, and it took away my chance of becoming a sportsman.

Previous to the date of my relief, a very singular incident occurred, while a third party, which, on account of hospital work, I was unable to join, were out after a cheetah. (I had the details from the men present, from W. himself, and from Ram Sing, the naigue of his company, who was in hospital at the time I left the regiment.) It occurred in this way: the cat had been tracked into a certain thicket, and it was expected that he would at any moment break forth. W. was about ten paces' distance from it, as was S. a little to the right of W. Both waited for some movement or sign on the part of the cheetah, but he made none At last S., losing patience, actually stepped into the thicket they had been watching. He must, indeed, have all but put his foot on the cheetah, who was crouching down, well gathered together, just about to make his spring. He took no notice of S., though close to him, but sprang at W., who was at least seven or eight yards off, whom he rolled over, at the same time knocking his gun out of his hand. Most luckily the beast rolled over also, but with the speed of light he recovered himself, and was about to mumble W.'s shoulder, when he received a stunning blow from a heavy bamboo club in the hands of Ram Sing, the naigue already mentioned, who had kept close to his Captain from the beginning. This saved W. at the instant, and the repetition of the blow drew the furious animal's attention solely to the naigue. He left W., and jumping on Ram Sing, knocked him down, tore both his shoulders, one with either paw, and then before help came detached the scalp from the poor fellow's forehead. At this instant he received a mortal blow from S., followed by a second ball from W. (who had recovered himself sufficiently to use his gun), which pierced his heart. At less than two paces off the beast lay dead beside Ram Sing, who was at once taken to the hospital. This brave fellow wanted to walk, and tried to do so, till it was evident that his strength was unequal to it. As they were bearing him along, fainting from the shock and loss of blood, he whispered, 'Aggur murgisto Ram Sing, mesaka ney. Captain Saib ne marre.' (If Ram Sing dies, what matter? the Captain is not hurt.)

As soon as the poor naigue reached the hospital a dose of brandy, a little disguised and given as medicine, quickly overcame the syncope, and Ram Sing opened his eyes, sat up, and when he saw W., who had walked by the side of his litter to the hospital, standing by his side, his eyes brightened, and he said, 'Saib ne marre?' W., who spoke Hindustani fluently, assured him that, thanks to his courage and quickness, he had received no hurt. Ram Sing was then told to lie down, and to be silent, while his wounds were attended to. This was by no means an operation without pain, but not a word nor a sound did the man utter. He had saved his Captain's life, all the regiment knew it, and he was a man of mark from that day forth. I verily believe that the pride and pleasure that he felt in what he had done repaid him a hundredfold for the suffering he had undergone; and as for the risk, he was too truly brave to think for a moment about that, and, more than all this, he loved and respected W. with a devotion that is not easy to describe. W. was always his hero, his idol; W. could never do wrong in his mind. W.'s remarkable bravery, imperturbable quietude in danger, together with his kindness and generosity, had elevated him into the position of a sort of demigod or superior being, and I truly and sincerely believe that almost every native man in the gallant —th would have laid down his life for W. without hesitation. The feeling displayed by these men brought strongly to my mind that shown by Clive's Sepoys at the siege of Arcot, when rice was so scarce that he feared he should be starved into surrender, and when there were 20,000 foes surrounding the place.

This incident closes what we have to present regarding Captain Whistler, one of the most noble-minded, brave and generous men that ever adorned the Indian Service.

No. III.

FROM my brother's memoranda, said the Doctor to the company on board the *Elephanta*, it would appear that several of the officers of the far-famed regiment, the 13th Dragoons, possessed merits considerably above the average. He gives sketches of most of them, portraits of a few. These I shall not attempt to reproduce, but I will venture to make some selections. He says :

' I found Colonel B., the officer commanding the regiment, one of the most courtly-mannered men I had ever met, and though his figure was by no means commanding, his easy elegant address was highly captivating, and his superior intelligence, marked by every look and word, gained respect at once, while the kind and urbane expression of his features challenged esteem and regard.' Within five minutes after his card had been taken in, and his name announced, my brother found himself, though previously a total stranger, chatting perfectly at his ease with his new commandant, such was the charm of Colonel B.'s manner.

Besides being the finished gentleman and accomplished soldier, Colonel B. was. a very successful water-colour painter, as was proved by the various specimens adorning his study. My brother had not himself been wholly unsuc-cessful in this walk of art, having gained some prizes at the

Society of Arts for his attempts; at all events, he knew enough of the art to appreciate the Colonel's beautiful performances, and he expressed his feelings freely and warmly, as well as in a way to show that he knew something of what he was talking about.

The result of the interview was that the Colonel took rather a fancy to the young assistant-surgeon who was to do duty with his regiment. On the part of my brother, the feeling was more than mutual, for the more he saw of his commandant, the more he liked and admired him. At the time I speak of, the 13th Dragoons were stationed at Bangalore, one of the most delightful localities in India, and I have already said that the native regiment, of which my brother was afterwards in medical charge, was stationed there also. The consequence of this vicinity was that in due course Colonel B. brought his wife to see my brother's wife, a visit which again in due course my brother and his wife returned. The ladies became friends, and the friendship has only been closed by poor Mrs. B.'s death. She was, at the time to which I refer, one of the handsomest, most queen-like women to be seen anywhere.

But it is rather of her gifted husband than of her that I wish to speak. Colonel B.'s talents were indeed so great and so various that they demand a far abler pen than mine to do them justice. Wit the most ready, sparkling, and unbounded, united with an unequalled address and manner, made him the most delightful companion that can be imagined. No company could resist his powers: laughter unrestrained and irresistible followed him wherever he went. I heartily wish I could recall even a few of the electric flashes of thought that, 'like orient pearls at random strung,' gave life and lustre, fire and fancy to his words. I fear, however, that I should only defeat my object if I ventured to make the attempt, I can never give the fitting time and place, the circumstance coincident, nor the look and manner that were so admirable and so appropriate.

On the occasion to which this extract chiefly refers, Lord Elphinstone, then Governor of Madras, and his friend Lord Cardigan, who was his visitor, were the guests of the regiment. Colonel B. was sitting at the mess-table between them in high spirits, his irresistible stories and anecdotes creating an atmosphere of merriment around him. My brother was not near enough to hear half that passed, but his eye took in the situation, and in spite of the noise, the clapping, and the laughter, his ear was very attentive and quick.

The first *morceau ragoutant* that reached him was Colonel B.'s account of what had taken place at Colonel C.'s public breakfast some four or five mornings before. Colonel C. was then the Commissioner for Mysore. While at breakfast, he received Lord Elphinstone's answer to an invitation requesting him and his friend, Lord Cardigan, to spend some time at Bangalore, and during their stay to give him the pleasure of being their host. The invitation had been accepted, and accordingly Colonel C. announced that the two noble lords would shortly be at Bangalore. There was a large party at the breakfast, among whom was Captain A., who was one of the Commission. As soon as this officer, whose intrinsic worth was not hidden by French, or, indeed, by any other kind of polish, heard the announcement, he broke out thus : ' Eh, sirs, twa lurds— twa lurds ! What'll I do, how'll I boo ?' a sally which occasioned no little merriment amongst those who heard it, and still more at the mess-table after the Colonel's recital, who followed it up by such a string of jokes and puns and telling repartees, that an old Bengal civilian, whose name was Potts, and who was the Colonel's *vis-à-vis*, appeared

thoroughly bewildered. He never uttered a word, but sat
looking from one to the other with his mouth wide open,
drinking in, as it seemed, the stream of wit, the like of
which he had never perhaps in his whole life heard before.
The old gentleman's behaviour afforded Colonel B. a good
deal of quiet amusement. Unnoticed, he made his friends
aware of what had attracted his attention, and then, as soon
as he saw that they were observing, he remarked to his
opposite: 'Mr. Potts, you're quite chatty,'* which, it is
needless to say, set the table off again.

When the laughter had a little subsided, Colonel B. recommenced by giving his guests a sketch of a certain Miss
B., a young lady between forty and fifty years of age, who
was a well-known character in the cantonment. He gave
them to understand that this young lady still *hoped*. She
could not, indeed, bring herself to believe that she would
always remain Miss B., and, in consequence of this settled
conviction, she not unfrequently afforded amusement to her
acquaintances. Remarks to this effect, whenever she indulged in them, appeared to yield the ladies considerable
enjoyment : 'You know, my dear, when I get married, or
when I have a house of my own,' etc. These unintentional
exhibitions of her hopes and wishes on the part of Miss B.
led to a good deal of harmless quizzing, and to numerous
inquiries, such as, 'On whom were her smiles chiefly bestowed?' 'Who was to be the happy man?' or 'Whether
this lucky individual had been fixed on?' 'When would
the ceremony take place?' and many more such seductive
and insidious questions, which led the dear innocent

---

* To those who have not been in India it is necessary to explain that
the word 'chatty' means in the Tamul language an earthen vessel or
pot, which, combined with the fact of the old gentleman's taciturnity,
being thus a silent receptacle of the flow of wit, made the remark doubly
telling.

into sundry admissions and confessions, tending to show that she had anything but a dislike to the holy state of matrimony, though she had not yet made her election. 'The state of affairs having thus been made sufficiently evident, several of the young scamps you see around you, who, as well as Miss B., are frequent visitors at my house, took it into their wise heads, for the sake of the fun, to declare themselves Miss B.'s admirers, partly with the sanction, at all events, with the tacit permission, of Mrs. B., who could not find it in her heart to object to anything in the shape of fun and frolic. So it has come to pass that a frequent amusement there is the violent love-making on the part of these young lads to this sweet young creature, who, to do her but justice, distributes her sweetness to A., B., or C. with an impartiality that really is quite charming. I sometimes fear that the young fellows are carrying matters too far with their protestations, their vows of devotion, their hopes of future bliss, their dread that she prefers another, their appeals to a cornelian heart she wears, which more than one of these describe as their mutual property, and a great deal more of like quality, which, with their kneeling and impassioned acting, is comical enough. Yet one thing to be remarked is, to my mind, more comical still—the more fervid the performance, the more the lady is pleased; but the crowning fun is that, under the continuance of the excitement, the dear old girl gets so dreadfully affectionate, that more than one of the performers has declared his conviction that ere long she will throw herself into the arms of one or other of them.'

'Well, B.,' said both his guests, 'you must give us an opportunity of being present at one of these scenes; we wouldn't miss the chance on any account. The fun must be "rich and rare."' 'Make your minds easy,' replied the Colonel; 'we'll have a rehearsal at which you shall be

present in a few days. Let me see,' added he, 'I'm not
sure that we can't manage it sooner.' 'The sooner the
better,' said his friends. 'There is the sham fight,' resumed
the Colonel. 'to-morrow, and it will occupy us from five a.m.
to about ten, which is the hour for breakfast with C. We
dine with General V. at seven p.m., but between breakfast
and dinner we shall have several hours free, say from
twelve a.m. to six p.m. Mrs. B. will order us a very light
tiffin at two p.m.—some ices and blancmange, *rien de plus*,
and then we can have, as an interlude before dinner, Miss
B. and her lovers. How will that suit you?' 'The very
thing,' said the ' twa lurds.' 'Nothing can be better.'
'That, then, is arranged,' said Colonel B., who continued :
'Now you would scarcely credit that anyone could be so
full of faith as this ancient young gentlewoman is ; but facts
are stubborn things, you know, and therefore stubborn
things are facts—at least, sometimes.' 'Ah, ha !' said his
guests, laughing ; ' breaking out of bounds, are you ?' 'No,
no,' returned the Colonel, 'only "verbum volans." But
these same young men, who are now making such violent
love to Miss B., played the lady rather a scurvy trick the
other day. They continued, however, to make her believe
that they were wholly innocent, and had had no concern
in it. They affected great indignation against the perpetrators
of the outrage, as Miss B. termed it, sympathized deeply
with her under the infliction, and vowed signal vengeance
if they could only find out the guilty parties. In a short
time the confiding fair one believed again, forgetting all
her suspicions and her anger, and now she listens with
obvious delight to the vows and protestations of her
simulating lovers.' 'She is truly, as you have mentioned,'
said Lord C., 'a guileless, confiding innocent ; but you
have not told us what the young deceivers did.' 'The
thing arose in this way,' said Colonel B. 'Some of our

young fellows, having heard that Miss B. expected a parcel from Madras, determined that she should have one with as little delay as might be. They first sent the parcel to Madras (to Oakes's, I believe), directing him to take off the wrapper with his address on it, and then to forward the parcel inside to the address written thereon. They further managed so that the said parcel reached Miss B. while she was at my house. Most of the young lads in the cantonment were there at the time, and a large gathering beside.'

' " Oh, my parcel, my long-expected parcel, come at last !" exclaimed the lady. " Oh, won't you open it ? Do open it, Miss B.," said numerous voices. " Let me help you "— from others. " But what is it ?" said Mrs. B. ; " is it anything that will break ? Be careful ; you don't know what it is." " It's only a silk dress, and some lace trimming." " Well," said one of the culprits, " whatever it is, they have wrapped it up well ; I think this is the tenth paper I have taken off." " Still more to take off," said another. " Very extraordinary ! What can it be? I'm sure it's not a silk dress ; I feel something much firmer and stiffer than a silk dress." " I tell you it's only a silk dress," reiterated Miss B. At last the boldest of the conspirators took off the last envelope of gauze paper, and exhibited *something*. As he did so he said to poor Miss B., " Surely this is not a silk dress, is it, Miss B. ?" " Oh, heavens !" screamed the astonished and horrified lady, running off at once into my wife's bedroom—" Oh, heavens ! I shall never recover it. Such an insult !"' ' But what *did* the parcel contain after all?' inquired the two magnates. ' Ah ! what did it contain ?' asked several voices. ' What do you guess?' returned the Colonel. ' Oh, we can't guess ; we give it up. Pray tell us '—from all sides. ' Well, then, what do you say to a pair of leather male garments, a pair of buck-skins— only a pair of buck-skins ? I can't describe them by the popular denomination; there would be breaches in my good manners if I did.'

While Colonel B. was running on in this way, the company, and especially the two young lords, were convulsed with laughter. As soon as Lord C. could speak, he said, with tears in his eyes, 'Oh, B., you'll be the death of us if you go on in this way. E. declares that his sides are so sore that it almost makes him cry to laugh any more, and I'm just as bad. But who suggested this delicate compliment to Miss B. ? I must have a glass of wine with him.' ' And I'll join you,' said his friend. ' Why, the truth is,' said D., ' there were three of us engaged in the matter, but which of us first thought of the leathers I can't say.' ' It is evidently a divided honour,' said the Colonel. ' I and Elphinstone will drink to you three,' said Lord C., and ' Hurrah for the buck-skins ! hurrah for the buck-skins !' was shouted on every side.

*   *   *   *   *

' I think it's high time for us to depart,' said Lady Jervois ; ' I'm not sure that we haven't stayed too long already. At any rate, it must be near eight bells.' ' I agree with you, Lady Jervois,' said Mrs. Smythe ; ' but really I did not anticipate that Dr. Ticklemore would be so minute in his detail. I can't help suspecting that he has been taking rather unwarrantable liberties with his brother's memoranda, and that his description of poor Miss B. is little more than a mischievous libel on that ill-used lady.' ' I'm sure, Dr. Ticklemore,' said Miss Perkins, 'that no correct unmarried lady would go on as you try to make out that Miss B. did.' ' Really, Miss Perkins and ladies all,' replied the Doctor, ' I do assure you I have taken no liberties with my brother's memoranda, and not for the world would I dream of taking any with such a lady as Miss B.' ' Good-night, gentlemen ; good-night, Dr. Ticklemore, with thanks for your narrative, or at least for part of it; but we must put you on your good behaviour for the future, or we cannot make a part of your audience.' 'Why, I haven't said anything that's not proper, have I?' 'No, no,' said Captain Ward; 'any exuberance in his descriptions he'll avoid in future, I'm sure. You pledge yourself, mind that, Ticklemore, on my guarantee.' 'Oh, certainly!' returned the culprit; ' I'm pledged, pawned, verbally and corporeally, to avoid all exuberance, though what kind of crime that is I don't quite know; *but it's all the same,' sotto voce.* ' Well, remember; you are only to be honoured with an audience on the promise of future good behaviour.' ' Aye, aye, sir,' said the nautical Esculapius.

*   *   *   *   *

' Well, now that the ladies are amongst the departed,' said Dr. T., ' I can finish the sketch my brother has given us of Colonel B.'s sayings and doings relative to Miss B. and the present of the leathers. Mrs. B., though she enjoyed the joke as much as any of the conspirators, took compassion on the wounded sensibilities of the lady, made her pass the night at the house, and kept her there as a guest for some days; in short, she did all she could to soothe and console. She would not allow anyone who called to be admitted, and when, after a day or two of seclusion, the Colonel met Miss B. in the drawing-room, he spoke to her just as if nothing had occurred to ruffle her feelings; he was ever kind and courteous to everyone, and unwilling to give pain. He would not, therefore, have made any allusion to what had recently occurred, but Miss B. felt her wrongs were too great to be passed over in silence, and her sorrows were too weighty to be repressed. With a flood of tears she referred to the outrage, the indignity, the insult that had been offered to her; it was cruel, it was unmanly it was cowardly, it was disgraceful. By-and-by she ran herself out, and began to speak of less poignant afflictions. It was not enough that she should be disappointed in receiving the dress she had been so long expecting, but she must, in addition, be subject to such vile treatment. (Sob after sob.) "Why don't you say something to soothe her distress, Dick?" said Mrs. B., "you can comfort so well if you will." "Can I?" said the Colonel. "*C'est bien*, madame." Then turning to Miss B., he said, "Indeed I sympathize with you deeply. Such a wicked present as you received would naturally cause much disappointment. Empty compliments always do cause disappointment; and then to have to appear before your friends without your dress must have given you deep mortification, although it is said that 'beauty unadorned is then adorned the most.'" "Dick, Dick," interposed Mrs. B., "how can you go on so?" "How could Miss B. go on so, did you say? Well, how she could is difficult to understand." "Oh, stop, will you," said Mrs. B., "you're a horrid fellow; you won't even listen to all Miss B.'s troubles and distresses." "What, anything more," asked the Colonel, "beside the costume of the Buffs, or the want of costume, that vexed her so much?" "Hold that mischievous tongue of yours and listen. Miss B. will be obliged when she leaves our roof to go and live in the Fort, because her nephew, Mr. H., has been ordered to reside there for the present." "And if it be so," replied Colonel B., "I don't see any serious hardship or misfortune in it." "No; but Miss B. regrets that she will be three miles from her friends; and there within the walls of the Fort she will have nothing to amuse her, nothing except the goats and kids, sheep and rams, and lambs, and the bare walls to look at." "Ah, now," said the Colonel, "I admit she is to be pitied; to have nothing to amuse her, nothing even to look at, except the naked walls and ramparts, is a sad and melancholy occupation. I feel for you deeply, Miss B."

'This meagre sketch of Colonel B. would be more im perfect than it is if nothing was said of his wonderful power as an actor. This, however, my brother passes over very slightly, and it is much to be regretted, as in some characters he was really inimitable, unapproachable. All the Falstaffs that the stage has ever seen were not so perfect in the conception and exhibition of the matchless wit of the fat old knight as Colonel B.'s. Many bigger and lustier men, properly stuffed out, would no doubt exhibit the figure which Shakespeare has given to the hoary sinner more adequately, but no one, I believe, ever came up to the Colonel in the rendering of every sentence and every word spoken by Falstaff. He made the author's meaning plain and intelligible to almost everyone ; his superlative acting explained what would otherwise have escaped notice, or have been misunderstood, or not understood at all. To read the play after having witnessed his portraiture of Falstaff was like looking at a butterfly's wing with the naked eye, and then viewing it under the microscope. My brother has some rather amusing remarks on the Colonel's powers and high qualities as an actor in other characters ; he mentions Tyke, Alapod, Touchstone, and many others, in all of which Colonel B. was very admirable. But a Bangalore audience, at the time to which my brother's memoranda refers, was little fitted to appreciate the higher walks of histrionic art. Farces, Bombastes Furioso, and such kind of entertainments were better suited to their mental calibre. He illustrates his meaning by the following anecdote : The Colonel's acting, though so truly admirable, had never elicited much applause until in one of his characters (I forget which) he had to bray like a donkey. This performance elicited uproarious and long-continued applause. The Colonel's only remark after this was, " He knew now what suited a Bangalore audience." This closes the sketch I have consulted of

this highly gifted and talented man. Both he and the
audience that excited his contempt have passed away,
almost all of them ; but all who ever knew Colonel B. may
well say, " When shall we look upon his like again ?"   Yet
though I am without the sources of information that I have
till now relied on, my memory would rise up in judgment
against me if I did not say a few words in illustration of the
undeviating kindness of heart, active benevolence, and unrivalled ability which so often prompted him to stand forth
as the defender of those whom misfortune, or even mo-
mentary culpability, had brought into grave trouble and
danger.   I shall never forget the impression made on me
merely by reading his masterly defence of poor Captain E.,
who was brought before a court-martial for being drunk
while on main guard.   I do not call to mind all the circumstances of the case, but I remember the prosecutor was
Major S., then commanding H.M.'s 39th Regiment, and a
noble regiment it was.   The facts connected with the charge
were chiefly as follows : Captain O. deposed that he visited
the guard at the usual hour, and the prisoner came forward
to give his report, but fell down on the ground before he
was near enough to hand it to him ; that he called to the
sergeant of the guard, who handed him the report.   Captain O. then asked the sergeant if he had seen what had
occurred ; the sergeant replied that he had seen it all.
Captain O. then rode to the quarters of the officers commanding the cantonment, and at once reported the circumstance.   Colonel L. then and there placed the defaulter
under arrest, and ordered Captain G., the next on the roster
for that duty, to relieve Captain E. immediately.   These
facts were all duly set forth in the various counts into which
the charge was subdivided, and were all proved by *viva
voce* evidence in court.   The prisoner had, by Colonel B.'s
advice, reserved his defence until everything that could be

7

urged against him had been stated, and, as it seemed, fully substantiated; he then recorded the plea "Not guilty," adding that he had placed his defence in the hands of Colonel B., who had kindly offered his assistance. The Court having granted Colonel B. permission to plead for the prisoner, the Colonel, having thanked the Court for having conceded to him the position he had sought, commenced his address something to this effect: As a British officer, he felt that discipline, the strictest discipline, was the life of an army, the great distinction between a *mob* and a *regular force*, and that it must be enforced on all occasions, and under every possible condition; that the pain and grief that a generous heart must sometimes feel in carrying it into execution must never for an instant be allowed to interfere or suspend, or to mitigate, the penalties or punishments awarded by military law for military offences. " With these sentiments firmly fixed in my mind, I should be the last man in the army to come forward to advocate any cause, or support any plea, that would in the remotest way tend to undermine or weaken or impair discipline. But, sir, discipline is not opposed to justice; discipline is the strong arm of justice; discipline without justice could not long exist, for then it would be injustice, and injustice would be a breach of discipline. Discipline and justice, then, must go together; they cannot be disunited. These principles, sir, are as old as the world, and as fixed as the foundations of the world; and, sir, in making this appeal to you, and to every member of this Court of Honour, I feel as sure of the response as if I saw every generous heart laid bare before me. You will all, without a doubt, uphold discipline, but you will not forget that to uphold discipline you must do justice; and to do justice you must take nothing for granted, you must insist on having proofs, undoubted, undeniable proofs; no suspicions or suspicious circumstances must be accepted as proofs. Did you, or could you, accept any such as proofs, you would not do justice, and consequently would not uphold discipline. If any one count of the charge cannot be distinctly and unequivocally proved, that count is doubtful, and the law declares that when there is a doubt the accused is to have the benefit of it. But why do I speak of law? Your own feelings will tell you most emphatically that you cannot condemn when you are in doubt. Now to apply these principles. The prisoner is charged with being drunk on duty—an unpardonable crime in a military point of view—and you have had it in evidence on oath that this unfortunate officer was so incapable that, when advancing to give in his report, he fell on the ground. This has been stated on oath by Captain O. and Sergeant Maguire, both witnesses of unimpeachable credit, and both without any adverse bias or leaning. But, Mr. President and gentlemen, we must not forget that opinions are not proofs. To prove that the fall and the incapability resulted from drunkenness we must have more than opinions. First, we must inquire if any liquor or spirit was drunk at the guard-room. The prisoner admits that he drank while on guard the quantity that you see is absent out of this small flask. It was nearly full when he left home, and the Sergeant found it on the table in the guard-room, with this quantity in it; this he has sworn to. Thus it is clear that Captain E. did not, out of this flask, while on guard, drink more than one glass of brandy, and he was there for six hours. The Sergeant has further deposed that no liquor except that brought in the flask by the prisoner was brought into the guard-room by any other person. How, then, is the drunkenness to be accounted for? One glass of brandy taken in six hours will not make any man drunk. There is the fall and the incapability, but one glass of brandy in the time stated will not account for these. If they cannot be attributed to drunkenness there must be some other cause. The prisoner will, if cross-examined, confirm what I have now to state. During the day of that night when Captain E. was to remain on guard, he had suffered more or less from neuralgia of the left side of the face ; he has, I may now state, ever since he was in Burmah, suffered at times from this complaint, and on account of this wearing and painful affection he has been obliged to take morphine and other narcotics to a great extent. He also admits that he had at times taken alcoholic stimulants in considerable quantity, and that shortly before going on guard he had done so. While on guard he further admits that he took several doses of morphine. To the combined effects of these remedies he attributed the fall and the incapability ; he was overcome by the action of stimulants and narcotics, but surely this is not drunkenness ? Dr. MacD. is also prepared to state on oath that he is fully aware of the fact that Captain E. has for a long time past suffered from neuralgia, more or less severe, and that he has on many occasions prescribed for him on account of it. These circumstances, I submit, relieve the case of its worst features, and I confidently appeal to the gallant officer who has felt it to be his duty to bring the charge into Court, whether he does not now feel that the case wears a new aspect ? Major S. generously and frankly admits that he is not now so certain of the prisoner's guilt as he was when he first took up the case. Nothing less was to be expected from his well-known character, zealous as he is that the reputation of his far-famed regiment, *primus in Indus*, should remain unsullied and unspotted. Earnest as he is to preserve its honour and its discipline, he is yet too magnanimous, too just, too truthful, to press his charge unduly. He has admitted that he is not now so certain as he was. What do those noble words

amount to? Do they not admit a doubt—a doubt entertained by a frank and lofty mind not shut against conviction? He says his opinion is not to decide. No, we know
full well for what purpose this Court is now sitting; we
know that a wife and family are now enduring the agony of
suspense; we know that degradation and disgrace, nay,
future poverty and misery, depend on your decision; we
know that though you, too, are zealous and eager to uphold
discipline, you are not forgetful of justice; we know that,
not less magnanimous and truthful than Major S., you will,
like him, not refuse to admit a doubt, where doubt really
is; we know to whom we trust, and if trust cannot be re-
posed in such an assembly of British officers, it is nowhere
to be found in the world! May I say one word more?
May that Great and Just Being before whom we must all
one day appear, direct and guide you so that your rest may
be sweet and unbroken, and never be disturbed by the
thought that you refused to a poor suffering brother that
justice tempered with mercy which we all shall one day
need, and all look to obtain, through merits not our own.'

A hum and buzz of applause ran through the Court;
then the President and members retired, and there was an
interval of silence and suspense. Whispers were the only
mode of communication employed. After nearly twenty
minutes had elapsed, a member of the Court opened the
door and directed Captain E. to attend him, that the
sentence of the Court might be communicated by the
President. It is not necessary to trace all the steps or
forms adopted by military tribunals; all that is needful to
record is that after a severe admonition, and the loss of
some steps in rank, Captain E.'s sword was restored to him.
Everyone in Court congratulated him warmly on his escape.
The poor man seemed stunned; he could only say,
'Thank you, thank you.'

Colonel B., who was overwhelmed by compliments and praises, as soon as he could disengage himself from the General and Major S., came up to Captain E., and hurrying him into his carriage, drove him away amidst the cheers of the assembly. But words are wanting to describe the meeting of the wife and the husband. The lady wished to throw herself at Colonel B.'s feet, but he would not suffer it. He placed her in her husband's arms, and then left them with their mingled benedictions making sweet music in his ears, and gratitude too great for utterance streaming from their eyes. Colonel B. directed his coachman to go slowly round the racecourse before he drove home. Is there a living man who does not envy him the luxury of that solitary drive? And what are the compliments and praises of the world compared to the approval of that still small voice that God has placed within our breasts?

Let us leave the excellent man of whom we have been speaking to the sweet converse with that silent voice. That the rewards he thus experienced were inexpressibly dear to him is proved by his practice through life. He stood forth on every possible occasion as the champion of distress, making his unrivalled talents the servants of his humanity, and the ministers of relief and safety to many who, like Captain E., had none but him to help them.

Who, then, knowing these things, can doubt that the soldier with his motto, " En avant," has found the path to realms beyond the sky, to fields of glory unprofaned by blood and death, but yet where few shall go before him?

THE DELIGHTS OF INDIAN MUSIC.

THE ladies, who were present the following evening when Dr. T. had narrated Colonel B.'s exertions on behalf of Captain E., were loud in his praise, and in their acknowledgments of the gratification they had experienced. Lady Jervois said, 'We can now thank you, Dr. Ticklemore, without any reservation, for assuredly you have afforded us a glimpse of a very fine character : but, like a beautiful dissolving view, you have not allowed us to dwell long enough on the picture.' 'Most true, Lady Jervois,' remarked Mrs. Smythe, 'we have not often the opportunity of contemplating such various gifts, such high intelligence, and such nobleness of heart united in one individual. I am grieved that you have not more to tell us of so charming a man.' 'Bella and I,' said Miss Perkins, 'are both of us quite in love with Colonel B. ; he must have been truly a delightful man.' 'Well, ladies, I am glad that my sketch of Colonel B. has not been unacceptable. I have a few words to say of Colonel MacC., who was a dashing soldier and a fine-looking man. These anecdotes, for they are nothing more, will just fill up the short time before we separate for the evening, and conclude the extracts I have made from my brother's memoranda, having reference to that glorious old Peninsular regiment, the 13th Dragoons. Colonel MacC.

was at the time referred to second in command, but he had originally stood before Colonel B., being his senior in military rank, and his name was first on the list for purchase, and both officers had lodged the sum required. Unfortunately for Colonel MacC., his father, on account of some temporary pressure, withdrew the purchase-money; and, still more unfortunately for him, during the term of withdrawal, which was to have been but a few months, the colonelcy fell vacant, and, as a matter of course, the officer whose money was ready was gazetted as colonel-in-command. This occurrence was unfortunate, not only for Colonel MacC., but for all parties concerned, and for the regiment, as in spite of every effort on the part of Colonel B., it caused something like a split, a division into two parties, and it produced a soreness and estrangement between the two senior officers. Military usage, and the polished manners of the higher classes, could neither support nor altogether conceal this feeling, which occasionally peeped out—at least, on the part of Colonel MacC., never on the part of Colonel B. It is true that he was the winner, and the old saying, "Those may laugh who win," was made good—not literally, certainly, for Colonel B. was far too polished to do anything of the kind, or to show anything in the shape of exultation; still the former cordiality was gone, and a studied politeness obtained in its place.

'Between these two gallant soldiers, there were other points of difference, which, while they were fast friends, were never referred to; but now that these mutual feelings were altered, these springs of strife did sometimes make themselves evident. A short explanation of what these were appears to be called for. Colonel B. was what the world terms a *novus homo*. It is true that his father was a talented professional man; it is true that his sister, by the attraction of her wit, grace, and beauty, coupled with a spotless name, had married an earl ; and it is true that he himself was a colonel of Dragoons ; but all this, which only proved that he and his belongings were far above their neighbours in much that was most admirable and estimable, went for nothing against the one overpowering fact that Colonel MacC. was a man of family. He could trace back his family name I don't know how far, his clan was mentioned in very old records, and he himself claimed an unbroken descent (though this, it seems, other gentlemen of the same name disputed) from one Roderick MacC., termed the " Red-handed," from the fact that his hands were never long free from this peculiar colour. This very noble gentleman was at feud with several other clans, and his exploits in the way of storming their strongholds, extirpating the former possessors, or burning them altogether in their dwellings after the storm, were greatly celebrated and admired by all his friends and dependents ; while by his neighbours of some other name he was as greatly feared and dreaded. The achievements of this most interesting character were lightened and alleviated by lifting cattle, or sweeping a particular district of everything movable.

' These frequent successful raids, varied only by the occasional abduction or violation of some unhappy female, put the finishing touch, the crowning halo, to the fame and glory of this superlative hero. That MacC., being a polished gentleman, not destitute of humanity, frank, and to the last point tenacious of his word, brave and generous, should consider his descent from the red-handed robber and murderer as a high distinction and a high honour may seem strange, but so it was.

' It is in all cases useless to argue against facts, and there are but few facts more distinct or positive than the pride with which the large majority of those whose birth enables them to do so deduce their descent from some iron-handed robber or murderer, provided he lived a long time ago. Time, it would appear, converts crime into virtue. If any warrior, knight, or lord committed, or attempted to commit, in these days, the crimes that his ancestors committed with impunity, he would be hanged or shot, and would, besides, incur the detestation of society.

'Colonel MacC. was proud of his name and his long line of ancestry, even though it included the red-handed gentleman, and many other smaller lights who did their best to emulate that worthy's achievements. Sometimes, when Colonel MacC. stayed longer at the mess-table than was his wont, he used to remark that the service had greatly deteriorated since he had entered it, and when the natural inquiry, "How so, Colonel?" or, "In what respect?" had been elicited, "the hidden anguish of his soul" would peep forth something in this wise: "Why, you see nowadays they put any man in command of a regiment. They only ask if he can purchase; if he can, the thing is settled, he gets the step. It signifies nothing whether his father was butcher or baker, tinker or tailor; if he can pay, he gets the step, even though it may be the command of the regiment; but in my young days a man's name did stand for something. They would not in those days have put Jack, Tom, or Harry in such a position, particularly when they had a man whose family was known, and who was in other respects qualified to take the command."

'Poor Colonel MacC.! he could not forget or forgive his supercession, but nevertheless he had many good qualities, and was a man to be liked and respected. He could also be generous even to a very contemptible character, as the following instance proves:

'Colonel MacC. was a thorough sportsman, an excellent man for cross-country, whether it was after a fox at home, or after a jackal in India; a capital shot, whether for tiger or elephant, or for partridge, pheasant, or snipe, and a man who, after his father's death, kept up a noble stud of horses. At Madras, at Hyderabad, at Bangalore, wherever there was a race, Colonel MacC.'s horses were entered. From inherited property, from being a bachelor, and from his position in the regiment, by which he received more pay than he spent, he became the richest man in it : he was, in consequence, enabled to indulge his desire to back his own horses, or to bet on others as he pleased, and this he did pretty heavily. At one of the Bangalore races, I cannot call to mind the year, Colonel MacC. had a bet of 3,000 rupees with a Mr. ——, an officer of one of the native regiments there stationed. The race came off. and the Colonel's horse won. Mr. —— immediately gave the Colonel a cheque on Messrs. Arbuthnot and Co. for the amount, and the matter was apparently settled ; but a few days after the Colonel received a letter from Messrs. A., stating that they had in their possession no funds belonging to Mr. ——. This personage, when called on to explain his conduct, pleaded that he thought the agents at Madras did that sort of thing. He wrote a very extraordinary letter, covering four sides of paper, and concluding thus : "That if they did not forgive him, to-morrow's sun should smile upon his grave." Colonel MacC. laughed immoderately, and when the other members of the racing committee, or most of them, said, "MacC., you must bring this gentleman forward," the Colonel replied : "Not I ; he's too paltry a creature for me to touch. Besides, he has afforded me a hearty laugh, which one does not enjoy every day. He will not show his handsome face amongst us again, that you may rely on ; and if he takes my advice, he will get himself moved out of Bangalore as soon as practicable." And thus the matter ended ; the Colonel lost his money, Mr. —— his character.

'About this time, or shortly after, it became known that a Highland regiment was to pass through Bangalore *en route* to Hyderabad—I should say Secunderabad, as the canton-ment is called—situated about three miles from the native city, Hyderabad. The natives, who had heard highly-laudatory accounts of the Highlanders, were greatly excited. The noble qualities of these soldiers on the field of battle were magnified in their minds, and the dress they wore was described as grand and beautiful, surpassing everything they had yet seen of the Europeans. Many thousands of natives went out several miles to meet the regiment on the morning it was expected to reach Bangalore, and their enthusiasm knew no bounds when they beheld the stature of the men, their kilts, their plaids, and plumes. At last, as the regiment approached the cantonment, the pipers struck up, and this so enchanted the natives that they were absolutely beside themselves with delight. The regiment was halted as soon as it was known that the General and staff, with all the *élite* of the station and a great number of fair equestrians, were coming out to greet them. Every company dressed up, leaving between them the exact distances prescribed. Every man brushed the dust off his brogues or sandals ; in short, everything was done that could be done to impress beholders.

'As the General and his party came in sight the pipes struck up again, and the regiment resumed its march. The General and staff drew up by the side of the road, and the regiment marched by, saluting ; after which, accompanied by the whole cortège—General, staff, officers, ladies, and natives—the corps marched on to the racecourse, where their tents had been pitched. " Really," said a young Scotchman, who had lately joined the 13th Dragoons, " if I wasn't a mounted man, I'd like to belong to a Highland regiment." " Well," said another, not quite so deeply smitten with the appearance of the kilts, "I dare say any one of their young ones will exchange with you if you only make the offer." "Aye, McDougal ; that will just suit you," said Vivian, "as you are such a devoted admirer of Signori Rossini, Verdi and Co." "I don't quite make you out," replied McDougal. "Why, don't you see," said Vivian, "you'll always have such glorious music ; the natives are so mad about the pipes that they one and all declare they never thought, before they heard them, 'that the English knew anything about music.'" The young Scot, who was an accomplished performer on the violin, and perfectly fanatic in his admiration of Italian music, did not at first seem to relish the joke ; but at last he joined in the laugh, protesting, however, that there was a time and place for everything, and that though the exquisite strains of "Lucia di Lammermoor" were fitter for the drawing-room or the opera, he would prefer the music of the pipes on the field of battle. "Well spoken, McDougal," said Colonel MacC. ; "you could not have made a better distinction."

'Comparisons of the music of the pipes with that of the natives furnished abundance of fun and amusement during the evening, reference being constantly made to the ignorance of the English as to music, which, in the estimation of Hindoo critics, was profound, and was only relieved from being complete by the unexpected sounds they had heard that morning. At last the subject was allowed to drop, being reserved for other like fitting occasions, while it was recognised, *nemine contradicente*, to be "an argument for a week, laughter for a month, and a good jest for ever."

'The provoking malice and wicked fun towards Scotchmen, of comparing the pipes with the music of the natives of India, cannot be apparent to those who have never been in that country. Therefore the following attempt to convey a faint idea of the peculiar attractions of Hindoo music has been inscribed — first with the view of enlightening minds (or ears) uninstructed by experience ; secondly with the view of giving point to the preceding remarks. The instruments on which native performers display their powers and skill are gongs and tom-toms, horns of different kinds, and sometimes a kind of hurdy-gurdy. I do not call to mind any others. By means of the gongs and tom-toms they mark time, and this is really the only approach (European ears being judges) to what we understand by the word "music"; but even this is so outraged by the stunning crashing noise made by these detestable contrivances, that the effect which would otherwise be produced by the regular recurrence of sounds at stated intervals is lost ; while the horns and the trumpets, if such a name is allowable, and the squeaking, shrieking, wailing, grunting sounds produced by the instruments referred to, make up a *tout ensemble* that must be heard to be imagined. Every performer plays his own tune, or rather produces a series of sounds one only more diabolical than another—if such assaults on the sense of hearing can be called a tune—on his own instrument, and every man performs in his own key. The result is the most hideous and frightful discord that can be produced. If the gongs and tom-toms are in the ascendant, the noise is deafening. If the small pipes and horns predominate, the conversation of cats in the gutter, or the howling of jackals, roving about at night, or the screaming of women and children, or all three mingled together, are simulated. A child, once very dear to me, described the effect produced on his ears by the performance of a number of native musicians in these words : " Oh, there's the crying band again !"

'Not long after the Highlanders had passed through

Bangalore, a young Scot, not a Highlander, was ordered to do duty with the 13th Dragoons, during the leave of absence granted to Dr. Clark, the regimental assistant-surgeon; two months later on his term of absence was drawing to a close, and consequently Dr. T., the temporary substitute, would, on its termination, be sent to do duty with an infantry corps, and lose the climate of Bangalore and one hundred rupees a month. All of these unpleasant consequences the said Dr. T. was naturally anxious to avert, or, at the worst, to postpone. He had, with this in view, some time back written to his friends at Madras to look about them and get him a strong letter to Colonel MacC.; they accordingly did so, and procured a *strong letter* from some Highland gentleman who either knew or boasted a fifty-ninth cousinship with Colonel MacC. The strong letter was presented the morning after its receipt with the required number of bows, and with the reverence supposed to be needful. All which I grieve to say were utterly thrown away on Colonel MacC.; he took the letter, and looked at the bowing youth who brought it, booted and spurred and buttoned up to the throat, with a scarcely concealed smile, pointed to a chair, and read his friend's communication. When he had concluded it, he refolded it, put it carefully on the table, and then, turning to Dr. T., said, " I fear Anstruther has put himself and you to trouble for nothing. In the first place, I never ask favours of anyone; and secondly, if I did, and you were my own son, I could not ask anything in the quarter you point at." Poor David T. was not a little taken aback at this rebuff, as the longitude of his countenance plainly announced; he got up, hoped he had not intruded, and begged to be excused if he had done so, made another of his best bows, and was about to beat a retreat, when Colonel MacC., whose somewhat sarcastic expression of countenance did not reach beyond the surface, said, "Sit down, Mr. T., I've something to say to ye. I can't serve you in the way that Anstruther asks, but maybe I can put you in the way of serving yourself." T.'s ears became doubly attentive. Colonel MacC. continued, "You have, of course, called on Colonel B. ?" "Yes, Colonel, but he was out." "Oh, you found him out! Well, you took a shorter time to do it than I did; but never mind that : did you leave a card for the lady?" "No, Colonel, I did not." "And pray, sir, why did you not? Don't you know it's your duty to pay your respects to your commanding officer!" "But so I did, Colonel." "But I tell ye, so you did not! There, now be off, and try to make out the riddle, which I can plainly see you don't yet comprehend. Try and translate it into practice. You'll find the advice good if you know how to use it."

'A great deal more was said, which I do not feel called upon to repeat. Poor David T. departed in a charming state of conglomeration, and he confessed to my brother, to whom, under the seal of profound secrecy, he reported the whole conversation, that when he left the Colonel's house he scarcely knew whether he was standing on his head or his heels. My brother, after indulging in a hearty laugh, asked him if he had yet paid one visit recommended to him. "No," said David, "I'll take care how I do that !" "But, then," returned my brother, "you won't be able to see Colonel MacC. again." "No," replied David, "I'll take care how I do that, too !"

'David T. was in many respects a very good fellow, but he took everything literally, and actually had, I believe, a sort of horror at a joke, particularly if he did not understand it, which was commonly the case. He was not a fire-eating Irishman, or he would have rivalled Sir Brallaghan O'Callaghan in the play, who says, "And if you shall say anything that I will not understand," etc. David, however, did not resort to the *ultima ratio* when he did not understand; he waited to have the joke explained. He had, perhaps, never heard that wit explained is no longer wit; but, whether he had or not, neither the wit nor the explanation ever seemed to disorder his equanimity. The only witty story I ever heard him tell, was one of Professor B., who was one of David's masters when attending the classes at Edinburgh. This gentleman was in the habit of enlivening his lectures by asking questions of his pupils. He had, on the occasion under reference, been using some mechanical illustrations to show that if the spring of a machine be wound up too tight, the whole apparatus will go too fast, unless a counter-balancing force be brought into play. Thus if the weights are not sufficient, the clock goes too fast; and on the other hand, if the weights are too great, the clock stops, or goes too slow. In the more perfect arrangements, a pendulum supersedes the weights, and can be lengthened or shortened to produce like effects. "Similar laws," said the Professor, "obtain in morals and in physics. If a youth is going too fast you put him under restrictions—in other words, you put more weight on him, and *vice versâ*. Now," turning round to one of the students, he said, "if you found a youth who was under your charge, a younger brother, for instance, not going quick enough, in fact—going decidedly too slow, what would you do?" "I wad shorten his pend'lum, sir," replied the unlucky wight. Here roars of laughter put an end to the sentence and the lecture; as this little anecdote puts an end to our further knowledge of David, who was a steady and solid practitioner of medicine, painstaking and zealous in his duty, a good husband, a good father, and a good Presbyterian. He died of cholera, poor fellow! at Trichinopoly, lamented by all who knew him, except the snipes, who certainly must have rejoiced when they heard of his death, since when alive he was never known to miss one of them.

'Most men who possess adventitious advantages, such as rank, wealth, position, and power, indulge in certain peculiarities of manner, speech, or habit ; and the reason is not far to seek. They are so independent that they consult only their own fancies. Colonel MacC. was no exception to the rule just noticed ; he had some peculiarities of manner as well as speech, and, of course, these were well known to the men of the regiment. Peculiarities of manner no doubt they caricatured amongst themselves, but could not show that they did so. With peculiarities of speech it was different, and the men hit on a method of amusing themselves with them that was certainly ingenious.

'Colonel MacC., it has been already said, was a capital horseman, and when out with the regiment always liked to see every manœuvre executed in the most rapid manner. Whenever the men were not quick enough to satisfy his judgment, he used to indulge in this form of reprehension : "Move, you beggars, move !" By degrees it became familiar to the men, and then they commented on it by purchasing a parrot, which, being a young and teachable bird, was not long in learning and mastering his lesson, "Move, you beggars, move !" The bird soon became proud of his proficiency, and wanted little or no coaxing to make him display it. At any time it was sufficient to say : "Good-morning, pretty Polly ! what does the Colonel say ?" to bring out, "Move, you beggars, move !" to the great delight of the men, women, and children of the regiment ; but every amusement or enjoyment has its drawbacks. On one particular occasion, when Colonel B. was on leave and Colonel MacC. in command, an inspection of barracks, hospital, etc., was ordered. Accordingly Colonel MacC., with all the officers present with the regiment, repaired to the barracks. While engaged in this duty everyone's ears were startled by the ill-timed sounds, "Move, you beggars, move!" No one took any notice, but glances were exchanged all round. By-and-by "Move, you beggars, move!" was repeated more emphatically than before ; this was too much for the Colonel, who called out, "Who is that? who has the audacity to interrupt the duty in this manner?" No one answered. "Sergeant-major," called out the Colonel, "who is that? I insist upon knowing! Tell me at once who it is that is guilty of this insolence? Whoever it is, put him under arrest immediately! What are you standing there for, like a fool? Did you not hear me say put the fellow under arrest?" "Yes, sir," said the Sergeant, "but I don't think it's any of the men." "Don't think it's any of the men; what do you mean? Is it one of the women or children that dares to act in this way?" "No, sir, it's none of the women or children." "Who is it, then? Take care, Hopkins, solitary confinement and reduction to the ranks will be unpleasant things for you to face after so many years' service; but it seems to me that you are going the right way to get them. Once more I say, who is it?" "I think it's the parrot, sir." "The parrot! What parrot? Whose parrot? Why don't you answer? Who owns the parrot?" "I think, sir, the bird belongs to the regiment." By this time Colonel MacC. had recovered his good-humour. "So it belongs to the regiment, does it? Well, take it away, and don't let it interrupt us again." Colonel MacC.'s good-humour on this occasion endeared him to the men so much that there was nothing they would not do to please him ; and though they kept the bird, they took the greatest care to keep him away or silent whenever the Colonel visited the barracks.'

THE PASSAGE-OF-ARMS BETWEEN COLONEL L. AND MRS. G.

DURING the year which passed before the Koorg War, and while Colonel L. was in command of the cantonment of Bangalore, a somewhat singular passage-of-arms took place between him and an old lady, Mrs. G., who was the widow of General G., who had, some six months before, died at Nagpore. This lady, having in earlier days dwelt at Bangalore, lost no time in quitting the dry, burning heat of the former locality for the delightful climate of the latter station. She had, through friends, secured a commodious bungalow, situated not far from the house afterwards occupied by the Commissioner for Mysore, and she had furnished her little house very nicely, and, in a word, made herself very comfortable. Having no family with her, her two sons being grown-up and both bearing commissions in the Company's Service, her means were ample for all her requirements, including her palankeen, carriage, and horses. Besides her pension she had her husband's savings, amounting to 8,000 Rs. or more.

She had inhabited the bungalow in question about three months, when she was surprised by a visit from the cantonment Staff-Officer, who came to announce to her that, by the new arrangement decided on by the General and officers commanding the cantonment, she would be obliged, on or before the 15th of the next month, to vacate her bungalow, as it, with several others, had been appropriated to the new staff-lines, and that he had come by order of the officer commanding the cantonment to give her due notice.

Mrs. G. replied that she was indebted to the officer commanding the cantonment for his politeness, but was sorry that Captain W. (the cantonment Staff-Officer) should have been put to trouble on her account. In a word, the politeness on both sides was perfect; everything was so sweet and agreeable that milk and honey could not exceed it.

The Staff-Officer—who was to the backbone of the unmitigated Pomposo breed, and who was generally known in the cantonment by the sobriquet of 'Immortal Jack,' being quite a young man at forty, dressing as such, although, to hide his premature baldness, he was obliged to wear a wig—retired quite delighted with his visit. He had sported his new staff uniform before the cantonment, and he had, as he thought, settled everything with Mrs. G., and so he reported to Colonel L.

Shortly after his departure, the lady sent for the house-man, who came at her call, making numerous profound salaams as he entered the house.

'Well, Vencaty,' said the lady, 'are you still desirous of selling your house? You told me when I first came here and took the remainder of Captain Turner's lease, if I recollect rightly, that you were willing to sell for 4,000 Rs. Is not that so?'

Now, Vencata-sawny, who was as cunning as a fox, having heard something of the projected staff-lines, answered with all the apparent simplicity of a child and all the practised skill of a lawyer: 'Missis please I sell. Missis like to buy, I like very much to sell.'

'Very good, Veneaty. You know my lease has only four years to run, and as I wish to make the house my own, I will speak to Mr. Cardoza, my lawyer, to draw up the necessary papers, and you can bring a vakeel, on your part, to see that all is right and just; and as soon as the papers are signed I will pay the money.'

'Missis very good lady. I do as missis tell. To-morrow I come—I and vakeel. Missis say what time.'

'Oh, you may come about ten o'clock; my breakfast will be finished before nine.' So Veneaty departed, after the usual salaams. Mrs. G. at once wrote to Mr. Cardoza, and on the morrow, a little before ten a.m., he repaired to his client's bungalow, and there found Veneata-sawny with his vakeel. A conversation something to this effect then took place.

The first question put to Veneaty by Mr. C. was: 'Have you obtained the General's permission to sell your bungalow, which is situate within the lines of the cantonment?'

'I had permission when I gave lease to Captain Turner five years before. Missis now got that lease.'

'That will not stand good now, I fear, as they are going to make new rules for the cantonment,' observed Mr. C.

'But, sar,' said the vakeel, 'Missis like to buy. Missis can sell again to Government.'

Now, this honest gentleman had ascertained that the utmost that could be got from the cantonment authorities, if they purchased, would be 2,000 Rs. He and his wily friend Veneaty were therefore strongly disposed to sell. Mrs. G. escaped the snare Veneaty had set for her through the caution of Mr. C., who ascertained the facts of the case at Captain W's office.

But though Mrs. G. did not buy, she held the lease of the house, and continued to inhabit it and to pay the rent as usual. On the 2nd or 3rd of the ensuing month, Veneaty again presented himself at Mrs. G.'s door with the usual salaams.

'Good-morning, Veneaty,' said Mrs. G. ; 'come for your rent, I suppose.'

'Missis please to give, I take.'

'Here it is; count it,' said the lady, 'and see that it is right.'

'What for I count? Missis never make mistake.'

'But you must count to satisfy me.'

Veneaty had done this with his eye the moment he saw the rupees on the table, but he said : 'Missis give order, I count.' And count he did, as slowly and deliberately as a child.

'Well,' said the lady, 'is it right?'

'All right,' said Veneaty. 'Missis please take receipt.' Mrs. G. did so, and locked it up in her desk.

She then expected that the houseman would take his departure, but he continued standing at the table without offering to go. Then the lady said : 'What is it now, Veneaty? I see you have something more to say. What is it ?'

'I no like to tell Missis ; I too much fraiding.'

'But what are you afraid of ?' said Mrs. G.

'Missis too much angry if I tell,' returned Veneaty.

'And if I am angry,' said Mrs. G. 'for I suspect what it is you wish to say, I shall not be angry with you.'

''Then I tell; but I too much sorry, not my fault.'

'What you want to say is,' said Mrs. G., 'that you want me to leave the house ; is it not ?'

'Missis never tell that word. I no want, but Mister Captain he too much want, therefore I tell ; he tell too much ; punish me you no leave the bungalow. What I do, I too much sorry.'

'Do not be afraid, Veneaty : he cannot punish you.'

'Missis how can tell. He tell Burra General Saib give order, and cantonment General Saib give order what I do.'

'You tell the Staff-Officer that you have asked me to leave the house ; that will set you right.'

'But Mister Captain too much bobbery man; every man too much fraiding him.'

'Never mind what people say ; you tell Captain W. that you have requested me to go out, and that I won't go.'

'No, Missis, I never tell that word. Mister Captain too much angry.'

'Very well,' said the lady, 'I will tell him myself; and I will also tell him that you have asked me to go out.'

'Missis too much good Missis, but I too much fraiding.'

'Well, Veneaty, never fear for me. I will take care of myself.'

Then Veneaty, with even greater reverence than usual, departed, thinking that Mrs. G. was a too-much brave woman.

Nothing fresh occurred till a day or two before the 15th, when Captain W. again made his appearance. Mrs. G. had in the meantime done nothing ; everything was in its place, even to the vase of flowers. After the ordinary salutations, the Captain said : 'I fear you are driving things to the last moment, Mrs. G. ; you have only to the 15th, by which time we must have the bungalow. I really fear you are putting yourself to unnecessary inconvenience.'

'Thank you very much,' returned Mrs. G. ; 'I have not been put to any inconvenience.'

'But I fear you will be, if you don't make preparations in time.'

'Oh, never fear,' said the lady; 'I shall make preparations in time—that you may depend on.'

'Then I will take my leave with many thanks,' said Captain W. ; 'you have relieved my mind very much.'

'You are very polite,' returned Mrs. G., 'but you have nothing to thank me for.'

'Oh, but indeed I have a good deal,' replied the Captain.

'Well, I am glad you think so,' said Mrs. G.; 'good-morning.'

'Good-morning,' said the gallant Captain, as he lifted his staff cap very gently for fear of displacing his wig, and galloped off.

On the morning of the 15th the same gallant officer appeared again, attended by a serjeant and several other people. He came to take possession of the bungalow, but this he found more difficult than he had anticipated. All the doors and windows were locked and fastened up except one window in the only upper room of the house, which was open, and at which Mrs. G. appeared.

'Really,' said Captain W., raising his cap, 'this is too bad, Mrs. G. You must pardon me for saying so, but it is too bad, after all the warnings you have had, and after the promises you have made.'

'I never made you any promise whatever,' said Mrs. G. 'You chose to put on my words a construction that suited your own ideas, and I tried to set you right; but you would not let me. I told you you had nothing to thank me for, but you persisted in doing so, somewhat to my amusement. Besides, I sent you word distinctly that I did not feel inclined to leave my house. Veneaty told me he had given you my message, but perhaps he did not speak the truth.'

'He did deliver your message, Mrs. G.,' said the Captain, 'but neither the General, nor the Colonel, nor myself thought for a moment that you really meant to act on it.'

'Well, sir,' said Mrs. G., 'you find your mistake; it is a pity that three such great men should fall into the same error, but by your own account so it is.'

'Well, ma'am, I am sorry you put me into such a painful

position, that I feel I have no alternative.   I must report your disregard of authority, and whatever happens, you must remember you brought it upon yourself.'

'Thank you, sir, for your advice ; but, really, unless the Colonel and yourself resolve to burn my house over my head and me in it, I don't see what is likely to happen.   I am a British subject, sir, although an unprotected woman. You threaten to break open my doors, and to expose my property outside the house, to be spoiled by sun and rain and night-dews ; try it, sir, and lay yourself and your gallant chief open to a civil action in the Supreme Court.   There the judges, thank Heaven ! care not two pins for your cantonment law.   You cannot bring me, being a woman, to a court-martial for disobedience to orders ; and I am advised, by those who do know something of law, that as I came here before your new rules were made, and besides hold a lease granted under cantonment law five years ago, you cannot legally turn me out.   Go home, sir, and think of some cunning way by which, as gentlemen, and men of honour, you can show courtesy and respect to an unpro-tected lady, the widow of a brother officer ; turn over in your generous minds how by violence and intimidation you can effect that which you cannot effect by law.'

Here Captain Pomposo, all but frantic, called out : 'Mrs. G.—Mrs. G., pray consider what you say, pray have——' But Mrs. G. refused to consider anything, or to hear any-thing ; she shut down the window and pulled down the blinds.   The 'immortal' had nothing for it but to ride to Colonel L.'s house and report the success of his under-taking.

When Colonel L. heard the result of Captain W.'s attempt to take possession of the bungalow, he was utterly con-founded—I might say almost horror-struck.   Resistance to military authority in a military cantonment had never, even in his dreams, assumed a tangible shape, or appeared even as a distant or possible contingency; and now he had to face it as a positive, undeniable reality. Actually in a cold perspiration he said, after pausing a minute or two : 'But what are we to do? I never met with such a case before, and never heard of such a case ; the thing is so preposterous and unnatural, as well as unprecedented, that I am really at a loss. If it was a man I had to do with I should know what to do; but really, independent of the scandal and absurdity of the thing, to engage in a contest with an old woman, and to run the chance of getting the worst of it, places me in a position I never for a moment contemplated. I am fairly perplexed, and truly would rather again face "la Vieille Garde" with Ney at their head than face this dreadful Mrs. G. Great pity women were ever admitted into cantonments ; they always give trouble and always cause trouble.'

'They did so in the first cantonment ever marked out, so we are told,' observed Captain W. To this the Colonel made no reply, not relishing even an approach to a joke on so serious and distressing a subject. After a silence of some minutes, during which the Colonel endeavoured to overcome his indignation, though with but partial success, he said : 'Send for the houseman.'

'When shall I tell him to be here?' said Captain W.

'Send an orderly to fetch him here at once,' replied the Colonel.

An orderly was accordingly despatched for Veneaty, who in due season arrived, puffing and panting in consequence of the rapid mode of progression insisted on by his military companion. When brought into the presence of the Colonel his nerves seemed to be greatly discomposed, nor did the Colonel's manner and mode of address tend much to reassure him. The first question put to him was :

'Are you the owner of the house now occupied by Mrs. G. ?'

'Yes, I am, General Saib.'

'Does she pay her rent regularly ?'

'Yes, General Saib.'

'Does she hold a lease of that house ?'

'She has taken Captain Turner's lease, General Saib.'

'When did she obtain that lease ?'

'Four months ago, General Saib.'

'Four months ?   Are you sure ?' ,

'Yes, General Saib.'

'It was not after the new rules were ordered, was it ?'

'No, General Saib ; it was more than three months before they were ordered.'

'Well, you see, W.,' said the Colonel, 'we shall gain nothing by parchment ; we must try something else.'

'Veneaty, when you want a tenant to go out, what do you do ?'

'If he no pay his rent, I get order to seize his property, then he pay or he go out.'

'But suppose he does pay his rent, and still you want him to go out, what do you do then ?'

'I give written warning to go out.'

'Then can't you do that with Mrs. G. ?'

'How can do that, General Saib ?   Mem Saib got lease.'

'Oh, I forgot that,' said the Colonel.   'What the devil am I to do ?'

'General Saib not know, how can I tell ?' returned Veneaty.

After a silence of some minutes, Captain W. said : 'In a case of like nature, or something like, that occurred at Bombay, they unroofed the house, and so got the tenant out.   Won't you do that ?'

'General Saib give order, I do; but Mem Saib, if she make complaint to High Court at Madras, what I do?'

'Well, Veneaty, you may go now; when I want you again I will send for you.' Then, turning to Captain W., he said: 'Before we act I must write to headquarters, and get instructions from Government. I must ask them to take the opinion of the law officers on this case, then perhaps we shall know what we are about.' So Veneaty departed, making profound salaams as he went out, rejoicing that he had not been required to take active measures against his tenant.

Three months elapsed before the Colonel received an answer to his letter of inquiry, and then the answer was not exactly what he wanted; but it gave permission to the local military authorities to direct the unroofing of the house if the occupant continued refractory after another warning, the Government being prepared to meet damages should any be awarded by the Supreme Court.

During the suspension of hostilities, Captain W.'s position was not in all respects a pleasant one; he was exposed to constant inquiries as to when active operations would recommence, how the fortress was to be stormed, and whether he was prepared to lead the forlorn hope. In fact, to the lookers on the whole thing was regarded as great fun. Nothing amused them more than to make inquiries on this subject, and few things annoyed the gallant staff officer more than to be questioned respecting it. His friends, good-naturedly, seldom lost an opportunity of doing so. On these occasions his usual reply was, that references had been made to headquarters, but that the law was uncertain. 'O-ho! is that it?' said one of these good-natured friends; 'then at least for the present you have yielded the field to the enemy? What a jolly old girl, that Mrs. G.! Upon my life she's a Boadicea, a Thalestris, a perfect Queen of the Amazons! To beat a general officer, a brigadier, and a staff-officer single-handed is really an extraordinary feat of arms.'

Captain W., who could not suppress his vexation, observed: 'You are talking a great deal of nonsense, Gunthorpe; the war is not ended yet. You had better wait till it is before you indulge in such idle gibes.'

'I fear,' returned Gunthorpe, 'if the war goes on as it has begun I shall have to wait a long time. But don't be crusty; I must have my laugh, and can't afford to put it off for the indefinite time you point to.' W. was vexed and sulky, but Gunthorpe would have his laugh, so the 'immortal' Don Pomposa rode off without making any reply.

At another chance meeting on the parade ground, the conversation again turned on the slow progress the besiegers were making, and the resolution displayed by the garrison.

'How long is it since the siege commenced?' said one. 'It can't be much less than six months,' said another. 'But it isn't a siege now, is it, W.?' said his quondam friend Gunthorpe. 'I should rather term it a blockade.' 'Oh, call it what you like,' returned W., 'that will make very little difference.' 'Certainly not, certainly not,' said G.; 'a rose will smell as sweet by any other name, you know. At all events, whenever you do obtain possession of the place so gallantly defended, you'll have to allow the garrison all the honours of war, that's certain. But do you know what I heard this morning?' 'How should I know?' returned W. 'Well, I suspect it will astonish you not a little. Mrs. G., it is credibly reported, to show her total indifference to all your proceedings, has determined to open a shop, and has already made arrangements for fitting it up.' 'Open a shop! Nonsense!' said W. 'True, I assure you,' returned his friend. 'But what kind of goods is she going to deal in?' 'Oh, everything included under the head of *stationery.'* 'Confound you, G. ! I thought some rubbish of that sort was coming.' The laughter of others showed that they relished G.'s small attempt. Then the party separated, all in high spirits and good-humour, except the 'immortal' Pomposa, who rode away swelling and ruffling his plumes, and vowing this, that, and the other. He thought of making an application for two months' leave of absence, but he remembered that if he got it he would have to forfeit half his allowances, therefore he agreed with himself that discretion would be the better part of valour. Nevertheless, he could not suppress a few kind wishes in favour of his friends, which, as they did not hear them, did them no serious harm.

Things went on much in the old way, until the arrival of the instructions from headquarters. Then active operations recommenced. Official notice was again sent to Mrs. G. that if she did not vacate her bungalow by a certain date, which was duly specified, orders would be issued to unroof it. Still the indomitable heroine took no steps to find another house, nor did she take any notice of the official warning.

When the period of grace was about to expire, Captain W., by the desire of the Colonel, wrote Mrs. G. a polite note, telling her that the workmen and coolies would be at her house on such a day unless she removed in time, but that both he and the Colonel hoped that Mrs. G.'s sense of propriety would save them the pain of enforcing a measure so repugnant to their feelings.

Mrs. G. replied to Captain W.'s note, with thanks for the intimation it conveyed, adding that as the roof was in want of some slight repairs, and that as she knew, when it was repaired, all the broken or injured tiles must be replaced by new and sound ones, the order was tantamount to one for repairing her roof, which she begged to acknowledge as it deserved.   As a lady, she could not raise her cap to the Colonel.   It was, however, scarcely necessary, as he had raised her tile for her.   This ran round the cantonment, while the laugh was all on the lady's side, and her pluck was universally admired.

By and by the day of fate arrived, so did the workmen and the coolies, with ladders and all other needful means and appliances.   Mrs. G., wearing a large pith hat, and farther defended by a large silk umbrella, having a long support that rested on the ground, came out, and pointed out to the men where they should commence their work. Veneaty was there, making pathetic appeals to everyone, as well as to his own throat, and uttering unceasing apologies. ' He too sorry.   He not do.   But too much fraiding,' etc., etc.   Numerous officers, some friends of Mrs. G., some strangers, but all more or less sympathetic and complimentary as to her courage and resolution, were assembled in and around her compound.   There was much talking and shaking of hands.   By and by jocose remarks and peals of laughter were mingled with the babel of various tongues and voices, and the whole thing seemed to be regarded by the majority as an excellent joke, Mrs. G. appearing to be in high spirits, as she talked to everyone, giving all to understand that her lawyer had positively stated that she was bound to make money by the proceeding, which she expressed her fixed intention to do, if only to read her special friends a lesson.

All this time, Captain W. did not appear.   Whether his conscience twitted him, or whether he feared the wit of his friends, is best known to himself.   Some assigned the one, some the other, reason for his non-appearance, and some said that both combined to keep him away.

The next morning, soon after gun-fire, Captain W. rode past Mrs. G.'s compound to ascertain if the orders had been duly executed. The lady was up and out, attending to her garden. As soon as she saw the gallant Captain she said: 'Good-morning, Captain W., won't you come in and have a cup of coffee?'

'No, I thank you,' replied the Captain, 'I'm on duty. I have to go to the artillery lines.'

'Oh, do come in,' replied the lady. 'I want to ask you why you were not on duty yesterday.' Captain W. coloured up, mumbled something, and was about to ride on his way, when his old tormentor, Gunthorpe, came up. After saluting the lady, he said to W.: 'Going to the artillery lines, are you? So am I. We'll ride there together.' So, raising their caps to the lady, they were about to start, when G. said: 'But isn't this a *moving spectacle?*' pointing to the tiles piled up on the ground. 'Whatever it is,' said W., again getting red in the face, 'it's no fault of mine.'

'I say,' said Mrs. G., 'it's nothing of the kind. I'm not thinking of moving—don't imagine any such thing—yet, after all, in another sense, it may be termed "a moving spectacle," inasmuch as it is most likely to move a good many rupees into my pocket. So you see, Captain Gunthorpe, that I have very good reason to be obliged to the Colonel and your friend Captain W.'

The lady and Captain G. were both convulsed with laughter; the latter, after a second bow, rode off with the Staff-Captain, who observed to G., 'You and the lady seem to understand the joke: I confess I can't see it.'

'Can't you? how odd!' said G., again bursting into a fit of laughter. Captain W. was sulky and silent, and little was said during their ride. When they reached the artillery lines, G. asked his silent friend to breakfast with him at the mess; but W. declined, stating he had yet to visit the canteen. So the gentlemen parted, and G. regaled his friends at mess with what he had seen and heard that morning.

Not to protract the story longer than needful, it is enough to say that the lady held out three months longer, during two changes in the state of her roof, which was first open on the north side and then on the south. She raised internal entrenchments of bamboo mats and cajans, which last she had to send some distance for. By these means, and the moving of her bed from this to that side as she found convenient, she defended herself against wind and rain and cold and sun most effectually; and though, as she observed, the polite attentions of her friends enabled her to converse with the stars more freely than she had been accustomed to do, she made no sign of capitulating; no white flag was seen on her battlements. She seemed, indeed, more active than ever. She drove out morning and evening, and whenever she met the Colonel or the Staff-Officer she saluted in the most obliging manner.

How long the siege might have endured it is impossible to say, had not the Koorg War unexpectedly put an end to it. Colonel L. was placed in command of the column that was to penetrate the Koorg country by Stony River, and therefore was shortly obliged to surrender to Colonel Burton his staff appointment as the commandant of the cantonment. Before he did so, however, Mrs. G. was seen at the band-stand, her coachman, her ghari-wallahs or grooms, and her horses, all decked out with large blue rosettes on their heads and turbans.

'Dear me, what is all this finery for?' said Miss Brown. 'Oh, I know. Mrs. G. is rejoicing that Colonel L. is going to Koorg.'

'Quite wrong,' said Mrs. G., who overheard her. 'It is on account of a matter of infinitely more importance to me. I have been awarded, independent of costs which will have to be paid as well, 5,000 Rs., as a compensation for the injuries I have sustained (so they put it). Now, isn't it good to get one's roof repaired for nothing, and then to get 5,000 Rs as a present into the bargain —isn't it good? So good that I could not help celebrating my victory and good fortune by a little outward display, as you see.'

By this time there was quite a crowd round Mrs. G.'s carriage, laughing, rejoicing, and complimenting her upon her success. ' But what will you do, Mrs. G.,' said Gunthorpe, 'if the new commandant takes up the cudgels, and continues the unroofing business ?'

' Oh,' returned Mrs. G., 'if he should be so very kind as to give me another opportunity of making another 5,000 Rs. I shall not object , I shall renew my conversation with the stars with unfeigned pleasure.' After this flourish of trumpets, and cheers from the ladies and uproarious laughter from the gentlemen, the old lady departed to take her accustomed drive round the racecourse.

It is almost needless to say that Colonel Burton declined to continue the war ; and thus terminated this famous ' passage of arms,' second only in interest to that of Ashby de la Zouch, recorded in 'Ivanhoe,' Mrs. G. having literally had her roof repaired for her for nothing, and having had a present of 5,000 Rs. on account of the proceeding.

It is said that the heroine, after her signal success, dropped her old coat-of-arms, substituting for her former crest a hen standing over two prostrate dunghill cocks, and for the three mullets on the face of the shield, several men thatching the roof of a house ; finally, for supporters, she had a brigadier and a staff officer. In place of her old motto, she had, ' I strive and thrive.'

On being asked why, being only Mrs. General G., she assumed supporters, she replied, ' My husband's family are

lineally descended from the King of Munster, so you perceive I am entitled to have supporters.' 'Well,' replied the
inquirer, ' you certainly found numerous and able supporters,
whether descended from the King of Munster or not.' 'Oh,
fie !' said Mrs. G., 'to try and throw a doubt on the validity
of my supporters.   Fie ! fie !'

MAJOR B.'S WELL-DESERVED DISCOMFITURE.

THE incidents about to be narrated happened during the campaign of 1834, undertaken against the Rajah of Koorg, whose atrocities could no longer be tolerated. The force ordered out for this purpose was divided into three columns : one under the command of General Waugh, a second under someone whose name we cannot call to mind, the third under that of Sir Patrick L., a thorough soldier, known afterwards as the hero of Koorg. The wives and other feminine belongings of the officers on duty with these three columns were left at Bangalore, from which station the several divisions started for the seat of war.

The desolate and distressed condition of these poor ladies, during the absence of their husbands, gave rise to those occurrences which the author has here endeavoured to describe, and from which the reader, it is hoped, will derive some amusement.

The solitary state of these fair sufferers naturally attracted the attention and commiseration of many of those gentlemen who were not employed on active service, and it was no less remarkable than beautiful to mark the constant devotion of some of them. It was indeed so remarkable that one of the ladies whose husband had not been ordered away, and who was at the time sitting by her side at the band-stand, observed, 'Who would not be a grass widow to get flowers and fruits from the Laul Baugh every morning, and such unfailing attention at all times ?   Surely the age of chivalry has returned.'

'I think,' Captain D. said, 'it is a pity that, with the age of chivalry, the husbands of the grass widows have not returned also.'

'That is a pity too, no doubt,' said the lively dame ; 'but in the absence of the legitimate comforters and protectors, isn't it charming to see how anxious most of the gentlemen present seem to be to make the ladies feel this absence as little as possible ?'

'Christian charity, Charlotte ; Christian charity,' said the gentleman.

'Well,' replied the lady, 'I hope it is ; but——'

'But what ?' said her husband, laughing.

'Oh, nothing ; only I hope they won't carry it too far. Some of them at least seem disposed to carry their charity (if that's the word, which I am by no means sure of) a long way.'

'If they carry it farther than they ought to do, isn't that the fault of the ladies ?' replied the marital speaker.

'William, you always take the part of the men, and it is not fair,' returned the lady.   'Look how Major B. besieges Mrs. W.'

'Well,' returned her husband, 'if he does she can force him to raise the siege whenever she pleases, can't she ?'

'I don't see it exactly in that light,' returned the lady ; 'I think gentlemen should not endeavour to do all the mischief they can, and then shelter themselves under the plea that ladies can, and ought, always to take care of themselves.'

'There is a great deal to be said, Charlotte, on both sides ; but tell me why ladies who have no fortunes to make, and whose election for weal or woe has been made years ago, continue to dress and dance, etc., just as they used to do when they were unmarried? Explain, if you please, the cause of these little performances before you utterly condemn the poor flies that are attracted by such Circean artifices.'

'Oh, William, I'm ashamed of you! You would go about to excuse the premeditated wickedness of men by trying to make out that the women are in fault in the first instance. I'm ashamed of you.'

'Ah, ma chère,' replied her husband, still laughing, 'however ingenious an attack may be as a defence, you have, in your ardour to defend your sex, forgotten to explain the spring of the *petits soin de toilette* that I referred to.'

'What nonsense you talk!' replied the lady. 'Are ladies utterly to neglect themselves, and to appear as slatterns and slovens, merely because their husbands are away?'

'I see,' said her husband, 'that it matters nothing whether menkind have the right on their side or not; womenkind ever have the best of it with their tongues.'

'It is nothing of the kind,' said the lady; 'we have the best of it because we're in the right and you are not.'

'That's a pretty flourish, Charlotte, but it will hardly account for the impression made on the whole cantonment; and if my memory does not entirely mislead me, I think I can remember that but the day before yesterday a certain vivacious, voluble little friend of mine' ('I'll pinch you, William') 'said that the "deserted wives did not at least mourn in sackcloth and ashes." Didn't that little friend of mine say something to that effect?' said her husband, laughing so much that he could scarcely speak.

'Oh, you're a horrid fellow, and can remember anything you please, whether it was ever spoken or not.'

'Oh, Charly, Charly! you must be in a difficulty when

you make such a dreadful charge as that, and, by innuendo. imply a doubt as to whether you ever spoke the words or not.'

'You've become a dreadful talker, William, and run into the greatest extravagance when you've nothing to the point to say ; but pray recall your faculties. Here comes young Johnson, who joined us but the other day.'

After the usual salutations to the lady and gentleman, the young ensign said : 'Oh, Mrs. D., there's such fun going on, that I must tell you of it.'

'Pray do,' said the lady.

'Just sit where you are and keep your eyes open ; in a few minutes you'll have Major B., in a handsome drag drawn by a pair of bays, with Mrs. W. by his side, drive by. Not to make the thing too particular, the old fox has got Mrs. Flower and my chum, Hopkins, in the back seat ; but it would do your heart good to hear how strong the Major is coming it with the lady by his side. I must say he's a man of metal. for every time he has out that same drag and bays, it costs him 25 Rs. ; old Brasher charges no less.'

Here Captain D. burst out into an immoderate fit of laughter, in which his wife, as it seemed almost against her will, joined, though in a subdued manner.

'Oh, don't laugh now,' said the youngster ; 'wait till you see the party and the dashing turn-out. They say the Major was never known to do such a thing before.'

By and by the drag and party appeared, greeted by bows and salutations from all sides. The Major, not at all dis-composed by the fire of small jests in the shape of com-pliments, inquiries, and hopes that he would never put down such a pretty turn-out, drove round the band-stand twice, and then pulled up by the side of Captain D.'s carriage.

'Upon my honour,' said Captain D., 'the regiment is very much indebted to you, Mrs. W., for having put the Major in the right way at last. No suggestions of ours were potent enough to induce him to sport a turn-out like that ; it really does as much credit to the regiment as to himself.'

'Oh, pray do not imagine that I had anything to do with it,' said Mrs. W. 'I knew nothing about it until the arrangement had been made. Had I known anything about it I would not have suffered Major B. to incur such expense on my account ; indeed, I have so much to thank him for that I was really vexed when I saw what his generosity and kindness had led him to do unknown to me. I declined at first to drive out in it, but I saw that he would think it ungrateful and unkind if I persisted in refusing to avail myself of what he was good enough to say would be a pleasure to him ; moreover, as I knew the expense had been incurred I no longer refused, and, as you see, here I am. Besides, since this morning's post another reason has urged me to show my sense of Major B.'s kindness and attention in every way that I could that was right and proper. I only stay one day longer at Bangalore ; my husband informs me that Colonel L. has granted permission to all the ladies left here to rejoin their husbands as soon as they can make arrangements to do so. I have already written to the commissariat officer to post bearers for me, and shall start early the morning after to-morrow.'

'Oh, Mrs. W., what terrible news this is for me !' exclaimed the Major. 'I wondered this morning, when I called, what urgent business you had to prevent you from seeing me, but now I understand it all ; you were packing up your trunks.'

'Yes, Major, I was packing up. Surely you couldn't think I would lose any time, when what I have been waiting for so long has come at last, could you ?'

'I suppose not,' said the Major with a very downcast air. 'But, you see, I have been hoping you would stay here a good while longer, and the blow comes suddenly upon me. I knew you would go one time or other, but I never thought it would be so soon.'

'And I never thought it would be so long,' said Mrs. W.

'But you don't really mean to be off the morning after next? Surely you can't mean that,' muttered or half whispered the Major, in a most imploring tone of voice.

'Oh, I can and do mean it most positively,' said Mrs. W., laughing in a most provoking way. 'I have ordered a set of bearers, and a masulchi, and shall be off by three o'clock —not five o'clock—in the morning.'

''That's too cruel of you, Mrs. W.; and to remind me of that sweet song I used to delight in hearing you sing.'

'Oh, I shall come back by-and-by, and then I'll sing it for you again,' replied Mrs. W., with a wicked smile that made all who saw and heard her, except the disconsolate Major, laugh outright.

'Ah,' said he, 'if I ever do hear you sing it again, it won't be the same song it was before to me.'

'And why not?' said the relentless Mrs. W., scarcely able to utter the words from suppressed laughter, which seemed also to have seized Mrs. D., Captain D., and the two younger fellows, Johnson and Hopkins. But the Major, indifferent to everything but his grief, only said: 'Well, Mrs. W., I will have a cavady cooly and the boxes filled with European articles got ready for your journey, and you must not deny me the melancholy pleasure of seeing you off, and saying farewell to you.'

Mrs. W., after a little struggle to overcome the former tendency, said: 'On no account would I hear of such a thing, Major. I'll wish you good-bye to-morrow evening, and as to the boxes, don't think of it. I have supplies of everything I can want on the road. Besides, I should have no means to carry them. I travel dawk.'

'Oh, well,' said the Major, 'I'll see to all that ; and don't suppose that I shall let you leave Bangalore without being up to see you off, at whatever hour it may be.'

'Well, Major B., I can't prevent you from doing what you say you will do, but I certainly think you'd be much better in bed.'

As the band began to play the National Anthem, the carriages began to move off, but the two young men stayed behind to talk over the scene they had just taken part in. They ordered their horsekeepers to take their bays home, and then leisurely walked on to the mess-room, indulging, as they sauntered along, in repeated bursts of laughter. Johnson, who first recovered himself, said, turning to his friend : 'Now, can you fancy that anyone could be so blind as our worthy, the Major ? The old fogey, in his latter days, has become so amorous, so demented, about Mrs. W., that he can't help making love to her before everybody.'

'That's plain enough, and patent to everyone who has got eyes and ears,' returned Hopkins. 'And to see how she treats him ! Upon my soul, it's the finest fun I've had since I've been here,' remarked Johnson.

'Why,' returned Hopkins, 'she laughs at him so openly that if he were not what he is, he must see it.'

'But he don't,' said Johnson, 'that is the best of it—he don't, and goes on worshipping, and never minding, in a way that's unlike anything I ever saw before. I won't say " more majorum," for that would be a libel on all other majors.'

'Well,' said Hopkins, 'that would require a free translation indeed to translate it into wit, for which I suppose it's meant. You ought to rejoice old Leatherum is not behind you : he would score up marks against you for which you would not be able to find a free translation, I suspect.'

'You and old Leatherum be hanged !' said Johnson.

'Thank you for nothing,' returned Hopkins. 'Hang "*odi profanum vulgus*" whenever you please, but as for me, I'm not inclined that way just now, so won't trouble you for any such delicate attention. Besides, I shouldn't exactly rejoice to see you turn Jack Ketch after bearing her Majesty's colours.'

'It would scarcely be needful, I suspect, if I gave you rope enough,' returned Johnson.

'You seem to be particularly attached to this line of illustration, Johnson, but as it is not altogether new, let's try something else.'

'With all my heart,' returned Johnson, 'but what line shall we take up ?'

'I don't know that we need take up any,' replied Hopkins. 'Suppose we get up on the morning after next in time to witness the parting between the Major and Mrs. W. ?'

'Why, you don't think old "Amoroso" will really get up after what she said to him, do you ?' said Johnson.

'I have a notion he will,' returned Hopkins, 'and if he does I would not miss the play for a trifle ; it will be truly affecting.'

'Oh, it will be grand !' said Johnson, 'but I wish the lady had not been in such a mortal hurry to get back to her husband. Three o'clock is an uncommonly early hour.'

'If we want to see what goes on,' observed Hopkins, 'we mustn't mind that. It is agreed that we turn out on the chance.'

'Agreed,' said his chum. 'I'll tell Veeratawny to call us at half-past two ; that fellow never makes a mistake. How he manages to wake whenever he is ordered to wake, I don't know ; but he does it, that I know.'

'He's an invaluable fellow,' said Hopkins, as he entered the mess compound.

The usual revolution of the hours brought round three

o'clock in the morning of the day named by Mrs. W. for her departure. Accordingly, her palankeen and twelve bearers were ready at her door, with two Cowry coolies and a masulchi. She was dressed, giving directions to her ayah, for whom a dooly had been procured, and who would reach the Bislay Ghaut, where the camp had been pitched, the day after her mistress. All the ladies who could afford to travel dawk agreed to go with Mrs. W., and consequently there were in her compound not less than four palankeens, four sets of bearers, cavadees, and masulchies. The ayahs were running about under unusual excitement, and the ladies were making the final arrangements in their palankeens.

Major B. now made his appearance, followed by a coolie bearing the box of European articles.

'You see, Mrs. W., though you are in such a hurry to run away from your friends, they are actuated by very different feelings, for which you are so hard-hearted as not to show the slightest sympathy.'

'Don't talk such nonsense, Major B., but like a kind, good friend go into the house and ask the ayah for my black bag. I've left it somewhere; I can't go without it.'

'Certainly, certainly,' replied the Major; 'happy to be employed in *your* service in any way.'

'Now that I've got rid of that tiresome old man,' said Mrs. W., 'run, Anawah, and tell my bearers to bring my palankeen over to this side of the compound, so that Mrs. F.'s bearers and palankeen may stand nearest to the gate.'

This arrangement having been effected, the torches were lighted, and the whole party was about to start, when the Major rushed out of the house, and ran up to the palankeen nearest to the gate, exclaiming, 'Dear Mrs. W., the black bag cannot be found anywhere. I am so sorry.' Then seizing the lady's hand, he pressed it to his lips. 'But, surely,' he said, still holding her hand, 'you won't be so obdurate after everything I've done to show how dearly I prize the smallest token of kindness from you, you won't, I'm sure you won't, deny me one farewell salute,' and at the same time he put his head into the palankeen to possess himself of the small token he had solicited. But before he could do so, the lady had saluted him with such a sounding box on the ear that he recoiled two or three paces, saying as she administered the sedative, 'Och, thin, you auld baste, get out of that!'

Screams of laughter from the other side of the hedge informed the discomfited would-be Lothario that there had been witnesses of his ignominious defeat, and while he stood with one hand up to the side of his face, paralyzed with mortification and vexation, the palankeens moved off. Then he heard one of the observers say to the other: 'Wasn't it a sounder!'

'That it was, and no mistake,' replied his companion. Then both broke into another fit of laughter. Who the two watchers were it is not necessary to say.

When the calling hours came round they had a charming little narrative for their friends, which flew round the cantonment like wildfire, to the intense delight of the hearers as well as reporters.

Lest the more sensitive, sympathizing half of the creation might imagine that, actuated by despair, the hero of this passing scene sought some tragic remedy to quiet his distracting sorrow, or like those youths that died for love,

> 'Wandering in the myrtle grove,
> His gentle spirit sought the realms above,'

as Mr. Pope tells us, it is satisfactory to be able to inform these sensitive souls that the Major did this literatim, for having evaded for three days any appearance at mess by reporting sick, he obtained three months' leave of absence to the Neilgherry Hills, said to be above 6,000 feet above the level of the sea.

When on the hills, the Major must be regarded as an exalted character, but let us breathe in the softest whisper that he was not. No, he was not a heroic specimen of manhood, that is the melancholy truth; and however distressing the fact may be to Paul de Koch (or his shade), instead of resorting for help to a bullet, or prussic acid, or a pan of charcoal, as all Paul's heroes and heroines did, he only fled to the hills from the looks and laughter of his companions.

THE RACE STAND AND THE FANCY BALL.

THE scene that now presents itself is that of the race stand at Bangalore. The ring, twenty yards distant, is just opposite, with the winning-post about four yards in front of it. All 'the beauty and fashion,' as the newspapers phrase it, are seated in the front rows of the stand, or are fast coming in. Old Tommy H., the General, is seated beside his beloved Anna, who is not merely General, but Generaless too. She is at least forty years younger than her husband, who cannot be less than seventy, while if she numbers thirty-two or three it is the utmost she can be rated at. She is a fine woman, with fine features, and withal, and in spite of the great disparity in years, a kind, loving, affectionate wife. It is no wonder, then, that the old man loves her— he says he cannot love her enough ; and truly the poor old fellow tries to act up to that saying. At a review, a brigade field-day or sham fight, Mrs. H.'s military ardour sometimes carries her away. She is a splendid horsewoman, and is seen galloping about at full speed from point to point, the Adjutant-General of Division sailing after her in the vain endeavour to keep beside her, while the General is trying to maintain his seat and a very gentle canter at the same time. To restrain the instincts of an admirably trained charger whose native fire has been cooled and partly tamed by fifteen years' service, is sometimes effected, but at other times with so little success that a horsekeeper, running on either side of him, is obliged to hold down his legs, and thus keep him in the saddle. The General is, besides, fully engaged in soothing the ungovernable creature by patting him on the neck, and speaking to him in the most endearing way, and these manœuvres seem to be perfectly well understood by the sagacious quadruped. The kind of conversation carried on between them was something after the following fashion : ' Wo ho, proud animal. Soh ho, my steed !'—Neigh, neigh !—' Soh ho, soh ho ! But why these bounds and curvets ?'—Neigh, neigh !—' There, there ! wo ho, noble beast,' the patting being all the time assiduously continued.

These exhibitions of horsemanship naturally amused all who beheld them, and led to a good deal of idle chaff and fun. Adolphe D., the Divisional Adjutant-General, was asked whether any order had yet arrived from headquarters to invest the lady in her husband's cocked hat, coat, and continuations, etc., and to clothe him in her petticoats, etc. ; for, if not, and the Arabs, who at this time mustered strong at Kurnool, should make a raid into the Mysore country, all the inhabitants of Bangalore might get up one fine morning and find their throats cut ; and a great deal more in the same strain.

However, as neither the old General nor his wife heard these stupendous efforts of wit, they were not rendered for ever miserable by them. On the contrary, sitting beside each other at the race-stand, they appeared particularly happy and comfortable. Pretty Mrs. D. was conspicuous amongst the ladies, she and her squire, Lieutenant M. of the Horse Artillery, being characterized as a particularly handsome pair. Unfortunately, they were neither paired nor coupled, Captain D. being the owner, or, it might be said, the reputed owner, of Eve's fair daughter.

It would be an endless task to enumerate all those who were present. First, all the sporting men were there, decked in hunting coats, buckskins, and top-boots. This list included Colonel MacC., Lieutenant M., H.A., Captain Venables, H.M.'s 39th Regiment, Long E. of 7th N. Cavalry, Suscat and Humphries of the N. Cavalry, Captain L. of the H.A., some strangers, sporting men, some civilians from Madras, and the Mofussil, several dragoon officers, and some few, besides Captain Venables, from H.M.'s 39th and the Native Infantry Regiments. Most of these occupied the ring, where the gentlemen who were to ride were dressing, or weighing, or being weighed. It was a busy, bustling scene. Some had field-glasses slung over their shoulders ; the greater number had notebooks in their hands.

The race-stand was now crowded with officers of all arms, some few civilians and ladies, many of them from Madras, Arcot, etc. The jockeys were many of them dressed and ready, whip in hand, for a final weighing ; the horse-cloths were being taken off the horses, and all began to examine the printed papers in their hands. Ten horses were to run. Lieutenant M., in jockey costume, now walked from the band-stand to the seat in the race-stand occupied by Mrs. D., who said : 'What is it, Frank?' ' I only came over to point out the horses to you,' returned her friend ; 'they are going to walk them about for a little while, and I'll stay with you till the first bell rings.' 'That's a good boy !' said the lady, looking at him as I should not have liked her to look had I been Captain D. But, alas ! alas ! *Hei mihi quod nullis amor est, medicabilis herbis.* So Ovid said years agone, and so he might say again could he again return to earth.

' Well, that beautiful creature is Colonel Cubbon's, and so is that.' ' And the dark gray, whose is that?' ' Oh, that is

Anatomy. Well, he's a handsome fellow, too, but in too good condition for such a name.' 'Whose horse is he?' 'He belongs to General Mrs. H.' 'Oh, really,' said the lady, 'what an odd name! But, no; it isn't. Nothing could be more appropriate for Anna Tommy.' 'Well done, Emma!' said her escort; 'that's capital. Isn't that good, Colonel Williamson?' 'What?' said the Colonel; 'I didn't hear.' Mrs. D.'s *bon mot* was repeated, and all who heard it applauded loudly. 'On my word,' said Colonel W., 'Mrs. D., you're a monopolist. The ladies say you have more good looks than should fall to any one person's share, and not content with that, you throw all your friends into the shade by your wit.' 'I'm *sure*,' replied Mrs. D., 'the ladies didn't say that; you say it for them. It would be only too delightful if it were true.' 'It is quite true, Mrs. D.; two delightful things are wit and beauty.' 'Oh yes; quite true if one possessed them.' 'Come, come, you're not going to outface me in that way,' said Colonel W., 'with such proofs before my eyes and in my ears.' 'Oh,' said Mrs. O., in a half whisper to Mrs. C., 'she has brass enough to outface old Nick himself; anyone with half an eye could see what she is, only these men, especially old ones, are such unutterable fools.' Mrs. D. probably heard something and guessed more, for she leaned back in her chair and laughed heartily; then, casting an expressive glance towards Mrs. O., she said: 'Who is it, Frank, that says, "The highest compliment one woman can pay another is when the one exhibits malignity and envy towards the other"—who is it?' 'I fancy,' returned Frank, 'you mean that clever sample of female vanity, Madame de Staël. But how did you make acquaintance with her? I thought you didn't care for that sort of thing.' 'I do read sometimes, Frank.' 'Yes, I know you do; I caught you reading the "Bride of Abydos" the other day.' 'Yes; I do read

Byron, and have the honesty and courage to admit that I do; others read, and deny that they do so. But I'm not going to fight with you now; this isn't the right time or place, sir. But I'm in high spirits this morning, and I ought to be, for I have won high compliments from Colonel Williamson—he who never speaks of our poor sex without bringing up all our transgressions, from that little mistake our unhappy great-grandmother made to the various errors, *faux pas*, or misdemeanours attaching to Madame de Maintenon or the Marchioness of H.'

'Well, "mera jan," I must run. I have scarcely time to weigh again and mount. They are ringing that bell with the utmost violence and impatience.' 'Go, then; mount and win,' said the lady. 'So I always do,' said he, whispering something in her ear. 'Begone, you wicked boy!' said she, laughing, but pushing him away. 'Now that there's a vacancy,' said the old Colonel, 'I'll occupy M.'s place, and repeat all those transgressions you refer to, solely, you know, to make myself agreeable.' 'That's rather an odd way of doing it, isn't it?' replied Mrs. D. 'It's something like beating one till you're tired, and then claiming credit for leaving off a minute or two.' 'No, no; it's a great deal more than that. I apply soothing plasters, don't I? and dress you very nicely, don't I?' 'Nothing of the sort. I have my ayah to do that; and if you're going to beat me again, on the strength of your nice dressing, I tell you I won't suffer it.' 'Well, then, just to please you, instead of dressing, I'll do the other thing, if you will only let me; in short, I'll do anything to please.' 'Well, then, Colonel W., you'll stop, if you please. I have, and you have, allowed your tongue greater latitude than ought to have been allowed, so if you please you'll stop now, and we'll talk of something else.' Old W. was quick enough to understand from the lady's tone and manner that she would resent any prolongation of the giff-gaff he had been indulging in, so, like an experienced warrior, he drew off his forces, and said : 'Come, then, I'll go on with the horses.' The lady, to show that she had forgiven the old sinner, said with an arch smile : 'I see how it is. Mrs. Williamson does not keep you at all in order ; she must do better in future, or I shall warn her if she doesn't. You're such an impetuous old gentleman that she'll have you paying adoration to all the ladies in the station.' 'Oh no,' returned old W., 'you wouldn't do that : have some compassion. Spare me that.' 'A-ha !' said Mrs. D., 'so I have found a crevice in your armour, have I ? Ha, ha, ha !' laughing maliciously. 'Well, sir, behave yourself, and try and control your juvenile impetuosity. Ha, ha, ha ! How M. will laugh when I tell him !' 'No, no ; you won't tell him—I'm sure you won't.' 'I rather think I shall,' said the lady. 'Are you afraid of twelve paces ?' 'As far as that,' replied Colonel W., 'I fear nothing, and I've proved that more than once. We can settle it over a handkerchief if M. likes ; but I am afraid to face the ridicule, the scandal, and the gossip that a meeting between me, a married man, and M. on account of a married lady, might and would give rise to. I confess I am afraid of that. Come, be generous, and don't say anything about my small delinquencies.' 'Well, sir, if you'll promise to behave yourself, I will for the present hold my tongue.' 'That's kind. Now we'll look at the horses.' So the horses were looked at and pointed out individually, and their qualities and prospects descanted on. By and by the start took place. M.'s horse Leander won ; Trojan, the horse backed by Captain Venables, second ; and Roderic, Colonel MacC.'s horse, third, the rest nowhere. Mrs. D.'s delight was inexpressibly great, and while she was talking with the utmost volubility she declared she had no words to express it.

In the midst of the glee and the rejoicing, M. made his appearance, but with a countenance expressive of anything but mirth and satisfaction. 'What's the matter, Frank?' said Mrs. D. 'Nothing,' said M., 'but that I have lost the race.' 'How can that be?' said the lady. 'Your horse came in first.' 'Yes; but when the jockey was weighed, it was found that he had lost weight.' 'Oh, how sorry I am,' said Mrs. D.; 'I could actually cry, I'm so vexed.' 'Don't do that, "mera jan," don't do that; I'd rather lose the next race than that you should do that.' 'Well, Frank, I won't if I can help it.' 'I am really sorry,' said Colonel W.; 'but how did it happen?' 'I can't tell, and the boy can't tell. He is a good lad, and is now doing what you were almost doing, Emma; he is crying his eyes out because he has lost the race and I have lost my money.' 'But how did it occur?' 'I suppose some of the shot escaped out of the shot-belt, though how they could I don't know. However it came about, it has happened, and I have lost the race.' 'Well,' said the Colonel, 'you take it very philosophically.' 'Why should I not do so? fretting or fuming won't help me. Losing my temper won't save me from losing my money.' 'True,' returned the Colonel; 'but few exhibit so much command over themselves.' 'Few are like Frank,' said Mrs. D. 'But how much weight did the boy lose?' 'I forget exactly; not many grains over allowances.' 'And must you lose the race for that? that is hard.' 'No, "mera jan," it is the law, the rule; and it is as fair for one as the other.' 'Why, then, don't they have a piece of lead scraped or filed down to what is exactly required, and then if it were sewn into the jacket it could not be lost.' 'Not a bad plan, Emma, truly; but it can only help us for the future; it cannot help us on this occasion.' 'What I can't understand is how Cubbon's horses, by far the best of those which started, did not win.' 'It was in consequence of their acknowledged superiority that they lost,' replied M. 'Isn't that a paradoxical remark,' asked Mrs. D. 'No, Emma,' said M.; 'they carried too much extra weight. I knew they would lose, and I told the Colonel so, and advised him to scratch them. I also said I thought that the committee had decided erroneously; but he was so good and so generous that he declared he would rather lose than spoil the race and the general pleasure. Oh, he is *primus et solus.*' All sung Colonel Cubbon's praises, and then all prepared for the second heat.

Not to make my story too long, it is merely necessary to state the facts as they occurred. Trojan was first. The little mare Kate (M.'s horse) came in second, but again M. lost through his jockey, this time evidently by villainy; the boy had chosen to lose his whip. This would not have occurred had the lad who rode the first race been allowed to ride the second, which M. himself wished. His wishes were, however, overruled by his friends; so the honest but unfortunate jockey was discarded and the scoundrel trusted, as too often happens in this world in more important matters. As he himself said, 'Fate was determined to win the race against him.'

Poor fellow! that day's sport made him an indebted and distressed man all his days. On the other hand Fate, or Dame Fortune was equally determined that Captain Venables should be a winner. First, the horse he backed so largely was an ugly, awkward, bony-looking brute that would never have had the ghost of a chance had not the committee, most unaccountably, at the last moment almost, doubled the length of the course. This enabled Trojan's wind and bottom to tell. Secondly, by another oversight, the weight named for him to carry was insignificant. For, by height, and size, and strength, he ought to have carried a stone more than he did ; but, in truth, his other qualities were overlooked ; his Roman nose and awkward appearance, together with his comparative want of speed, which was well known, deceived the members of the committee. He was scoffed at as a competitor, and was generally put down as nowhere in the race, and consequently the bets and odds were heavy against him. Had it not been for the double course, which made the stretch close on three miles, the knowing ones would have been quite right ; but the alteration, which was purely accidental, upset all their calculations. Still, had it not been for the first jockey's accident and ill-luck, Leander would have won. As it was, Captain Venables won everything; his gains were calculated at more than £2,000, and, as everyone said, lucky it was for him that he did win. Had he lost, he had nothing, absolutely nothing, to offer in the shape of payment but his commission.

All the senior officers of the 39th had been constant and earnest in their remonstrances and entreaties to Captain Venables to draw back, and not to involve himself to such a perilous extent ; but all to no purpose. An obstinate fit of deafness, and, as it was looked on, madness, seemed to have got possession of him. He would hear nothing, see nothing, and say nothing except, 'Well, we shall see,' and such like cool, determined phrases. Everyone set him down as an obstinate madman, whose ruin was certain. Major S. said to him after a long, earnest, and fruitless remonstrance, ' Well, Venables, I shall be sorry, after twenty years' service, to see you carrying a musket, but there's nothing else before you that I can see.' ' But,' replied V., ' I can see something else, Major ; you will never see me carrying a musket.' ' I hope not,' replied the Major, as he walked out intensely disgusted and disappointed.

The real meaning of the expression was not understood

till after the speaker's death. Then, as members of the committee appointed for that purpose were examining and noting down his effects, a bottle labelled 'Cyanide of Potassium' was found; it contained fully two ounces, not having been opened. This of itself might not have excited much suspicion, as several officers were then amusing themselves with learning how to plate copper and other articles, for which the salt in question was largely used; but that it had been obtained for another and far more deadly object was made clear by a book found near the bottle. This was the last edition of Taylor on poisons. The section on prussic, or hydrocyanic, acid and its compounds had evidently been carefully studied; there were many marks and annotations in the handwriting of the winner of the race in pencil, and one which explained the writer's feelings and intentions so plainly as to remove all doubt from the minds of the committee. The words were these, after underlining the quantities required to kill an adult, ' But, after all, I may not require it.' The Father of all mercy graciously removed him from the world without having the contemplated crime to answer for.

The manner of this unfortunate man's death was as follows : After the second heat, when all doubt was removed, and it was certain that Trojan had won so largely, Captain Venables flushed up so as to appear almost purple in the face. My brother was standing directly opposite in the race-stand, and at the time watching the winner. He beheld the extraordinary flush mentioned, saw it gradually fade and pass away, and a deadly paleness succeed to it; finally, he saw the most extraordinary changes take place. The officer's face became brown, leaden, almost green. and at last a little flushed ; then he tottered, and would have fallen but that a friend held him up and supported him until a palankeen could be found ; into this he was placed and conveyed home. Dr. Davis, the assistant surgeon of the regiment, was sent for; he directed his patient to take a glass of hot brandy-and-water directly, to be undressed, and put to bed. The report spread everywhere that Captain Venables, the winner of the race, had been so overcome by the excitement as to be seriously ill; that he had drunk a glass of brandy-and-water, had been put to bed, and was not to be disturbed till to-morrow. Few except my brother thought that anything beyond over-excitement was the matter; but he had closely observed the extraordinary changes exhibited by the poor man's face, and feared a fatal issue. Almost every other person said: 'Oh, he'll be all right to-morrow. Oh, it's nothing but over-excitement; he knew if he had lost that he would have to sell his commission, and have to serve in the ranks, so, after all, his being upset by his wonderful escape and good fortune is nothing to be wondered at.'

This being the general opinion, little more was said or thought of Captain Venables; but there was great stir and bustle amongst the young people, and especially amongst the young ladies, nor indeed was the stir and excitement confined to the young people. A fancy ball, to follow on the evening of the races, was too important and rare an occurrence to be lightly passed over. This momentous consummation to the races had been announced more than six weeks before, so tailors and a variety of curious artificers had been busy during the month. Ladies and gentlemen had also been unusually busy. The result of all this preparation was a very splendid collection of fancy costumes and groups taken from Scott's novels, as well as from the more sober though less delightful pages of history. Some of the groups and costumes were so exceptionally good that they really deserve a passing notice.

Of these groups Queen Elizabeth and three ladies of her

court, in the costume of that day, with their grand ruffs, farthingales, and trains were very effective. Their four cavaliers, all habited in the well-known dress worn by Sir Walter Raleigh, formed a much-admired set for a quadrille. Queen Mary and her four Marys, with cavaliers wearing Highland dresses, formed another set for a quadrille, and were much admired. Another group habited as Virgins of the Sun also attracted much notice, the leader being Mrs. W. This naturally gave rise to several facetious remarks, which I leave to the imagination of the reader. Then after the groups there were several couples, which elicited marked applause. Mrs. C. and Mrs. M., as two Greek ladies, were greatly admired. Then Mrs. L. and Mrs. C., habited in the costume worn in the reign of George I., were acknowledged by all to be capital, and won universal admiration. Miss S., whose fine figure, beautiful complexion, and good-natured face must not be omitted, habited as a flower-girl, won many admirers. Other young ladies were seen disporting themselves as Persians, Circassians, Swiss maidens, sylphs, and vivandieres, and were all more or less admirable, and when mingled with the requisite number of Turks, Greeks, Hungarians, devils, and scaramouches, made up a beautiful and interesting *mélange* of characters. But the admired of all admirers was Mrs. S., in Scott's too charming character of Rebecca. To very handsome and expressive features, and to a tall, faultlessly graceful figure, this lady added the appropriate beauty of a brunette. Her dark eyes were fringed with long silken lashes ; her long and luxuriant dark tresses, partly escaping from ribbons and turban, fell in natural curls on her neck and shoulders, and, seen through her gauze veil, formed a wealth of beauty which set off and enhanced the witchery of a bust that Leda herself might have envied. Her costume, closely copied from the description given in ' Ivanhoe,' completed the enchantment wrought by her appearance. Her elegant little feet and slippers, almost concealed by her full silken trousers, when they did appear, gave a provoking glimpse of that perfection of form which her dress concealed. She was by all admitted to be the cynosure of all eyes.

But where was the Bois-Guilbert who ought to have been her cavalier? Ah, where indeed? 'Tell it not in Gath, speak it not in the streets of Ascalon.' The Bois-Guilbert, who was to have been personated by her husband, Captain S., was unable to stand or even to articulate; he was lying on his bed, partly undressed, almost unable to move, and in a pickle that cannot be described. Poor Rebecca! her sorrowful expression of countenance was felt too deeply to be regarded as acting, or if it was it was acting with an aching heart. Unhappily the condition in which Captain S. was found was almost a nightly occurrence; and yet this very man, when sober, was without exception the handsomest and finest man in the cantonment.

The sensitive mind recoils with indignation, disgust, and horror from the picture presented. God's grandest gift to man, his intellect (which, far better than any trivial anatomical distinction, distinguishes him from the beast), wilfully, wickedly, and wantonly thrown aside to gratify the lowest of all propensities. But the drunkard does more than this. It is a libel on the beast to say that the drunkard makes a beast of himself; he makes himself worse and lower than the beast, for the beast does not get drunk. It is only man who gets drunk; it is only man who dares to insult his Creator in this detestable manner—who dares to fling back in His face his best gift, and who thus displays, at one time and in one act, his disobedience, his wickedness, his folly, and his ingratitude. And if we now inquire how a persistence in drinking ends, the hospital, the gaol, and the workhouse answer. While, during life, as the man

pursues the dreadful downward path, he forfeits every kindly
feeling on the part of those who once loved him, and would
have done their best to serve him, in death he is remembered only as 'that drunken fellow' So-and-so. Some
former friend, who knew him before he had yielded to this
enthralling vice, may say perhaps: 'Well, I am sorry for
poor ——. I knew him when he was as nice a fellow as
you could wish to see; and to think that he, or such as he,
should be among the victims of the Vampire Drink, is very
sad; I cannot bear to think of it.' This is the career of
the drunkard in this world. What it must be in the world
to come, when he must give an account of his life, is dreadful to reflect on.

If the drunkard is a married man, his offences and his
wickedness are greater still; all that applies to the unmarried
man applies to him, and in addition cruelty of the worst
kind—cruelty so heartless and so unnatural that, though
we know it, we can scarcely believe it possible. The fiercest
and most ravenous beasts of prey (though not gifted with
human feelings and intelligence) do not desert their mates,
nor their young; but the drunkard who is married not only
deserts both, but will, to gratify his filthy passion, drink
away his income, drink away his status in society, drink away
his future prospects, and thus reduce wife and children from
the position in which they were born, and had heretofore
moved, to want, penury and degradation. Still not contented, but prompted by the horrible love of drink, the
married drunkard deprives his wretched, miserable wife of
the trifle she earns weekly, striving to stave off actual starvation, sells or pawns everything the unhappy pair once possessed, and the wife dies in the streets of starvation, cold,
and misery. This is the natural result of drunkenness when
observed in its effects on the classes that live by their daily
labour. Let us trace in a higher grade the effects produced

by indulgence in this baleful habit. The drunkard before his marriage manages to conceal his practices not only from the young lady he woos to be his wife, but from her friends. He, however, soon shows his colours. If in the army the natural consequence is that he drinks himself out of his commission. By the generosity of his Colonel and brother officers, he is allowed to sell, and the proceeds are made over to his unfortunate wife, who is deeply compassionated by all the regiment. And shall this mean, selfish wretch, who has wrecked the peace and prosperity of those whom he has sworn to love and cherish—sworn on the altar of the Most High—not be answerable? Shall he who has kept his holy marriage vows by bringing privation and misery on those who should be nearest and dearest, not be answerable? Innocence and virtue toiling in distress appeal to Heaven strongly. Man may disregard, but there is One who will not disregard—One who has said: 'Come unto Me all ye that labour and are heavy laden, and I will give you rest.' A mother toiling to feed her children—toiling in an altered and reduced position, to which she has been brought by her drunken husband—is too sad, too noble a sight, not to attract the eye of mercy. If the destroyer has one spark of human feeling left, the knowledge of what he has done must be like the fire of hell in his heart and brain; but words in such a case are vain. 'Vengeance is Mine, saith the Lord, and I will repay,' and to the Lord's vengeance such men must be left.

The effects of drunkenness, as exhibited by married and unmarried men, have been drawn from instances unhappily too well known to the author. Let us look now at the effects of this national sin, this degrading, despicable form of selfishness, regarded from a public point of view. What do the public prints tell us? What do we read of every day? Is there a crime that can be named that cannot be shown to have originated in drunkenness? Wife and child murder are actually common as one of these results. The vile husband comes home drunk, a quarrel ensues between him and his wife, and she—perhaps with her infant, or little boy or girl—is kicked to death by the infuriated savage. And what is too often the result? If the human brute expresses sorrow, and says he had taken a drop too much, he is allowed in some way or other to escape. Either the coroner and his jury bring in manslaughter, or the sapient judge and jury, by whom the ruffian is tried, find some legal reason to let him off, or the jury refuse to hang. They are too pitiful, but they have no pity for the unfortunate woman and her child or children. Drunkenness, as it is now regarded, is positively a protection to the murderer. Let us see how it acts in cases of less enormity than murder. Someone, man or woman, is beaten or kicked within an inch of his or her life, and the excuse invariably is that the beast had been drinking. Magistrates almost always ask this question. Policemen never fail to state that the man was, or was not, drunk. If the statement is that he was not drunk, it invariably acts as an aggravation of guilt; and, *vice versâ*, if the culprit is pronounced to have been drunk, it is at once received as a palliation. That which in common-sense is a positive crime, *per se*, is made by irrational custom to lessen and mitigate a greater crime.

The plea put forward to defend this practice is this: Would you punish severely the man who, from the influence of seductive company, or from any other cause, happens to get tipsy, even if he should commit manslaughter or other serious offence while under the effects of vicious stimulation? Certainly not. But this is mere sophistry. It is not an accident we have to consider; it is that of men who night after night deprive themselves of their senses by drink. In this case it appears clear that the fact of the man being drunk is a serious addition to his crime, as he has wilfully, and with his eyes open, deprived himself of his senses. This portion of the subject is too wide, too vast, for me to enter upon, as it necessarily touches the legal aspect of the question ; and there are no doubt numberless legal gentlemen, gifted with fine and acute intellects, who are fully equal to the determination of the intricacies and difficulties of the question.

To the reader, the author feels that he owes an apology for having in a light work, devoted chiefly to the worship of Momus, been led to say what he has said on legislative matters ; the delict was not intentional, it arose naturally from the incident related, and from consideration of the dreadful evils of intemperance, and the defects of the statutes passed in reference to it. Yet, if from the melancholy details recorded with reference to gambling on the racecourse, and the miserable instances of drunkenness brought forward (which, be it remembered, are cases actually observed), one solitary individual be induced to reflect on the life-long misery which almost surely will result from pursuing either of these baneful paths, and he by this means is led to pause in his ruinous career, the effects of the fault may perhaps go far to obtain pardon for it. Nor can the author think that because his principal object is to amuse, he should altogether be debarred from sometimes assuming a graver tone. Examples of individual sorrows, failings or crimes, ought not to be altogether useless, seeing that they are pages of individual history, and all history we know teaches by example.

Having now offered his apology, and recorded his plea for a favourable judgment, his long digression draws to a close, and he returns to the fancy ball, the description of which was interrupted by feelings excited in consequence of the condition recorded of Captain S. Let us now forget the unhappy man, and mingle with the gay crowd.

It has been before observed that the ' Virgins of the Sun ' attracted a good deal of rather quizzical notice on account of their leader, or high priestess, or whatever else she may have termed herself. Now it so happened that this lady unintentionally afforded new cause for the same sort of notice. She wore, as all the young ladies in her train did, a veil attached to her head-dress, from which it descended to her feet, falling in graceful folds about her person. As the room became warmer, in spite of the punkahs which were kept constantly going, for the dancers—among whom Mrs. W. (the *quasi* virgin) had distinguished herself—the veil became unbearable. Mrs. W. rejoiced in rather a superfluity of flesh ; she was a sanguine, full-blooded woman, with a large endowment of adipose tissue. We would on no account be so vulgar as to say that she was a fat woman ; all that can be asserted, with due regard to the *bienséances*, is that she was decidedly, very decidedly, stout. The heat, the dancing, and the lady's full temperament, made the veil insufferable ; it was accordingly laid aside, then at once were displayed charms that it is most difficult to do justice to. A dress laced in to the last point of endurance, and at the back so liberally cut down that the view afforded was unusually extensive, may give some notion of the length and breadth of the prospect. The heat, the exercise, and the constitution of the lady may, to those who have carefully studied such natural phenomena, suggest that a lovely roseate hue, a truly infantine tint, overpowered the native alabaster of the skin. The effect of the painfully heroic efforts to obtain a waist had produced a strong line down the spine, and had, moreover, accumulated masses of roseate adipose tissue on either side of that line. The *tout ensemble* presented such a comical resemblance to something that may be imagined though it may not be uttered, that the whole room was in a titter.

'Did ever you see anything like it, in your life?' said
Mrs. C. 'Why, to tell you the truth, my dear, I think I
have,' said Mrs. O., laughing immoderately; 'have not you?
Think now!' 'Oh,' said one of the young ladies. ' I never!'
'On my life,' said old Mrs. Fitslik, 'it's like nothing in the
world but a baby's ——.' 'Well,' replied Mrs. O., 'if it
is, it must be an unusually well-developed baby: but I
suppose " Virgins of the Sun " may have unusually developed
babies, if they have any.'

To repeat one hundredth part of the light sarcasms and
gibes and ironical praises of Mrs. W.'s liberality, beauty, and
good taste, would be impossible. The universal inquiry
was, during the evening, ' Have you seen Mrs. W.'s infantine
back? if you haven't, you had better do so without loss of
time, for I'll be bound you'll never see anything like it
again, except you go into the nursery.' These, and innumerable others like these, formed the staple of the chat
amongst the fairer half of the creation, and from these
the talk of the gentlemen may be surmised. Some of
the remarks, no doubt, were witty and caustic enough; but
as the author has gone quite as far as he desired on the
broad gauge in order to expose a special instance of bygone
female vanity and folly. he begs to relegate the sayings of
the male observers to the *Greek Kalends*.

The lights and shades of a ball, and especially of a fancy
ball, have ever been to the author, who was not a dancer, a
source of amusement. The wonder, embarrassment, pleasure,
and delight of the neophytes, who made their first appearance on the scene, was to him very interesting and sometimes entertaining; as were the rivalries, flirtations, dis-
appointments, and vexations of the more experienced
practitioners. It would serve no purpose but to fatigue the
reader to go into the details of these lights and shades.
Everyone can picture to her or himself the usual occurrences

of a ball—the eagerness of the young gentlemen to obtain
as a partner for the valse, or the polka, or the galop, some
particularly good dancer, or some particularly pretty girl,
and the extraordinary ingenuity and tact displayed by the
young ladies in avoiding and getting rid of those they did
not wish to have for partners, and in waiting for, in piqueing
or punishing those men whom they did wish to secure. Bless
their sweet faces ! all they did was equally remarkable.

WORSHIPPING TITLED FOLK.

THE little *plaisanterie* about to be narrated took place at the house of the officer whose amiable disposition towards those under his command, and particularly towards my brother and Mrs. B., has previously been shown.   Fortunately for all parties, the unhappy temper referred to was not always present, and, as this veritable history will prove, Colonel G. could make himself agreeable and join in fun and mirth as pleasantly even as Mrs. B. herself, who planned and originated *le petit jeu* now to be described.   The frolic was suggested by the extreme love and reverence displayed by a young lady, then staying with Captain and Mrs. C., for titles and titled personages.   The whole conversation of this young lady, a Miss Freeman, was made up with what Lord —— had thought, or said, or done ; and how Sir George had remarked, with his usual good sense, so and so ; and how the young Marquis of —— had been so funny about the horses, and how the ladies present had been so much amused, etc.

An exhibition of Miss F.'s feelings, likings, and instincts, took place at Mrs. G.'s house on the occasion of a morning call.   Mrs. B., who happened to be there at the time, and who really had seen a good deal of high life, was so much amused that unintentionally she communicated her own feeling to Colonel G., who, we have seen, by his dexterity in turning the tables on poor Mrs. B., was by no means destitute of acuteness or satirical power. He soon comprehended the situation, and did his best to aid Mrs. B. in drawing out Miss Freeman. The conversation proceeded in a manner that may be guessed at by the following imperfect report :

'Well, but, my dear,' observed Mrs. B., 'I should like to hear some of the funny talk of the "most noble" youth that amused your lady friends so much ; can't you tell us something of what he said ?'

'Oh,' replied the young lady, 'I don't remember all he said.'

'But,' returned Mrs. B., 'we don't ask for all ; can't you tell us something of it ? You surely must remember something, and then perhaps we should be able to guess at something more.'

After a pause Miss F. said, 'I remember, amongst other funny things the young Marquis said, speaking of all the girls present, that "the young fillies were rather a promising lot taken altogether."'

'Did he really say that ?' asked Mrs. B. ; 'very amusing wasn't it, Colonel G. ?'

'Amusing and complimentary too,' returned the Colonel.

'He must have been a delightful young man,' remarked Mrs. B.

'He was indeed, Mrs. B.,' said the young lady.

'But, come, tell us something more ; don't be so stingy with your recollections : pray give us a little more.'

'I wish I could,' returned Miss F., 'but I've such a bad memory. Oh, I do call to mind. He said Miss Marks "went right well on her pasterns."'

'What an amusing fellow !' said the elder lady.

'You can't think what an amusing creature he was,' continued Miss F.

'I begin to have some notion,' replied Mrs. B.

'Oh, but you don't know what he said of Miss Smithers.'

'How should I?' returned Mrs. B. 'I wasn't so fortunate, you know, as to be one of his intimate friends.'

'That's true,' said Miss F.

'But,' continued the elder lady, 'let us hear what he said.'

'It was so funny that we all laughed.'

'How tantalizing you are! Why don't you repeat it, that we may laugh too?' said Mrs. B.

'Well,' replied Miss F., laughing, 'he said "she was bluff in the hocks."'

'Said "she was bluff in the hocks!"' said Mrs. B., as soon as she could recover from her laughter (in which her friends joined). 'No wonder you were all charmed with him; it is scarcely possible to imagine a more fascinating or witty young gentleman. But what did he mean, my dear, by bluff in the hocks?'

'I'm sure I can't say, Mrs. B.; but I know everybody thought it very funny and very amusing. I don't think anyone knew exactly what he did mean, but everyone laughed most heartily. I know I did.'

'Truly,' said Mrs. B., 'a more convincing proof of wit than that I can scarcely imagine; it must have been superlative when it amused everyone though no one understood it.'

'It must not only have been superlative, but amazing,' observed Colonel G. 'I only wish I could get people to laugh on such easy terms; but I suppose being a marquis goes some way.'

'Very likely,' said Mrs. B. 'What do you say, Miss F.?'

'Of course it does. I should say it would go a very long way,' said the young lady.

'It is greatly to be regretted,' remarked Mrs. B., 'that

we have no such witty young marquises in this part of the world.'

'Yes,' said Miss F., 'that's what most makes me regret coming to India; we find no people here with handles to their names.'

'Come, come,' said Mrs. B., 'you must not exactly say that; we had Lord E., and his friend the Earl of C., here but a very short time ago.'

'Ah, but there's no one of that rank here now,' returned Miss F., 'and I really don't care much to meet those who are not in some way *distingué*.'

'That's to be expected,' replied Mrs. B. 'Being yourself, by your natural refinement of mind, so *distingué*, you would, as a matter of course, like to meet distinguished people; we will see what we can do to introduce you to someone with a handle to his name. There are two or three officers belonging to the class you admire so much about to join the 13th from England, and as soon as any one of them arrives, I'll make it my business to introduce you.'

'Oh, how very kind of you, Mrs. B.! I thank you very much.'

Mrs. C. and her guest now rose to depart. As soon as they were gone, Mrs. B., Colonel G., and his wife all indulged themselves in an unrestrained fit of laughter. 'I really have more than half a mind to play that girl a trick,' said Mrs. B., 'to punish her for her insufferable affectation.' 'On my word she does her best to make herself ridiculous.' 'Several of my servants are sick, including the cook,' said Mrs. B., 'or I'd give an evening party, and introduce some of our young fellows as people of rank.' 'Let that be no obstacle to the fun,' said Mrs. G. 'I'll give the party; do you introduce your friends.' So the two ladies and Colonel G. engaged heartily in the plot.

In due season invitations were issued to 'a select circle

of friends,' as the stereotyped saying has it, which included the C.'s and Miss Freeman, to an evening party to meet Sir Charles Oakley and Sir Hubert Stanley. Great was the excitement amongst all invited to know all about the strangers, of whom they had never heard.

On the evening named, the guests arrived, and as they did so Colonel G., who was waiting in the hall for that purpose, cautioned everyone to say nothing if, in the strangers, they happened to recognise faces with other names than those adopted for the evening. Everyone saw there was some frolic *in hand* or *on foot* (if the latter phrase pleases better), and immediately everyone entered into it so far as to resolve to observe all but say nothing.

Mrs. C. and Miss F. soon made their appearance. Captain C., for some reason, did not go, which, as he was a man of sour disposition, inapprehensive of a joke, was lucky. By and by Mrs. B. and the guests of the evening—or, rather, the guest, Sir Hubert being sick—appeared. ' Indisposed to come, I presume,' said Colonel G. ' So I told him,' returned Mrs. B. As the drawing-room door opened, a half-caste ' writer,' dressed in livery for the occasion, announced Mrs. B. and Sir Charles Oakley, who immediately afterwards was formally introduced to Mrs. G. Irrepressible was the tittering amongst those who recognised in Sir Charles the jolly, fat, good-humoured Lieutenant Mac- —ny of the 13th Dragoons ; but under Colonel G.'s sharp supervision all held their peace. Sir Charles was in high spirits, made himself very amusing and agreeable, and was for the evening a real ' live lion.'

As soon as the introductions were over, Mrs. B. called Miss F. to come and sit beside her. Sir Charles was at the time standing near her chair, and a good deal of fun seemed to be going on between them, if that may be inferred from the laughter.

'You know the Marquis of Sevenoaks, I hear, Miss Freeman,' said the Baronet; 'an old schoolfellow of mine at Eton. Many a thrashing he's had from me. I was in the upper forms, and the Marquis was my fag.'

Miss F. opened her eyes very wide, and then exclaimed: 'Oh, but you're joking, Sir Charles! Surely you can't mean that you thrashed the young Marquis of Sevenoaks?'

'Why not, Miss Freeman? All fags get their share of licking, and why shouldn't he?'

'Oh, but it's so cruel; and the Marquis must have been quite a little fellow then. It's shocking to think that the bigger boys should have the power to thrash the little ones, and actually be allowed to do it, and in this case to a boy of such high rank—a Marquis. I really can't think it; you're trying to possess me' ('Upon my life!' said Mac——ny, 'I'm not') 'with absurd notions and imaginations. The idea of thrashing a young scion of nobility, quite as a matter of routine, as if he was no better than a tinker or tailor! It's quite preposterous and revolting, and seems almost an act of profanation! I never can believe it.'

'It's a pity, then, you didn't hear the young beggar singing out when he had to hold up.'

Poor Miss Freeman! all her ideas suffered a dreadful kind of revolution. She was in a sort of stupor; her brain was in a whirl. Could it be possible that a young Marquis could be thrashed at the pleasure of an elder boy merely because that boy sat on another form? To be called a young beggar besides, and to have his sufferings actually made game of by a mere baronet, it was all so dreadful, so astounding, and so utterly opposed to all her preconceived notions, that she was lost in amazement.

'You say, Miss Freeman,' said the Baronet, breaking in on her silent contemplations and reflections, 'that the fagging seems to be a matter of form. Well, so it is as to the seats of the boys, but not at all a matter of form as to the smart of the stripes ; that depends on strength of arm.'

' Whatever it depends on,' said Miss F., ' it's very shock-ing to hear; but I'm persuaded you're hoaxing me. I'll never believe that a young nobleman of such high rank would or could be used in such a way.'

' Very sorry you don't believe,' said the Baronet, ' but all the same it's true ; and, after all, his allowance as fag was nothing to what he used to get from old Thwackum regularly every day. Spoony, as the young hero was then called, used to get it regularly for his parsing, and whenever he saw the cane coming he used to begin to blubber, to the great amusement of old Snuffy, which was Thwackum's common appellation. The old fellow on these pleasant occasions used to become facetious, and, after his fashion, witty. Spoony in those days was marked pretty strongly by the small-pox, and whenever the tears filled the little pits caused by the pock marks, Snuffy used to say : " What, Mr. Puteus, the lord of the wells ! Why, my little conjuring wand is as potent as the rod of Moses in raising the waters, and in setting the streams a-flowing. But why begin before there's need ? The pleasure's to come, you know." The reason he called him *Puteus* was that this is the Latin for a well, and so afforded opportunity for his allusions, and at the same time for a vile attempt at wit, *i.e.*, to call him *Mr. Beauteous.*'

' Can it be possible,' said Miss F., ' that anyone could be so cruel, cowardly, and fiend-like as to rejoice over pain, and make fun of a poor young fellow he was going to punish ? I cannot believe it '

' Don't, then,' said the heartless Baronet, turning away and laughing, ' but nevertheless it's fact, pure and simple.'

Sir Charles then sauntered away, leaving Miss Freeman

considerably mystified, and in an unsatisfactory state of doubt as to how far she was to believe the various unpleasant statements made by her new acquaintance.

Mrs. B., the Colonel, and Mrs. G. were at this time making themselves very merry, but their conversation was carried on in so low a tone of voice that nothing reached Miss Freeman's ears. She was in a melancholy mood, thinking of the sufferings the young Marquis had undergone, the enormities of those who had caused them, and whether all or the greater part of what she had heard was not pure invention; and, finally, that the Baronet wasn't half so nice as the Marquis. But, then, how could he be, being only a Baronet?

While she was communing with herself, Mrs. B. returned to her former seat. As she resumed her place she said: ' And how do you like Sir Charles, Miss Freeman?'

'Oh, I like him of all things,' replied the young lady, 'only I wish he would not speak so unkindly of the Marquis.'

' I fancy he only tells you,' replied Mrs. B., ' what is common at all our public schools, particularly if the boy spoken of does not happen to understand his syntax (I think they call it) well. But,' continued she, ' I don't perceive that you are making any approach to a more cordial footing.'

' I wish I could,' returned Miss F., 'but I don't know how to manage it.'

' I am surprised at that,' said Mrs. B., ' since you have been so intimate with so many titled personages; but I will try if I can't help you.'

' Oh, Mrs. B., if you would I should be so grateful.'

Mrs. B., as soon as she caught his eye, beckoned to Sir Charles. When he came up to her, she said: ' I thought you were to be in waiting on me, sir, for this evening; but I find you're a very careless squire.'

'Haven't you elected me for your knight? How, then, can I be a careless squire? But *mille pardons,*' continued the gentleman, 'I do confess to a temporary dereliction.'

'Which,' returned Mrs. B., 'if I were not most royally disposed I should not forgive so readily.'

'I think if I were forgotten so I would not be so merciful,' observed the young lady.

'Why, what would you do under such circumstances?' asked Sir Charles. 'Would you order the culprit to be shut up in the Tower? or would you order him to be beheaded at once?'

'Not being a Queen,' returned Miss F., 'I would not resort to such measures.'

'Then what would you do?' continued the gentleman. 'Would you have a riband or a silk cord tied to the rover's leg or arm, and fastened by the other end to your fan or your waistband?'

'No,' replied Miss F., 'I would not do that.'

'No! Then what would you do?

'I think I know what I would do,' returned Miss F.

'I say,' said Mrs. B., 'for the sake of similarly neglected ladies, do inform us.'

'Yes,' said Sir Charles, 'it would only be fair to tell.'

'I think,' said Miss F., whispering the words into Mrs. B.'s ear, 'I would try and retain him by the language of the eyes.'

'Oh,' said Mrs. B., laughing, 'but all ladies may not have such proficiency in that language as you may possess.'

'I have a notion,' said Miss F., 'that most ladies understand that language, and all, I fancy, do employ it sometimes.'

'But,' inquired the Baronet, 'what's the dodge? Put us up to the dodge, Miss Freeman.'

'Oh, I can't do that,' said the young lady, looking at the gentleman in a sort of languishing, sufficiently expressive, way.

He then, turning to Mrs. B., said : 'Come, Mrs. B., won't you tell us what this knowing dodge is ?'

'No, no ; don't tell, Mrs. B. !' exclaimed the young lady ; 'pray don't. I beg you won't.'

'Miss Freeman is inclined to trust to the power of invisible chains, that's all,' said Mrs. B.

'Oh, that's it, is it ?' said the Baronet. 'I should fancy such chains very infirm, and little to be depended on—in fact, I should regard them as utterly worthless and flimsy, except, indeed, they happened to be that kind of flimsy that the fat old banker's widow hung round the neck of young Lord Manners ; that might hold.'

'And what kind of chain is it that you describe by this word flimsy ?'

'Don't you know ?' replied the gentleman. 'I thought everyone knew that.'

'He means a chain of bank-notes,' said Mrs. B. 'A bank-note is with men on the turf, and other classes less respectable, termed a "flimsy."'

'And that's the meaning of a "flimsy," is it ?' said Miss F.

'Yes, my dear,' returned Mrs. B. ; 'that's the meaning.'

'And that's the sort of chain that would, in your opinion, be of force sufficient to restrain a wanderer from straying, is it, Sir Charles ?'

'If it is,' interposed Mrs. B., 'I for one don't agree with him. Experience tells us that all such chains are scarcely ever found binding.'

'But what a mercenary view to take of the matter ! I'm sure, Sir Charles, that's not your belief in your heart of hearts. I'm certain you have too much chivalry in you to think so.'

'Well, I don't know,' returned the Baronet ; 'I've always thought I had a great deal too much heart, but at any rate

I'm sure I haven't more than one. As to the chivalry, if we get a chance at the Russians I may perhaps find out if I've got any, and so perhaps may they.'

'I think, Mrs. B.,' said Miss F., 'I begin to understand your friend Sir Charles ; he is one of those who delight in making themselves appear worse than they are, and not only worse, but the very reverse of what they are.'

'Take care,' said Mrs. B., 'that you don't pursue that style of reasoning too far. By following it up you might invest him with all the attributes of an 'Admirable Crichton,' and, after all, find out that he is only Sir Charles Oakley.'

'Oh, but,' said the Baronet, 'she says she has found me out, and thus indirectly asserts that I am supporting an assumed character.'

'Oh, Sir Charles !' exclaimed the young lady, 'how can you say so? I only said that I thought I began to under-stand you.'

'Well,' returned the gentleman, 'isn't understanding me finding me out ?'

'Oh, but !' returned Miss F., 'you put such a different construction on the words ; and I never said or thought you were supporting an assumed character.'

'Didn't you ?' said the Baronet, laughing ; 'I thought you did, and if you had, only conceive how wrong you would have been.' The laughter seemed infectious, for Mrs. B. restrained the tendency that beset her with no little difficulty. 'But didn't you say,' continued the Baronet, 'that I was one of those who delighted in making myself appear worse than I was, and not only worse, but the reverse of what I was ; and if that is true, is not that supporting an assumed character ?'

'Oh !' replied Miss F., 'you do twist things in such a way, you know I only meant that you might be what I supposed, in spite of your seeming.'

'It seems, then, after all, Miss F.,' said Sir C., 'that you have not found me out, since you persist in believing me to be not only a dragoon and a baronet, but a chivalrous, unselfish, unmercenary sort of fellow, with more hearts than one.'

'More hearts than one was entirely your own, Sir C.,' said Miss F., 'made out by an obvious perversion of language; and with regard to the other matters, I suspect I'm not so wrong as you try to make me appear.'

'It's very ridiculous, isn't it, Mrs. B. ?' said Sir C.

'What's ridiculous?' said Miss F.

'Why,' replied Sir C., 'it's very ridiculous to me to find myself ranked so high without deserving it, and credited with a lofty, unmercenary character, because I alluded to the power of bank-notes, to say nothing of being also credited with possessing more hearts than one; while, at the same time, it is asserted, or insinuated, that I am supporting an assumed character. All this is charmingly ridiculous to my mind.'

'Well, well, it's useless for me to say anything; you will have it all your own way, Sir Charles,' said the young lady, 'and you have managed to misinterpret everything I have said in such a comical manner that I own it is very ridiculous.'

'Capital!' said the Baronet; 'then after all we do agree, which, considering that we have differed in everything, is in itself sufficiently ridiculous, and will, I trust, afford us both ground for laughter for many a day to come.'

'As for me,' said Mrs. B., 'I'm sure the remembrance of this evening will afford me food for laughter whenever it recurs to my mind; and now I'll wish my friends good-night; and then, Sir Charles, I shall be obliged if you'll order my carriage.'

So the party broke up, the secret having been thoroughly well kept, thanks to the vigilance of Colonel and Mrs. G.

As soon, however, as Mrs. C. and her charge departed, there was a general unloosing of tongues, bursts of laughter were unrestrained, and there was much rejoicing over the fun of the evening, and much fresh merriment. The next morning, rather before the customary hour for visiting, Mrs. B. and Lieutenant Mac——ny called on Mrs. C. and Miss Freeman, for the purpose of enlightening them as to the playful deception that had been practised on the previous evening, which Mrs. B. confessed she had originated. Miss Freeman was at first a little put out, and Mrs. C. was extremely astonished; but very soon both ladies yielded to Mrs. B.'s fascinating manner and strong feeling for fun and frolic, aided by the dragoon's rollicking good-humour and handsome apologies; in short, they were so pleased with their visitors that they quite forgot every feeling of annoyance, and agreed that as the gentleman had supported his assumed character so well, he was still to be 'Sir Charles' with them, as it is hoped he will be with all who love a harmless joke.

A REMINISCENCE OF TRICHINOPOLY.

To make a scene is generally considered, and really is in most cases, an unfailing method of affording amusement to the bystanders, and as this amusement is always at the expense of the actors, such performances are very generally avoided. No one willingly, except under unusual and extreme provocation, will run the risk of making himself ridiculous, which making a scene almost always involves. For these reasons exhibitions of this kind are rare, very rare. The fiat of polite society has gone forth ; this fiat announces that performances of this kind are forbidden, tabooed. Who is there that has not repeatedly heard, in his or her younger days, that so and so, or anything of that kind, 'is a breach of etiquette ;' 'the refinement of the age does not permit it ;' or 'good taste and good manners will not sanction such expressions of feeling,' etc. ? Yet, notwithstanding all these clearly defined laws, unalterable as those of the Medes and Persians, we know that scenes in high life, as well as in low life, do occur ; and sometimes even in military life, despite the stringent restrictions of discipline which are superadded to those already mentioned.

Having by accident, or by good luck, if the reader prefers the latter phrase, been present at an exhibition of this nature, which occurred many years ago at Trichinopoly, and having been much diverted by it, I have endeavoured by the aid of my pen to present it to the reader. I feel painfully the impossibility of conveying by this means what should have been witnessed to be fully appreciated—the looks, the tones, the expression of the faces, the actions, and the attitudes, cannot be given by the pen ; and in the attempt to describe them, the essence of the fun, the humour of the scene, evaporates. Even were such a thing possible, the repetition of such a scene would be tame compared with the original performance. On all these accounts, I trust that the shortcomings of my attempt will be judged with generosity and with leniency. In this hope, I shall strive to the utmost with the difficulties of my task, so that if I cannot achieve success, I may at least fail with some degree of credit.

I shall now, as the first step in the execution of this my self-appointed task, endeavour to describe as accurately as I can the actors and the scene. But it is needful for the full understanding of the comedy that I should also explain (so far as I am cognizant of them) what the circumstances were that led up to it. The actors were Lieutenant-General Blundermore Bluster, K.C.B., commanding the southern division of the Madras Presidency ; and Colonel Prolix Pertinacity, C.B., and V.C. commandant of H.M.'s —— Regiment of Infantry, stationed at Trichinopoly.

The General was a man of large and burly form, six feet two inches in height, and of proportionate bulk. His countenance expressed unmistakably the high estimation in which he held himself and all his belongings, even his goods and chattels—everything, in fact, that was *his*, and, above all, *his* views and opinions. These last he seemed to regard almost as things sacred, and not to be questioned. With this was conjoined a manner that expressed a sort of lofty indifference, if not contempt, for all surroundings, both men and things ; regarding all those who ventured to differ from him in opinion on any subject as guilty of gross impertinence, as well as bereft of common-sense, the fact of the disagreement proving their folly.

Colonel Prolix Pertinacity was a red-haired gentleman, who stood five feet four inches in his shoes, with a broad bald head, bull neck, and massive shoulders, of greater bulk even than the General's, and of such corpulent body that he could almost say with Falstaff that it was a long time since he had seen his own knee. His countenance expressed unconquerable determination, but was nevertheless frank and open when not under excitement; it was also evident that he possessed a fiery, quick, irritable temper, and an undaunted, immovable disposition.

From these outline sketches of these two officers, it may readily be inferred that they did not and could not agree. There had been, indeed, during nearly two years constant misunderstandings and altercations between them, causing unpleasant references to higher authority. Colonel Perti-nacity considered himself ill-used, oppressed, and tyranni-cally dealt with; the General complained of disrespect, and unmilitary conduct almost amounting to insubordination, and generally of behaviour to the prejudice of good order and military discipline. He had on several occasions sent the Colonel home with a public reprimand, and had threatened ulterior proceedings. In reply to the references that had, up to this time, been made, it appeared that his Excellency the Commander-in-Chief of the Madras Army did not take exactly the same view of Colonel P.'s conduct that General Bluster did; at all events, nothing very serious came of the General's references and complaints, and Colonel P. always returned to his duty without having received any damaging reprimand or 'wigging' (as the phrase is) from the higher powers. He was advised to be more cautious and circumspect in his behaviour towards the General in future, and to avoid if possible any expression capable of misconstruction, and, finally, not to insist on his own view of affairs so determinedly as he seemed to have done, etc., etc. What was said on these occasions to General Bluster was only known to himself, and perhaps to his staff; but as he did not communicate the contents of all the letters received from the Chief, it was strongly surmised that these letters were not all sugar-candy. However this may have been, the general opinion of the officers in the cantonment, and of the society at large, was rather in favour of the Colonel, although some took the part of the General. The argument used by these persons was usually something to this effect: 'Why does Colonel P. persist in maintaining his opinions when they differ from those of the General? If he is ever so right, what does it matter? Why does he not suffer the old gentleman to have his say without contradiction? What can the opinions of any such grand sample of bombastic self-sufficiency signify?' To this it was replied by those who took the part of the Colonel that so long as the General's remarks applied to abstract opinions, or to things in general, it would be wise on the Colonel's part to hear and say nothing; but that the General did not confine himself to any such line, or, indeed, to any line at all, but in the amplitude of his observations frequently made assertions that bore hard on others, not merely in their capacity as officers, but as men, many of whom, having received a much better education than the speaker, were in a manner called upon to admit his assertions as facts, although they knew the statements to be erroneous.

Instances of this love of dictation, and the determination to lay down the law on all subjects, whether military or not, were constantly occurring, not seldom to the discredit of the General's scholarship. One day he downfaced young Arnold on a point on which the 'sub' was far ahead of him. The youngster was saying something about platinum to some of the other young lads, who, though they may have been well up in Euclid, and in fortifications, and could give you back accurately all that they had learned about 'momentum, velocity, and the square of distances whether inverse or not,' were not quite so well up in physics or chemical analysis. In reply to one of these young gentlemen who had been asking questions about platinum, Arnold stated that it was an elementary substance, adding that it was one of the sixty-three such substances.

'Hulloa!' cried the General. 'What's that you say, Arnold—sixty-three elements? I fancy your elementary education has been rather neglected, my lad. Don't you know, having so lately come from school, that there are only four elements—air, earth, fire, and water? Why, they knew that as far back as the days of Aristotle!'

Poor Arnold, not knowing the General's ways (he had only just joined), unconsciously replied : 'They don't teach that nowadays, General.' One of the young men who had been at Sandhurst with him whispered Arnold not to say anything ; but he, knowing no reason why he should be silent, replied as I have stated, and thereby drew on himself the extreme anger and indignation of the General. 'Do you mean seriously to tell me that, sir? Do you mean to say that the small men of these days pretend to be wiser than Sir Isaac Newton, the greatest philosopher the world ever produced? He never said that there were sixty-three elements, and you, a youth not twenty, just free from the pedagogue's ferula— you pretend to be wiser than that great man, and all your seniors beside.'

Arnold was going to say something, when luckily the General stopped him with a violent gesture and angry visage, saying : 'Go home, sir, and if you learn nothing else, learn a little respect for your superiors.' Poor Arnold was kindly hustled out of the mess-house where this little episode occurred, lest, as one of his friends from the Land of Cakes said, 'waur should come of it.'

The General seemed to be partial to Aristotle and his philosophy, although he was not able to read the easiest class-book in the original language. He had, however, made acquaintance with the famous old Greek through the medium of translations, and was ever ready to do battle in his defence.

He fought furiously on one occasion to prove that Nature abhors a vacuum, and stormed so violently against those who expressed any doubts as to the accuracy of the dogma, that the innocent old philosopher, who had been at rest since the days of Alexander, might really have thought that his disciple meant to harry him out of his grave, such was the din and uproar made. And when the doctor of the regiment presumed to suggest that Torricelli had proved that it was the pressure of the atmosphere that had produced the phenomena that Aristotle had mistaken for Nature's abhorrence of a vacuum, the unfortunate man received such a torrent of abuse, delivered with such tremendous emphasis and vociferation, and such tremendous gestures, that he was glad to make his escape, as soon as he could find an opportunity, without saying another word. But he did not depart without receiving a closing broadside from the General. 'I should advise you, Mr. Cutter, in future,' said the General, 'to be cautious how you expose yourself to the ridicule of your friends, and to beware of venturing on such a palpable absurdity as to compare a paltry Italian fellow, like your Torricelli, with one of the sages of antiquity; perhaps I might say, considering Aristotle as the founder of the syllogistic method of reasoning, the greatest of those great men.'

Cutter departed, after making his salute, a wiser and a

sadder man, whispering to the Adjutant as he went out: 'O tempora! O mores! Well, he did not eat me alive, which I thought at one time he was inclined to do.' As Cutter left the mess-house, the General observed: 'What a silly conceited little fellow that is to presume to enter on subjects of which he evidently knows nothing! I shouldn't wonder, in his impudence, that this little carver of human flesh would impugn the syllogistic method, although it has been adopted and followed at both our great seats of learning and knowledge.'

'I greatly fear, General,' said Wagner, the Adjutant, 'that if you question him you'll find Cutter as much a heretic in this matter as in that of the vacuum.'

'Oh, he is, is he?' said the General. 'Well, tell him to dispute the following: "All men are liable to error; in other words, all men are more or less unwise and foolish. Cutter is a man, therefore he is unwise and foolish." There,' said the General; 'let him digest that at his leisure.'

'I heard him the other day,' said Wagner, 'trying to apply the syllogistic method to a saying of some old fellow of Crete, who said that "all the Cretans were liars," and he bothered me by asking whether the Cretan spoke the truth. I told him I couldn't tell. "Not tell?" said he. "Why, if the first proposition was true, then the gentleman who announced it, being a Cretan, must be a liar; and if that proposition was not true, then he was equally a liar for having spoken a falsehood." I confess I couldn't make anything more of it; but perhaps, General, as you understand the syllogistic method so well, you could make something of it.'

General B. looked hard at Lieutenant Wagner, but for a time said nothing, and then said: 'Well, I'll think of it.'

Wagner during the whole time preserved a most imperturbably serious countenance. When the General was gone, Archer, the Quartermaster, said to Wagner: 'Well, you have the cheek of the devil, Wagner; but take care that you don't one of these fine days come to grief. I half suspect that at one time he thought you were laughing at him.'

'Laughing at him!' exclaimed Wagner. 'How could you imagine such a thing? I'd as soon laugh at a boa constrictor when he had his folds round me.'

'Well, well,' returned Archer, 'so be it; but pray be careful, and remember that however ridiculous his pretensions to learning or science may be, he'll be a very ugly customer to deal with.'

'Ugly enough, certainly,' added Wagner, and then walked off. And so this dialogue ended.

On another occasion a very hot passage of arms occurred between the General and Colonel P. on the then vexed question of the relative superiority of the two arms—cavalry and infantry. The great improvements made since that day in the manufacture of small arms have put that question to rest, but at the time here referred to there were high authorities and great names on both sides.

General B., who had been a cavalry officer, insisted vehemently on the superiority of mounted men, declaring that it was simply nonsense to dispute the point, and that a cavalry charge would always break any square or infantry formation if made with sufficient impetuosity and pushed home as it might be. At first no one, as most of those present knew the General's amiable temper and pleasant mode of arguing against those who differed from him, said anything. The General, taking silence for consent, rattled away at a great rate, bespattering all who could entertain any other opinion than his own very handsomely—blind and prejudiced buzzards, owls who loved the dark, gentlemen whose long ears betrayed their nature, etc., etc. 'Well, at least it's satisfactory to find,' he concluded, 'that I have knocked the nonsense out of some who formerly held opposite opinions.'

This was too much for poor Colonel Pertinacity, who could hold his peace no longer. 'If, General Bluster, your remarks have any reference to me, which I can hardly suppose, I am still unwilling to let you think that I have altered my opinion as to the superiority of infantry over every other arm used in modern warfare.'

'Well, sir,' said the General, 'I can only say I am sorry for you; I had incautiously given you credit for being wiser.'

'And I, in reply,' said the Colonel, 'beg of you to reserve your sorrow, as I do not think that I stand in need of it in the slightest degree while the Duke of Wellington and other great men are of my opinion. You may well spare your sorrow.'

The General, under great excitement, very red in the face, exclaimed: 'The Duke, sir, has never expressed any decisive opinion on the subject. Show me where he has done so.'

'He *has* expressed a very decisive opinion by his deeds, General,' replied Colonel P. 'Our squares at Waterloo resisted all the desperate charges of the French cuirassiers and other kinds of cavalry.'

'And if they did, sir, what's that to the argument?' replied the General. 'If the French had been in square, and our cavalry had been numerous enough, and had charged them thoroughly home, the opposite result would have been obtained.'

'It might have been so, General,' observed the Colonel, 'but I don't admit that it would have been so.'

'Of course you don't,' said the General, with a withering

sneer; 'I never expected that you would. But you are not ignorant, I suppose, that one even of our regiments was nearly cut to pieces by the French cavalry at Quatre Bras?'

'True, General, I am not ignorant of the fact; but you seem to have forgotten that this occurred because the regiment was charged before it had time to form square.'

'And I say,' shouted out the General with an infuriated look and manner, 'that if the charge had been made, as it ought and could have been made, that the result would and ought to have been the same.' (The Colonel shook his head). 'It is useless to shake your head, sir. Independent of the common-sense of the thing there are proofs without number to be adduced that show the superiority of the cavalry arm over the infantry. You are fond of examples and of authorities? Pray how did Condé win the battle of Rocroi, and how did he break the Spanish infantry, considered then the best in Europe?' And with a triumphant laugh: 'Tell me, sir, how did Bonaparte retrieve his lost battle of Marengo? Was Kellermann's charge one of cavalry or infantry? Tell me that, sir.'

Colonel P., however, stood his ground firmly in spite of this deluge of words and array of facts; and without imitating the General's insulting manner, said: 'The battle of Rocroi was fought in days when the mode of warfare and the power of the weapons used was very different from those now employed; it is for these reasons scarcely applicable to the argument.'

The General laughed, saying: 'Of course you think it inapplicable; but, come, sir, what do you say to the charge at Marengo—was that inapplicable too?'

'No, General, certainly not; but it was made under most favourable circumstances for its success. The Austrian troops were in such an extended and attenuated line that they could make no adequate resistance, and the French squadrons rode through them as they would through a field of stubble.'

'As I would ride through you and your infantry people,' added the General, 'if they were opposed to me.'

The Colonel, whose blood was now thoroughly roused, laughed scornfully, saying : ' I should be sorry for your own sake, General, and that of your men, that you should try such an experiment, for you would never live to try another ; aye, even if we were in line ; but if we were in square we should drive you before us like chaff before the wind.'

'Very good, sir, very good,' said the General, scarcely able to articulate from rage. 'Go to your quarters, and remain there till I ascertain from the Chief if he approves of such language and behaviour to the officer commanding the division.'

The Colonel was about to reply, when a man of herculean strength, Captain Carter, Adjutant-General of Division, acting as if by order of the General, said : 'You are to come with me, Colonel,' and actually by main force almost carried him out of the room. As he was forcing the Colonel away, he whispered : 'Are you mad ? Do you want to give him such an advantage over you as will end by depriving you of your commission ? For God's sake, Colonel, collect yourself; he'll stop at nothing now.'

This encounter between the General and Colonel Pertinacity caused another reference to the Chief of the Madras Army, a man of great experience, enlarged mind, and kindly disposition, who entirely disapproved of the conduct both of the General and the Colonel. To each of these officers he gave very sound advice, strongly urging on them the necessity of altering their behaviour towards one another. The Chief added his hope that he should not again be troubled by any such unbecoming and indecorous altercations, but that if, contrary to his instructions and commands, there should be any recurrence of such doings, it would be his duty to submit the whole matter to the consideration of H.R.H. the Commander-in-Chief of the British Army.

As well might Mrs. Partington with her mop attempt to stop the ocean's incoming tide, as the Commander-in-Chief of the Madras Army attempt, by command or recommendations, to restrain and subdue the angry passions of these two disputants. His advice and injunctions, embodied in the words self-control, common-sense, and good temper, were thrown away upon them. Both parties prepared long statements setting forth their views and feelings, and explanatory of their real or supposed injuries. Both prayed that these papers might be laid before H.R.H., along with such remarks as H.E. the C.C. of Madras might please to make. The General's statement was little more than a recapitulation of what he had said before. The Colonel's was also in great part a recapitulation, one passage excepted, which so forcibly expressed the writer's feelings as to deserve quotation. It was introduced as the climax of a long description of his wrongs and sufferings, and it was couched in these words : ' I do assure your R.H. that an angel from heaven could not serve under General Sir Blundermore Bluster.'

These papers, after more than one kindly attempt on the part of authority and of friends to prevent their going forward, were at last sent home, and in due time we shall see what H.R.H. thought of the proceedings they set forth.

In the meantime we will for the present remain with General Sir B. B., and listen to the remarks he is uttering as he stamps about the mess-room. He did not even wait till Colonel P. was out of it before he turned to Wagner, and said : ' Really, in the whole course of my experience, I never knew anything to equal Colonel P.'s behaviour ; one would almost think that he was bereft of his senses. I do not say anything of his disrespect to me—that must be left to the authorities to pronounce upon; but to make such an *exposé* of his ignorance and want of knowledge on matters pertaining to his profession is not only lamentable, but in the highest degree absurd.'

'I cannot help thinking, General, that such exposure is absurd,' replied Wagner.

'Absurd, indeed,' said the General, 'absurd and ridiculous.'

'Yes,' answered Wagner, 'very ridiculous; I fancy we all thought so.'

'Of course you did; I don't see how you could think anything else. And before officers immediately under his command, too; it's much to be lamented, but, notwithstanding, I can't help saying it is very ridiculous.'

'No doubt, General, truly ridiculous.' Wagner was now almost *in extremis;* something affected his articulation so that he could scarcely speak, and it seemed that it would have been impossible for him to have sustained his part much longer. Luckily the General himself came to his relief in an unexpected way. 'Wagner,' said he, 'you're a very sensible fellow, come and dine with me to-morrow at 6.30 precise, and I'll give you a glass of burgundy to moisten your clay with.' Wagner replied by a very low bow, and without raising his head managed to get out, 'Very happy, General.' Then waving his hand to all present with a 'Good morning, gentlemen,' the General departed.

As soon as his carriage drove off every soul in the mess-room indulged in repeated bursts of laughter; Wagner more uproariously than any of them. After the cachinnation had subsided, one of them said: 'There must be something in your face, Wagner, that fascinates and blinds old B., or he certainly would have seen that you were laughing at him; this is the second time you've done it.'

'And,' continued Wagner, 'got an invitation to drink burgundy to reward me; but it's not my face, man, fascinating as it may be, that has done it; it's his own superlative conceit and ignorance that have blinded him. But, by Jove! I was nearly overpowered this time. I don't think I could have kept my countenance another minute to save my existence.'

'Don't tempt fate again, that's my advice,' replied his friend. 'Drink the old fellow's burgundy whenever he gives you the chance, but don't laugh at him before his face any more; for, if he detects you, you'll find he'll ruin you; conceited and of meagre attainments though he may be, he knows military law, and how to work it against anyone who offends him. Men of his stamp, who have little or nothing but their physical strength to boast of, never forget or forgive being laughed at. He never stopped till he got poor Banter out of the service. Remember, it's not worth while to give up your commission for a laugh.'

'Well, Archer, I am schooled, and promise to be careful, and, as you advise, never to laugh at him again before his face. Good manners be my speed; but you don't object to my doing it behind his back, that's some comfort.'

'So ho!' said Archer, 'you're quibbling. I want you to keep out of danger; you know best whether laughing under any circumstances at a man like that, considering his and your position, will help you to keep out of danger.'

'Amen, so be it!' said Wagner. 'I'll henceforth be as grave as an owl, and as silent as a clock that isn't wound up.' So ended the colloquy between the young Adjutant and his friend Archer.

Shortly after the scene just described, General B. was ordered to act for General Somers in the Presidency

Division. This was joyful news to all stationed in the Southern Division, and the reverse to those stationed in the Presidency Division.

Within a month after General Bluster had taken up the command at the Presidency, the season for making his tour of inspection arrived, and he accordingly visited in succession all the stations within his range; amongst the rest that of Wallajahbad, forty miles from Madras, but once a frontier station, at the time spoken of merely a sick depôt for the Company's invalid officers and Sepoys, who had returned sick from foreign service, or for troops suffering from fever and other complaints which induced the medical officers of their regiments to recommend them a change of climate.

When the General visited this cantonment there were only two effective officers in the station, the Doctor and the cantonment Adjutant; the two others were non-effective—invalids, Colonel H., commanding the cantonment, and Lieutenant C., who sometimes put the company of invalid Sepoys stationed there through their drill. The Doctor and the Adjutant had work enough on their hands, as there were often 600 men on the sick list, sometimes more than 1,000; but no other person had anything beyond the slightest routine work to do, and very little of that. Colonel H., though married, was a man who thought of little else than gratifying his animal passions—*more canino*, the expression of his features plainly demonstrated these propensities, and his language, which was scarcely ever anything but obscene, fully confirmed the facial indication.

On the occasion of the General's advent, this pleasant gentleman invited the Doctor and his wife and Lieutenant C. to dine with him, to meet the General. I give these paltry details because it affords the reader an opportunity of seeing General B. in private society, and in the company of ladies. Mrs. H., during the dinner, and as long as she stayed afterwards, said very little. Colonel H. said nothing, except to agree with the General whatever the subject or statement might be. The Doctor's wife was the only person who maintained anything that might be called general conversation. The Doctor himself at first said very little, having had at his hospital a small sample of General B.'s amiable temper and manner.

This little display arose thus: The General asked how many sick he had (the report had been placed in his hands almost immediately after he reached the hospital; this he did not look at, but after folding it up placed it in a letter-case carried by an orderly). The Doctor answered: 'Nearly 700, General.' 'What do you mean by nearly, sir?' said the questioner. 'Answer my question, and state the precise number.' 'Six hundred and seventy-nine, sir,' replied the surgeon. 'How can that be, sir? You have nothing like that number in hospital.' 'No, General, only 130, which is all the hospital will hold without injurious crowding.' 'Oh, that's all it will hold, is it? But I see some empty beds; how do you account for that?' 'Patients dismissed this morning, General.' 'But you say you have near 700 sick, and only 130 in hospital; what do you do with the 500 and odd remaining?' 'They are on the convalescent list, General.' 'On the convalescent list! I ask you what you do with them.' 'They live in the Lines, General.' 'And do you visit them in the Lines?' 'When any of them are ill enough to require visiting in the Lines I do visit them, and then send them into hospital. Those who suffer from chronic ailments, or from debility, attend at the hospital as desired.' 'As desired!' repeated the General. 'Pray, sir, what kind of phrase is that? What am I to understand by it?' 'As often as is considered desirable, General.' 'D——n it, sir, what *do* you mean? Do you mean once a day, or every other day, or twice a week?

What do you mean? Why don't you try and speak plain English?' 'Some of them do come every morning, some every other morning, some twice a week, and some once a week,' replied the Doctor. 'Upon my word, sir, you have a nice way of doing your duty, seeing your patients once a week, and the others as you please, in order to shuffle through your work with the least trouble to yourself.' 'Pardon me, General. I try to do my work conscientiously, without any reference to personal trouble.' 'No, sir, I won't pardon you; but I'll make you do your duty as it ought to be done. Now mind, sir, I will not allow any convalescent list, and you see every one of your patients every day. Mind that, sir.' 'Very good, General, but where am I to see them? The hospital will not hold more than 130.' 'Don't attempt to make idle objections, sir; it's your business to find a place to put your patients in. Indent on the commissariat for hospital tents. Ask the cantonment Adjutant for help; he can, I dare say, find some unoccupied building, or can obtain the use of tents. What do you say, Adjutant?' 'It was formerly, General, the practice to use tents for this sick-depôt, but when the hospital was built this practice was ordered to be discontinued, as the outlay for the purchase and wear and tear of tents was very considerable.' 'And pray, Adjutant,' said the General, looking disgusted, 'why did you not tell me that before?' 'This is the first opportunity I've had to tell it, General.' 'Well, however it is managed I will allow no convalescent list. You, sir,' turning to the Doctor, 'do you hear that?' 'I hear, General.' 'And mind you obey it, or it will be worse for you.' The Doctor bowed, but made no reply.

The General then departed with Colonel H. The cantonment Adjutant lingered behind to whisper to the Doctor: 'Don't be uneasy; you'll see this will be only a flash in the pan. The good folks at headquarters won't sanction the extra expenditure that this impracticable old gentleman wishes to lead them into. He wants to make the regulations for effective men applicable to a sick-depôt, and you'll see he'll be overruled. Good-bye.'

With the remembrance of the General's pleasant manner in the morning fresh in his mind, it is not to be wondered at that the Doctor was taciturn during the dinner; but being an easy, good-tempered little fellow, he accepted the General's challenge to a glass of wine as a sort of apology for his rudeness at hospital, and began to keep his thoughts under less restraint; and as the wine circulated after the departure of the ladies, the conversation turned on the behaviour of a certain General Lloyd. This, not supposing he should give offence, the Doctor condemned from beginning to end somewhat freely. Whether it was that General Lloyd was a countryman, or whether the wine began to tell, or whether it was merely the inherent temper of the man which excited his determination to lay down the law on all subjects, or, as his victim, poor Banter, said of him, that 'he would not allow anyone to call his soul his own,' I am not able to explain; but certain it is that the Doctor's expression of opinion excited his anger and indignation in a high degree, which he gave vent to in the following manner:

'On my life, sir, you are a modest young man,' was his opening speech, which he continued thus: 'Your own profession and your own duties are not enough for you to attend to, but you must entertain your seniors and superior military men, whose experience and rank and knowledge of military matters should give some assurance of their competence to understand and judge in such a case, with your sapient notions; you must give them your views and opinions, and on matters which neither your education nor training can possibly give you the means of judging or criticising justly. In taking upon you to pronounce on the conduct of a General of Division, in the presence of an officer of equal rank, you assume a position that is highly disrespectful and offensive, and in doing so you have exhibited your ignorance no less than your conceit and presumption. You, a subaltern, not a military man even of the lowest grade; you, who are merely a carver of human flesh, your assurance is astounding !'

The Doctor, who had until now exhibited remarkable command of temper, could bear no more. He said: 'General, I thought I was at a private party, where freedom of opinion was allowed, and not in the orderly-room, in speaking of General Lloyd. I meant no offence to anyone; certainly not to you. If I have given you offence, I regret it; it was wholly unintentional. With reference to being a carver of human flesh, I do dissect or carve, as you please to term it, dead human flesh to learn to heal and cure live human flesh. But are not those who wield the sabre only to maim and kill live human beings more truly carvers of human flesh than medical men are?'

The General absolutely foamed at the mouth with rage and fury. He had been a dragoon, and had on several occasions wielded his sabre with most unsparing vigour; he therefore felt the retort keenly. His eyes glared, and he looked like a tiger going to spring. Whether he would have proceeded to assault and battery is uncertain : but Colonel H., going at this moment round to the Doctor, said : 'I have forgotten Mrs. H.'s request— I ought to have told you before—that she is by no means well, and wishes to see you as soon as you can leave the table. She was ill before she rose from her place; pray go at once.' Accordingly the Doctor left the table at once.

Having seen General B. in the mess-room, at the hospital,

and in private society, we trace him again to Trichinopoly, and again in the mess-room of H.M.'s —— Regiment. He had returned to his old division when relieved from acting in the Presidency Division by the return of General Somers, and we find him again in the mess-room, where all his old acquaintances and Colonel P. were assembled, in order to hear the decision of H.R.H. the Commander-in-Chief of H.M.'s Forces. It was to be read out in the presence of all officers bearing H.M.'s commission who might at the time be in Trichinopoly.

This decision of H.R.H. was just what might have been expected—calm, wise, authoritative, and, though severely minatory, in the end generously lenient. It was too long to be given verbatim, or even in detail; a brief abstract is all that can be attempted. It expressed the extreme displeasure of the Chief towards both the General and Colonel P., and his surprise that senior officers should not know how to restrain their irascible feelings towards one another when they must be aware that concord and harmony were essential to the preservation of discipline and the welfare of the service at large. So strongly did H.R.H. condemn such evil example that he had determined to remove both offenders from the army, and nothing but the fact that they had both fought and bled for their sovereign and their country induced him to forego the infliction of a punishment which was fully deserved. H.R.H. added that he felt offended and indignant that his time should have been taken up in reading long statements relating to such trivial matters as personal disputes. He was resolved that nothing of the kind should occur again without bringing down immediate removal from the service. He had been asked for a decision on the merits of the case. He would give no such decision. He found so much to blame in the conduct of both officers that he would not waste his time in sifting and weighing their conduct so as to determine which of them had behaved the worse. He enjoined strict attention to the advice offered some time previously by the Commander-in-Chief of the Madras Army, and especially to that contained in a letter from that officer under date so-and-so. Finally, that he should regard a strict adherence to those recommendations as indicative of a desire to carry out his injunction to preserve discipline and concord, and *vice-versâ* in the case of any departure from, or any non-adherence to, them. He concluded by informing them that their conduct would be under strict supervision for some time to come.

When the General ceased there was a stir, and evident rejoicing amongst all present. The admirable sense and sound logic of the despatch, with the extreme kindness and leniency of the decision, was the theme of eulogy with all, and warm congratulations, both to the General and Colonel P., were offered by all who were on terms to do so.

After the excitement had a little subsided, the scene occurred which led the writer (who was *en route* to Madras, halting three days at Trichinopoly) to investigate and make inquiries. Thus he became acquainted with the antecedents of the officers who figured in it.

It commenced in this way : The General, after having read out the C.C.'s communication, continued for some minutes silent, walking up and down with the despatch in his hand. At length he stopped, and spoke to the following effect :

'Gentlemen, I can fully understand the generosity of H.R.H. as shown in this despatch. I admire and appreciate his delicacy and his kindness. He would give no decision on the merits of the case. No, no ; how could he, having in his magnanimous clemency decided not to inflict the punishment due to ill-regulated and ill-considered behaviour?' (Sensation amongst the officers present). 'For myself, gentlemen, I am quite willing and content to bear the share of blame that has been awarded to me, in the thought that, by doing so, I have helped a brother officer out of a very dangerous position.' Signs of impatience on the part of Colonel Pertinacity, of which the General took no notice, but continued thus: 'Yes, gentlemen, I say, under the circumstances adverted to, I willingly—nay, cheer- fully—accept the share of blame attributed to me, and am resolved to set the example in obeying and following out the advice tendered by his Excellency the C.C. of this army, especially since my attention has been so pointedly directed to it by the recommendation of H.R.H.

'Colonel Pertinacity, you have heard what H.E. the C.C. of Madras says, and also what H.R.H. says respecting it? I trust you will meet me half way in showing obedience to it.'

'Most certainly, General B. I shall pay the strictest obedience to it, in spite of the one-sided remarks you have thought proper to make in your present address, in which, I must in my own defence say, you were not borne out by the despatch you hold in your hand.'

'Oh, Colonel P!—Colonel P.! is this the way you carry out H.R.H.'s instructions? You provoke me beyond endurance; but I will not say another word that is calcu- lated to bring on a rejoinder. In spite of what has been said, I believe you do mean to obey H.R.H., therefore I offer you my hand.'

Now, to the understanding of the pantomime that followed it is needful to state that the General stood at the top of the room, and on either side stood seven or eight officers disposed according to their rank. On the right hand, at the head of those on that side, stood Colonel P., distant from the General about three paces. The General, holding out his hand, made a step towards the Colonel, repeating: 'Colonel P., here is my hand.' But the Colonel made no sign of acceptance, and when the General approached nearer to him, he put his hands behind him, and, as the General followed him, backed down the room in that position, bowing to the General, and saying as he did so: 'You must excuse me, General B.; I cannot take your hand.'

'Come, Colonel. What, will you not obey the orders of H.R.H.? Come.'

'No, General B.; I cannot take your hand. I am nowhere called upon to do that by H.R.H., but I will obey to the last point all I am called upon to do.'

The moving scene continued, both the retreat and advance, and appeared to the lookers on so intensely comical that they scarcely dared to look at one another.

While the retreating Colonel was reiterating his determination to obey the orders of H.R.H., and exclaiming: 'I will obey—indeed I will. On my honour, General, I will obey!' Wagner whispered to the officer standing nearest to him: 'Private theatricals—kiss and be friends. Acted for the first time by field officers for the amusement of a select audience.'

'Hush! Hush!' said Archer.

By this time the two performers had approached the lower end of the room, where Wagner was standing; the short, fat Colonel, with his hands behind him, his dress coat-tails spread, one on either side of that portion of his person rendered prominent by his bowing posture, and not posterior but anterior by the back step mode of progression. The sight presented was altogether too much for Wagner's equanimity. He again whispered to Archer: 'Heaven preserve us! I have served in the trenches at Sebastopol, and thought I was acquainted with every kind of explosive missile, bomb, and shell in use; but anything so large and formidable as that now slowly ricochetting this way I never beheld. Pray God its force is spent. If an accident should occur, only think what would be our fate!'

'Hold still, Wagner! Will you never get sense?' retorted his friend.

At this point the General, beginning to perceive the absurdity of the situation, ceased to advance, and, drawing himself up stiffly, said: 'You refuse my hand, Colonel Pertinacity? So be it, then; you ought to know the responsibility you incur by this line of conduct, and I shall press you no further. I waived my rank for the sake of peace, and to set you an example which, I am sorry to see, you are unable to appreciate.' So saying, and with a salute to all present, he marched off, as Archer said, 'with the honours of war.'

'No, no,' said Wagner. 'With the honours of peace. And a more entertaining *piece* I must confess I never witnessed. What I endured in conquering my desire to laugh no one can imagine; but, say as you will, I don't believe all the sufferings of all the martyrs were anything to be compared to it.'

These private theatricals were, so far as ever I could learn, never made known officially to headquarters; but it was strongly suspected that the details of the performance somehow or other oozed out, and found their way to the ears of authority, for within a week after the date on which this remarkable *pas de deux* had been exhibited in the mess-house at Trichinopoly, General Somers was posted to the Mysore Division, and General B. was appointed to the Presidency Division, as it was said, that he might be under the eye of the C.C., on the principle that induces men to put a severe muzzle on a savage and intractable dog. Colonel Pertinacity was, not many months afterwards, placed in command of a regiment ordered to the West Indies.

CURIOUS MOPLAH CUSTOMS.

THE deed of violence which forms the basis of this narrative took place at Tollicherry, or rather in that district. How it was that my brother came to be stationed there will appear in due course. We left him at Bangalore, from whence he marched with his regiment to Secunderabad. He had not been there many months when an order was received directing the regiment to proceed with all possible speed to Scinde, where troops were urgently required. Some weeks before the order in question reached Secunderabad, my brother, finding that the climate of the Deccan did not agree with him, had applied for and obtained medical charge of the Zillah of Tollicherry ; but as soon as he heard there was a chance of being engaged in active service, he had applied for permission to throw up the Zillah and to proceed with his regiment, and this was granted. He had, consequently, marched with the regiment from Secunderabad to Doolia, a distance of 600 miles, on the road for Scinde. The men had shown the best spirit, urged by their officers to do their utmost, and knowing that they were going to serve under Sir Charles Napier. They had accomplished the distance in an incredibly short period, but all their exertions, as it turned out, were of no avail. Sir Charles had fought his grand battle of Miani, and the regiment was no longer wanted.

With this chilling news came the order to halt and to divide. One wing was to remain at Doolia, the other to proceed to Assurghur. There never was such a melancholy change among officers and men as that produced by this order. Previous to its receipt there was not an officer or man on sick report; all were in the highest spirits, and, in spite of fatigue, earnest to get on, lively, cheerful, and happy. In a few hours there was neither a happy face nor a cheerful voice to be seen or heard. Disappointment, vexation, and dejection were on every countenance. In a few days half the regiment was in hospital, and nearly half the officers on sick report. My poor brother had a sad time of it; besides his own share of vexation and disappointment, he was worked off his legs.

Now he renewed his application for the Zillah of Tollicherry, which, in consideration of the proper feeling he had displayed, was again bestowed on him. To reach this station, from the place where he then was (Doolia), he had to travel 200 miles to Bombay, and from thence to proceed by sea to Tollicherry, a distance of about 800 miles. At that time the south-west monsoon was close at hand, and my brother, consequently, found it very difficult to procure a vessel that would undertake the voyage. At last, by paying double hire, he chartered a *Satamar* (called by the natives a Fatty mary), the owners and the serang engaging to take the risk, which in the sequel proved to be so fearful that it seems a miracle how ship or crew ever lived through it.

On the day that my brother set sail from Bombay the sky was, after mid-day, more or less overcast; towards the evening the sun appeared through the dense atmosphere to be almost of a blood-red hue, and the edges of the clouds of a deep copper colour. A little later the sun became to a great extent obscured and hidden by a mass of clouds, so much tinged by dusky red that the dark gray tone was almost extinguished. As the mighty orb sank below the horizon, the red, crimson, and copper tones quickly disappeared, except on the under surfaces of some clouds high above the sea-line, and darkness spread with extreme rapidity over everything, while a low moaning and fitful whistling of the wind seemed to presage a struggle of the powers, which from the beginning of the world has been attended with such fearful results. The aspect of the heavens, the moaning of the wind, and the uneasy motion of the waters, were not lost on the serang and his native sailors. They took in all sail except a small triangular one, a sort of apology for what we call a mainstay sail, to enable them to keep the ship's head to the wind. They then lashed the salankeen to the deck, and awaited with awe the bursting of the storm. It commenced with a perfect deluge of rain, blinding flashes of long-forked lightning, followed almost instantaneously by such rattling sharp crashes of thunder as for a time to take away the sense of hearing.

Sea and sky were wrapped in total darkness, when not illumined by the zigzag lines of lightning. The wind now increased, and the sea became dangerously rough and angry. Had the wind gone on increasing, bark and crew must have perished; but mercifully. It did not, its low muttering, moaning, or occasional whistling note was heard at intervals; still it never blew hard and furious as it threatened to do. The darkness, the downpour of rain, the lightning and the thunder, continued, while now and then a sea, and constantly the spray, swept over the vessel; for though the wind did not increase, the sea had been so raised, and the waves had become so threatening, that during two hours, while the worst of the storm lasted, my brother expected every moment that some overwhelming sea would whirl the unhappy *Salamar* into the depths below.

The storm had commenced a little after the sun had gone down, and darkness had covered everything; then the furious rain descending in sheets of water, with lightning streams and deafening thunder, had continued at short intervals for three hours, and the sea had got up. Everything depended on the increase of the wind, and for two hours more there was nothing less than the prospect of instant death present to the minds of all on board. Shortly after midnight the violence of the storm began to abate; the wind, instead of increasing gradually, subsided; the rain was less like a deluge; the flashes and streams of lightning were less frequent and less vivid; the crashes of thunder less sharp, and evidently more distant; but the sea did not go down. Nevertheless the magnitude and the violence of the masses of water that rose and fell were less appalling and less frequent.

It was now about half-past two, and there was an interval in the fall of rain (the first that had occurred). The sea no longer came sweeping over the deck, though the spray still kept everything wet, but the worst was over, and my brother had lain down to sleep. He was awakened by the serang with a native compass in his hand, followed by a sailor who was holding up a lantern to enable my brother to see the card. The vessel had been running down the coast, not very far from shore; but now a new peril presented itself.

The darkness was less complete, and was rapidly becoming less and less : this change enabled the natives to perceive something white not far ahead : they knew at once that it was the foam of breakers caused by a reef of rocks, on which if they kept their course they would certainly strike. They could not sail towards the land, as the coast is rock-bound almost everywhere, and they dreaded pointing the head of the ship out to the broad ocean. It is ever the custom with native mariners to hug the land, so in their distress, and seeing the breakers ahead, they had come to ask directions from their passenger, though they knew he was a hakim and not a sailor; but such was their respect for the knowledge of Europeans, that they thought he must know what was best to do. My brother at once directed them, in spite of their fears, to point the head of the brave little craft that had stood the storm so well out to sea, and such was their confidence in his wisdom that they at once did as he desired. Having thus avoided the rocks, and seen the head of the vessel pointed away from land, my brother again lay down to sleep.

Two hours had scarcely elapsed before he was again awakened by the serang with the compass in his hand. It was now light enough to see everything with perfect ease. The sea all round was comparatively calm, but the land was not to be seen. This it was that had again excited the fears of the crew, and had led them to appeal again to the European. On learning the cause of their fear, my brother directed them to put about and steer towards the land; they again obeyed, and again he went to sleep. At about half-past six a.m. he was awakened by sounds of rejoicing and singing, which he soon found arose from their sense of security, thankfulness, and gratification, at having again caught sight of the land. The sun was shining with power renewed, and everything was dazzlingly bright; even the light reflected from the sea was too much for the eye. The serang, however, soon rigged up a double awning which kept a part of the deck in shadow. This permitted my brother to take his breakfast comfortably. About midday they made the port of Goa, where he landed, but stayed there only to dine. In a couple of hours they were again at sea, and in two days more anchored at Tollicherry.

As soon as his trunks were landed, my brother made the serang happy by a present of 5 Rs., and the sailors equally so by another 5 Rs., to be divided amongst them. While waiting at the Bunder-Major's office for bearers to carry himself and the palkee to the doctor's house, a peon, with spotless garments of white save a red shawl twisted round his waist, bearing an ebony sort of curved staff covered almost all over with silver, presented my brother, after many profound salaams, with a note from the First Judge of the Circuit, requesting that my brother and his wife would give him the pleasure of their company till they could find a house to suit them. This princely man added that he had ordered a suite of rooms to be got ready for their reception, as well as rooms for the children and the servants ; finally, that he had sent two sets of bearers to bring up the palankeens, and that the peon would procure fresh sets of coolie bearers to bring up the children and the ayahs, as well as means for forwarding the luggage.

On perusing this note, my brother jumped into his palankeen, which the Judge's bearers shouldered at once, and almost ran with it to the Judge's house, anxious to be the first to tell him that they had brought the new 'hakim saib.' On getting out of the palkee, my brother found Mr. V. waiting in the hall to welcome his guests. His first remark was, while extending his hand to my brother : 'But where's Mrs. —— ?' The story of the going on active service, as it was supposed, and the impossibility under such circumstances of taking his wife with him, had then to be told. Mr. V. listened to the explanation, and then said : 'But where is she ? Have you left her at Secunderabad all this time ?' 'No,' replied my brother, 'she and the children have been staying at Anot, where her brother (in medical charge of the 5th Cavalry) is stationed.' 'And when do you expect them here ?' continued the Judge. 'Why,' returned my brother, 'that depends, I believe, on the safe accomplishment of a certain trouble that married people are occasionally subject to.' 'Oh!' said Mr. V., 'that's the state of the case, is it? Well, it can't be helped, I suppose; you must make yourself as comfortable as you can here till the lady arrives.'

Mr. V. was not only a thorough gentleman in manner and exterior, but truly so in feeling; no one could be more unmindful of self, or more disposed to make everyone forget that he occupied the first position in the district. Frank, sociable, generous, and hospitable, as well as lively and good-humoured, he was a noble specimen of an Englishman, and a typical example of the best kind of the old Indian burra saib, a class that even in those days was fast disappearing, and cannot, I believe, now be found. My brother stayed with this kind and generous man during more than two months, and then he only succeeded in effecting his departure on the plea that he must prepare his house for the advent of his wife.

While Mr. V.'s guest, my brother made the acquaintance of all the European residents at the station, paying and receiving the customary visits, all which matters of form my brother heartily detested; but the Medes and Persians of old were not more rigid in their laws than Anglo-Indians are in the matter of paying and returning visits. My brother, therefore, obeyed the *lex non scripta* with as little delay as possible. He first made his bow to Mrs. A., the wife of the second Circuit Judge, a lady of whom it was whispered that she wore certain portions of costume generally considered to be *propria quæ maribus*. However this may have been, her husband, Mr. A., was a most kind and excellent man. Mrs. H., the wife of the third Judge, with her husband, both became valued friends. Both are doubtless gone to the 'better land,' therefore it would not be kind or wise to grieve for them.

Next to the Circuit Judges comes the Zillah Judge, who

was also a married man; consequently, to his house the hakim's palkee wended its way in due course. He found this lady so rigid in her religious opinions that she would not allow of any difference. On making this discovery he congratulated himself that she did not possess the power to enforce conformity; visions of solitary cells, bread and water, and other more dreadful pains and penalties, forcing themselves on his mind. Her husband seemed to be so far in leading strings as to have no opinions except those held by his wife; though, independent of this little weakness, he was very probably a good and estimable man. The expression of this gentleman's countenance was, however, usually so lugubrious and unhappy that my brother observed, when speaking of him: 'If his religion has the effect of making him as miserable as the expression of his features indicates, I very much doubt if it be the true religion,' and certainly the Zillah Judge's melancholy face did *countenance* such an opinion.

It is now time to speak of Mr. G., the sub-collector, who was as unlike Mr. H., the Zillah Judge, as it is possible for one man to be unlike another. Mr. G., to begin with, had no wife to save him the trouble of thinking on important matters, and was as good-humoured, jolly, and generous, as the other was melancholy and penurious. He was, moreover, as fond of fun as the other was fearful of it. H., in short, was a killjoy, and G. was a lovejoy. The consequence of these differences was that H. was not, generally speaking, a particular favourite, and G. was.

The list of officials closes, I think, with the Master-Attendant, or Bunder-Major, as he was popularly termed. This old gentleman had been captain of a merchant vessel, and was therefore, by courtesy, always called Captain B. He was a red-faced, jolly-looking old tar, really good-natured and kind-hearted, but one who murdered his mother tongue at times in rather a determined manner. The letter V seemed to be particularly obnoxious to him. When speaking of a gentleman named Vaughan, he called him ' Waughan.' Or when speaking of several articles of different qualities, he expressed himself thus : ' Oh, there was a many on 'em of wery warious qualities !' The poor man had evidently come from before the mast, but he had the manliness not to deny it, or be ashamed of it ; and he was, despite the murders he perpetrated daily, a sort of privileged character, and to a certain extent a favourite.

Those not belonging to the list of officials may very soon be disposed of. Old Mr. B., a retired civilian, and his son, Henry, occupy the first place. The father was a jolly old *bon-vivant*, and had in his younger days, so it was said, been somewhat gay, if the word be accepted not in its literal sense, but in that in which it is usually employed in polite society. His son was a chip of the old block, and a bit of a scamp into the bargain. Mr. G., the German missionary, concludes the catalogue. This individual was in high favour with Mrs. A. and her husband, and with Mrs. H. and her husband.

The catalogue of European residents being concluded, it remains to notice the Eurasians, the greater number of whom were descendants of Portuguese and natives. Most of these were mean, degraded, lazy individuals forming a section of the population not very much respected. Some, no doubt, were respectable persons, acting either as writers (clerks), or tradesmen, tailors, carpenters, etc. There were some few of the Eurasian class descended from Englishmen and native women, who were also employed as writers in the Circuit Court.

One of these, a Mr. James, occasioned considerable amusement, both to the First Judge and to my brother, by presenting to the former a petition for a fortnight's leave of

14

absence. Mr. James had found out that Mr. V. and his guest made it a regular practice to take an hour's constitutional walk every morning between 4.30 and 5.30, *i.e.*, before the sun became unpleasant. The petitioner had made use of the opportunity afforded by this practice to prefer his request, which, as he removed his hat and made his best bow, he presented in the form of a petition, his face all the while radiant with smiles. Mr. V., without opening the paper, said : 'Well, Mr. James, what is the purport of the petition?' 'A supplication for leave, sir,' replied Mr. J., 'for a fortnight's leave.' 'This is a very unusual application, Mr. J., at this period of the session.' 'Yes, sir, I know it is somewhat unusual,' replied the petitioner ; 'but still, sir, for the reasons assigned, I hope you'll be kind enough to grant it.' 'Well, what are the reasons?—state them.' Mr. J. had all this time been smiling blandly, and looking persuasively suppliant. Now he looked, in addition, not a little sheepish and ill at ease, shifting the weight of his person from one foot to the other. At last, he said : 'Would your honour cast your eyes on the paper?' 'What is it?' said Mr. V., 'are you ashamed to tell me?' 'No, sir, I'm not.' 'Then, why don't you tell me? The sun will be getting hot, and I can't delay my walk homeward any longer. Either tell me at once, or present your petition in Court before the business begins.'

Mr. James, thus urged, smiling more than ever and looking more sheepish than ever, confessed that he wanted leave to get married. 'To get married!' repeated Mr. V., with almost a scream of laughter ; 'surely, Mr. James, you don't mean that?' 'I beg you'll pardon me, sir, my proposals have been accepted, and the day for the ceremony has been fixed.' 'The day has been fixed, has it?' said Mr. V., greatly amused ; 'why, I should have thought, Mr. James, at your time of life you'd have given over all thought of such matters.' 'No, I haven't, sir,' replied the victim of the tender passion. 'No, you haven't,' said Mr. V., with renewed laughter. 'Why, what may be your age? It's in the register, you know, so you may as well tell it.' 'Why, sir,' said this ardent sample of humanity, 'I think I shall be seventy, or near it, next birthday.' Here my brother could contain himself no longer, and joined Mr. V. in a most uproarious fit of laughter. When the cachinnation was over, Mr. V. said: 'On my word, Mr. J., you are a most inflammable individual. Pray, how long has your first wife been dead?' 'Nearly eight years, sir, and I've been alone all that time.' 'Oh, you've been alone all that time, have you?' gasped out Mr. V. as soon as he could speak. 'It strikes me that, at your time of life, if you kept alone a little longer it would be no great punishment; but you ought to know best about that. Pray, who is the lady who is anxious to have such a blooming bridegroom as yourself?' 'Miss Lucretia Pereira, sir; her father is a very respectable man, sir.' 'No doubt of it.' returned Mr. V.; 'but who is he? you don't mean the head writer in the Zillah Court?' 'Yes, I do, sir,' simpered Mr. James. 'Mr. Pereira! why, his daughter can't be sixteen.' 'No, sir, I don't think she is more than sixteen.' 'And you are seventy,' said Mr. V. 'Well, all I can say is that you are a bold man, a very bold man, and I fear you will repent your boldness; but I will not stand in the way of such a courageous young hero. I will grant you the leave you desire; but tell the registrar to enter it, as well as the name of your substitute, which, by the way, you have not mentioned.' 'Oh, thank you, sir, thank you, it's young Mr. Pereira!' 'Well, well,' replied the Judge, 'now you have got your leave, let me get home.'

As Mr. V. and my brother walked homewards they indulged themselves with various jocose remarks at the expense of the amoroso. 'The old idiot,' said my brother, 'he deserves all that's in store for him.' 'The whole thing is comical enough, truly,' said Mr. V.; 'but, notwithstanding, I am, in spite of my laughter, sorry to see an old man, hitherto accounted respectable and well-conducted, laying up misery for himself at the close of his career.'

For the sake of getting rid of Mr. James and his bride, though it anticipates the dénoucment considerably, I will state now what happened five months after the date of the said Lucretia's marriage. At that time she presented a little Miss James to her husband, who blandly remarked, in reference to the occurrence: 'That it was an extraordinary instance of what does sometimes happen, and of the wonderful powers of nature.' Mr. G., who happened to be present when the news was reported, made a somewhat cynical remark, which my brother declares he could never quite understand, though, in illustration of his meaning, Mr. G. indulged in making sundry grotesque contortions of his features, and in applying the index finger of the right hand to the side of his nose; which departure from strict decorum must, my brother presumed, be set down to his love of fun, and keen appreciation of the ridiculous.

This young person's career was what might have been imagined from its commencement, and more than fulfilled my brother's anticipations. The wretched old man died within a year from the date of the event I have recorded.

Let us now pass from the consideration of the Eurasians to that of the native races to be found at Tollicherry. The Hindoos there located are called Nairs and Teers. They possess good features, and are well formed and proportioned. They seem to have the same usages as other Hindoos, the same kind of temples, the same division into castes, and the same reverence for Brahmins, snakes, and monkeys.

The costume of these people, as far as relates to the men kind, does not differ much from that of the male Hindoos of other parts of India; that of the women is a little peculiar, as they wear nothing over their shoulders or busts. Their dress consists chiefly of a cloth, which they wrap round their waists so as to form a becoming sort of petticoat, or what serves the purpose of one. In the absence of any upper garment, they set a grand example to the great majority of the ladies of this and other civilized countries, where these feminine divinities use every conceivable art and contrivance to help to display the last hair's breadth that custom will allow.

The dwellings of the Nair and Teer people are pretty to look at, as they all have a small piece of ground that is well cultivated. They grow cocoa-nut trees, and other palms, pepper, vines, and plantains; and those who possess a larger portion of land raise rice and other grains.

The Mussulman population are not very numerous, and the greater number of these are shipowners and traders to the Persian Gulf, Arabia, and the Red Sea. They possess, many of them, considerable property, and inhabit large upstair houses which, according to native ideas, are very convenient and highly respectable, but unfortunately are not clean. The Bazaar men mostly inhabit huts like those to be found all over India. The dwellings of the Moplahs, a sort of cross breed sprung from Arabs and the natives of this coast, are like those of the Mussulmans, but inferior.

For the due understanding of the tale I have to tell, it is necessary that I should describe the manners and customs of the Moplahs in detail. I shall, therefore, return to them by-and-by. At present it will be convenient to finish the enumeration of the native inhabitants. It would indeed be a poor sketch of the place that did not bestow some notice on the numerous pariah dogs that roam about during the day, or the jackals that do the same by night, making it hideous by their howling, and dangerous too, as they generally go about in packs, tearing over the place, flying over the roads, which are narrow and mostly sunk between opposite banks which are about 6 feet high. In their spring over these roads, should a man be riding along (unless he is very quick), his head being slightly above the height of the banks, he is sure to be bitten; and if it was only ear, or nose, or cheek that suffered, though an unpleasant infliction, it would not be of any serious consequence. But this is not the case; these howling devils, in their snap, generally convey the poison of hydrophobia. Those who get this dreadful disease in this direct way are, however, few; it comes to man through the pariah dogs, who are frequently bitten by these mad jackals, and who, having themselves become infected, convey the poison by their bites to men.

During the first year of his residence at Tollicherry, my brother reports that seven Sepoys died of this incurable malady. The number of villagers and country people who died of it in this time was unknown. The authorities did all they could to keep down the number—I might say the swarms—of pariah dogs. The sub-collector, in this respect a man of dogged determination, was very diligent in collecting tongues and tails: for every pair of which he paid an anah. This practice was resorted to every hot season, and continued for more than three months; so that the dog-days, in this part of the world, last longer it would seem than they do elsewhere. But jackals and dogs form only a small part of the native inhabitants of Tollicherry. My brother says, 'I do not include in my list domestic animals such as horses, oxen, buffaloes, goats, sheep, or even donkeys, which we all know are common enough everywhere; but those ugly and deadly things not met with everywhere. In all the backwaters, rivers, and marshes, there are numerous muggers, or alligators; and some of these monsters are so large and so powerful that they have been known to drag down into the water, in spite of the poor animal's utmost efforts, a full-grown buffalo.' My brother witnessed an occurrence of this kind, as he was driving in a buggy within sight of a backwater. He was too far off to render the poor creature any aid; he was besides without weapon of any kind, though nothing but a good rifle would have been of any use.

In the sea all along this coast sharks of all kinds abound; and on and in the land there are snakes, scorpions, and centipedes innumerable. Of the birds, my brother says little or nothing, as they did not to his eye differ much from those met with in other parts of the country. There were kites and crows, those invaluable scavengers, and many smaller birds which he did not notice. He concludes his list of native inhabitants with the monkeys, which were very numerous; differing much in size, shape, and colour. He describes a monkey standing about 3 feet high, and black all over, except the white ruff under his chin, as a very fine and handsome specimen of the race, and of a species differing from the rest of the quadrumana.

By using this word species, I fear my brother has exposed himself to the wrath of the infallible Dr. Darwin, who, in his wonderful scheme of development by evolution, has stated that the quadrumana are our immediate progenitors. He has not, it is true, explained from which kind of monkey man is developed; nor how it happens that there are not as many kinds of men as there are of monkeys; or whether his friend ' Development' doubles up all the monkeys, great and small, black and brown, before she makes a man. All this, and much more, it is true he has not explained, but he has told us that our earliest ancestor or progenitor is an Ascidian (a cell), and that in a long course of ages, by the agency of his gossip ' Development,' the cell becomes this, that, and the other, the penultimate change being into a monkey, and the ultimate into a man. Harlequin's wand does nothing comparable to this. To convert a cell (a mere bag) into a man was reserved solely for 'Madame Development.' After effecting such wonders, it would be little short of high treason towards the man who discovered 'Madame Development's' powers, ungrateful, insulting, and a *sell*, indeed, had my brother omitted to take some notice of our immediate progenitors. I hope, ladies and gentlemen, you are none of you Darwinians; if you are, what a profane and sacrilegious infidel must my brother appear! Yet even here I espy some comfort if you, as well as being Darwinians, are also of the 'advanced platform,' as the phrase is in the wisdom of this nineteenth century; because then you will have mercy on me, as an insane person. Almost all murderers are, by the advanced wisdom of this same century, put down as insane, and are not to be hanged, as they deserve to be, but are to be maintained at the public expense; *i.e.*, at your and my expense—though we may have wives and a dozen hungry children to provide for—in order that the murdering gentleman may have time to repent; in other words, that he may have another opportunity of imbruing his hands in another victim's blood. 'Oh, by all means abolish capital punishment!' said the witty Frenchman, 'only let the murderers set the example.' Well, sir, or madam, I hope now you will not be less merciful to me, even if you be a Darwinian, than the wise men of the advanced platform are, or would be, to the murderer. So with renewed hope, having finished the catalogue of the native inhabitants of Tollicherry, I will proceed with the promised details respecting the Moplahs.

With such superlative examples of grace and beauty as those constantly observed among the daughters of the three British Isles, and the almost irresistible power exercised by these 'Queens of Creation' over the opposite sex, we need not call in question the effects recorded of this same irresistible power in ancient days. Jove himself, it is said, could not resist the exquisite form of Leda. Troy was besieged for ten years, and destroyed at last, to recover a matchless but naughty Greek lady, who ran away from her husband with a handsome scapegrace called Paris. Antony lost the dominion of the world for Cleopatra's smile. And, coming nearer to our own times, Diana of Poictiers at sixty, so historians tell us, retained so absolutely the affections of a king of France, that he simply doted on her ('doted on her simply' would be the better form of expression). And Ninon de L'Enclos, at seventy, drove all the young bloods of Paris demented by her beauty, which, it is positively affirmed, far surpassed that of all the younger ladies who approached her. One of the greatest of the Mogul Emperors, Jehangire, was so enchanted by the charms of a Turkoman maiden, who, when she grew up, was called 'Mhere ul Nissa,' the sun of women, and was afterwards the far-famed Nour Jehan, that he committed a dreadful crime to obtain her. This lady, in the early bloom of beauty, had been brought to Delhi, was seen by Prince Jehangire, and in both bosoms a mutual passion was kindled. But she had in her infancy been betrothed to Shere Afkun, a Turkoman of noble birth and distinguished merit. According to Indian notions nothing should be suffered to interfere with the fulfilment of such a pledge, and therefore the reigning Emperor (the celebrated Akbar), from a high sense of what he believed to be right, over-ruled the wishes of the lovers, and insisted that Mhere ul Nissa should be married to Shere Afkun. Jehangire bore his despair and disappointment as he best could, until, by the death of his father Akbar, he became the Emperor of India. Then power, united with his grief and passion, overcame his better nature, and he had the unfortunate Shere Afkun murdered, and at the same time he got possession of the person of Mhere ul Nissa. But for years the guilty monarch sued in vain. At last the lady consented to be his wife and the Empress of India.

All this proves that the dominion of beauty is confined to no hemisphere, and specially serves to introduce the present narrative, which relates to a part of India which, of all others, from the debilitating nature of the climate, and the peculiar customs of the people we are to speak of, would seem to be the least likely to furnish a tale of love and passion. But however unlooked for or unexpected the usages or customs on which a story-teller founds his narrative may be, or however unusual the circumstances arising from them, he cannot be held responsible for the facts or their results, so long as it can be proved that the said usages and customs do really exist.

In the present case the Moplah customs and usages referred to practically obtain over a considerable part of the western coast of India, *i.e.*, from the country of Mangalore, and from some distance north of it, to Cochin, and some distance south of it. In short, these customs are known and followed wherever the race has spread. For the details of the murder committed by these Moplahs my brother's notes are clear and precise, and for the particulars respecting Aminè after her return to her own country he declares that he gives the account as it was given to him by a Mussulman pilgrim, who, many years after the date of Aminè's death, passed *en route* to Mecca through her native place. The Mussulman pilgrim was a merchant of Tollicherry, who, being naturally interested in her fate, from knowing how barbarously her husband had been murdered, collected all the information he could from those who had been about her. He had it written down, and on his return to India forwarded it to my brother, who was then at Madras. My brother had it translated from the Persian into English, and has embodied it in the present narrative.

The Moplahs are, as aforesaid, a sort of cross-breed sprung from the seafaring Arab traders and the native women of the west coast. The children of these alliances settled on the coast with their mothers. Hence the Moplah race. They are men of large frame, and particularly strong and powerful. They are either cultivators of the soil, or merchants trading by sea. Some of the headmen among them are possessed of large estates, employ numbers of servants, and own numerous herds of cattle, flocks of sheep, and goats, with some horses and donkeys. Others possess Patamars and Dhonies. All cultivate the soil. Of this class of wealthy proprietors two individuals, at the time referred to, were generally regarded as chiefs or headmen. Both were almost equally wealthy, and equally looked up to by their neighbours. The younger of the two, although a Moplah, was a remarkably fine handsome man, retaining something (though not enough to spoil his good looks) of the Arab or Jewish cast of feature. He was of a disposition more frank and joyous than is usually met with among Arabs or Moplahs; his name was Lutchmon Sing. The other, called Saul Jan, was not so tall by four inches as his neighbour Lutchmon Sing, but he was larger in the body, broader in the shoulders, and was in all respects an amazingly powerful man. He exhibited the reserved, morose disposition characteristic of the race.

Before the occurrences in which these two men were the principal actors are spoken of, it is necessary to notice, as briefly as possible, the peculiar customs of the race in reference to women. With respect to property, or in fact anything they happen to covet, the Moplahs entertain the most advanced notions, and, with regard to the other sex, opinions and customs that are, to say the least of them, most singular. Any Moplah gentleman may visit any other Moplah gentleman's wife whenever he pleases; all he has to do is to leave his shoes outside the other gentleman's door. When this signal is made, no husband dare intrude. The visitor may stay the whole night, or as many hours as he chooses; it is all one. No person can enter the house, nor is such a thing ever thought of, till the visitor's shoes disappear. Whatever the husband may suffer, or however desirous he may be of standing in the visitor's shoes, it cannot be done, and it is bootless for him to complain. Under all circumstances he must restrain his feelings until the visitor removes his shoes. Well, the reader will probably say this is a very pretty and a very moral custom indeed, but is it really a fact? It is indeed. The reader will then probably inquire if the man aggrieved has no redress. Certainly he has, according to Moplah notions, complete redress. Has he not the right of returning the gentleman's visit, and of leaving his shoes outside that gentleman's door as long as he pleases? The Moplahs declare that all visits of this kind are punctually returned, so you perceive the politeness is mutual, however widely spread. Moplah notions of politeness and etiquette are very enlarged, it must be confessed, and thoroughly communistic; they have nevertheless certain advantages. For instance, the husbands are never troubled with sons to provide for, as all the children are, in every sense, the wife's children. In fact, no child knows who his or her father is or may have been. These are secrets, probably known to the ladies; but no one has the effrontery to make impertinent inquiries, consequently Moplahs never think or speak of their fathers, only of their mothers.

Whence this highly modest and delicate custom has been derived my brother has been unable to ascertain. 'If,' says he, 'I might offer a suggestion, I should say that it might be derived from an extended study of zoology, particularly of that wonderfully intelligent, faithful, and valuable race designated canine, as well as of that of our immediate progenitors, the quadrumana, amongst whom very similar usages obtain.' On this point the opinion of Dr. Darwin would be invaluable. The suggestion he has offered is to a certain extent confirmed and borne out by the common remarks of the vulgar, who, besides being ignorant of zoology, are ill-minded persons, who declare that these Moplahs one and all are 'dirty dogs,' which it is obvious can only be true of half the race. But it is wise and safe not to carry the scrutiny too far, lest we should be led to apply an ill-sounding name to the other half. Of the dogs of this race it has been already stated that they entertain notions prejudicial to the general safety of life and property. They never probably heard the noble axiom of Louis Blanc and his worthy compatriots 'Propriété est le vol'—but they certainly acted on it so thoroughly that to obtain anything they valued and wanted, or that the headmen whose retainers they were wanted, they plundered or took life without hesitation Witness the numerous cases of murder, gang robbery, etc., etc., which were, at the time referred to, continually occupying the attention of the courts throughout the Moplah range of country.

In illustration of the various amiable qualities of these Moplahs, my brother instances a case in which he had to give medical evidence. Early one morning the body, or more properly the mangled remains, of Lutchmon Sing, who has been already mentioned as one of the two principal headmen of the district, was brought to his door to be examined and reported on. He found that after the poor fellow had been knocked down and stunned by a blow on the head, proved by the smashing in of his cap, a severe wound of the scalp at the top and back part of his head, and a fracture of the skull, his body had been almost cut, transversely, into two parts. The spine, with some spinal and lumbar muscles, were all that held the two portions of it together. The muscles of the abdomen, as well as the lower part of the large lobe of the liver and the colon, were divided.

It was a piteous sight. Here was a fine young fellow in the prime of life, who was a favourite with all the Europeans, and with most of his own countrymen, brutally murdered, without any apparent cause. And what made everyone sorrow the more was the fact that he had been recently married to a Persian lady, whom, after a devoted court and worship of more than two years, he had at last succeeded in winning, and had brought home and located beyond the Moplah bounds in a stronghold situated in the hill country, but at no great distance, his holding being within the Manantoddy district.

It was evident that the division of the chief parts of the trunk had been effected by some sharp and powerful cutting instrument, most probably by one of those sharp toddy knives or bill-hooks which all jungle-men in India carry. The murder, it was supposed, had been perpetrated at the instigation of the rich Moplah named Saul Jan, whose lands were situated at no great distance from those of the murdered man, Lutchmon Sing. These two headmen, it was well known, had been at feud for a long time, ostensibly on account of some adjacent lands lying between their respective estates; but it was whispered that the murdered man's shoes had on one occasion (some two and a half years since) been found outside Saul Jan's door, and that he (Saul Jan), from circumstances to be hereafter explained, had not been able to return the visit. Be this as it may, the visitor's body was, after this occurrence, at the distance of time specified, found in the condition described.

A Hercules of a fellow, named Kulmuck, with a most villainous expression of countenance, who was an outdoor or field servant to Saul Jan, was with some others brought up before the Zillah Judge on suspicion of being the actual murderer, or at least of being a principal concerned in it. Some parts of this man's cloth were stained with blood, as was the handle and broad blade of his toddy-knife; his right hand was also stained with blood, and the palmar surface of the index and second finger of the right hand were slightly torn. It would appear that, even before he had washed the blood stains from his hand, or knife, or cloth, he had gone to the hut of a fellow-servant, a constant companion, and had there indulged himself so largely in drinking arrack that when the peons found him he was almost insensible, unable to speak, or stand : and lucky for them that he was in this state, as otherwise his toddy-knife would probably have been so used as to have saved some of them all further worldly care. Even without a weapon of any kind, manacled and pinioned, the peons shrank from him, and actually seemed afraid to touch him, so well were his strength and ferocity known.

When asked by the Zillah Judge how he accounted for the blood on his cloth, toddy-knife, and hand, he stated that, just before he had lain down in his comrade's hut, he had killed a shark, and had at the same time torn his hand. He further stated that parts of the shark would be found in his own hut, which was not more than a quarter of a mile distant from the one in which he had stayed to drink. Certain of the peons, who had been ordered to go to his hut, there found parts of a recently killed shark, which they brought into Court. The Judge asked the prisoner what took him away from his own hut, and for what purpose he went to the other man's dwelling. He said at once that he had heard of the chatty of arrack, and had gone there to get his share of it. The fishermen, who had seen the shark caught and brought home, were called into Court, and all agreed as to the time (about 6 a.m.) when Kulmuck had been seen with his prize. The peons had accurately noted the time when they found him all but insensible from drink, viz., about 5 p.m. They knew well that such a bullock of a fellow would not require more than three or four hours to sleep off a debauch, and allowing him to have been drinking two or three hours, there would remain no less than four hours to account for. The prisoner admitted having been in the fields, but he said that, instead of having been in that part of the jungle where the body was found, he had gone in another direction; and he mentioned some paddy fields through which he had passed, and others in which the men were ploughing with their buffaloes. On inquiry all these circumstances were found to be correct, and they considerably narrowed the time to be accounted for. Still there was an interval of some two hours, or at least an hour and a half, of which no sufficient or satisfactory explanation could be got at. The suspected man merely said that he was in the jungle, looking for a kind of lizard of which the native hakims make a certain kind of medicine, which they set great store by.

The Judge and the whole Court were at fault. The case was adjourned, and the prisoner remanded. The cloth and the toddy-knife, and the blood washed off by my brother into a broad-mouthed stoppered vial, with distilled water, were all placed in a box, and locked by the Judge with his own hands; then a broad piece of tape was placed round it, having the Zillah Court seal affixed at either end of it. The Judge then publicly placed the key of the box in my brother's hands. Finally, a peon carried the box into his private studio, or temporary laboratory. My brother then wished Mr. H. good-morning, and went home to set about the investigation which it was his duty to make.

This he found very laborious, as the modes of examination were necessarily repeated for the stains on the cloth, the handle of the knife, the blade, and the blood washed off into the stoppered bottle. The last named he examined first, being fearful of those changes which in a tropical climate take place very rapidly, and so greatly alter and distort the appearance of the blood globules. By his celerity he prevented any such change, and thus obtained capital specimens, which dried on the slides, and were available for evidence in Court.

To return to the Court. The things to be examined, having, as aforesaid, been consigned (under seal) to my brother's charge, and the prisoner having been placed in strong quarters, under ward changed every eight hours, while the Judge and his subordinates are seeking for further evidence, let us look into the history of the feud that, it is not denied, did exist between Lutchmon Sing and Saul Jan. This, it was said, arose from the rival claims of the parties to some lands situate between their respective holdings: their claims had been before the Court on several occasions, and had passed from the Zillah to the Higher Court. The case was supposed to be in train for decision, but scarcely for settlement, as it was known that both litigants were resolved to appeal to the Supreme Court. Thus the litigation might last for years. All this was publicly known, and it would satisfactorily account for the feud and the ill-feeling, but not for the murder; even Moplahs do not usually murder because they are legal opponents. The acknowledged feud was, therefore, regarded as insufficient to account for the extreme measure resorted to, and as a natural consequence suspicion took possession of the minds of those who were cognizant of the case that there had been some other unknown cause at work, and that to it the commission of the crime must be attributed. At the same time that this suspicion began to manifest itself, a whisper was breathed that there was such a cause. Spoken very cautiously at first, and in altogether a vague and indefinite way, after a time the whisper grew into something more tangible, assuming shape and form ; it became at last a direct statement that the murdered man had violated the laws and usages of the Moplah race, inasmuch as he had married a wife of another nation, and had kept her away in a sequestered district of the hill country. where he had purchased another holding, and a dwelling, or rather fortress, which had formerly belonged to a Poligar chief, who had been a follower of Sevagee. This dwelling, it was further stated, he had repaired and embellished for the lady he had brought from beyond the sea. He had also furnished his house with all that his wife could wish for, and had garrisoned it with a number of servants and retainers (almost all of whom he had armed with firelocks and rifles, as well as with shields and scimitars), so that, his gates being strong and his walls high, he could defy any assault except that of heavy artillery.

But why had he taken all these precautions and spent so much money, and why had he taken his stand so far beyond the Moplah country? This proceeding was considered by the Moplahs, one and all, as an outrage ; an insult to the men, and a crime of the deepest dye, as opposed to the recognised custom, for which nothing less than death could be awarded as sufficient punishment. Several Moplah men stated these opinions unreservedly in open Court ; though all positively denied having administered the punishment, or having been instigators or accessories to it. After long-continued denials and evasions, and a most ingeniously protracted display of fencing, it was at last brought out in evidence that Lutchmon Sing, some two and a half years ago, had paid a visit to Saul Jan's house, and that his shoes had been left outside the door for some hours ; this, it may be remembered, has been already noticed. After this fact had been established the Zillah Judge asked if Saul Jan, then under examination, had not, according to the Moplah customs, returned the visit of Lutchmon Sing. At this question Saul Jan broke out into the most ungovernable rage, cursing and swearing and wishing he could murder Lutchmon Sing over again. All this surprised the Judge, but he vainly attempted to obtain from the man, who had exhibited this paroxysm of rage, the meaning of it. He sullenly refused any explanation, accompanying his refusal by gross abuse, saying that he would not eat dirt to please the white Kafirs, the Shitan ka butchey logue, the heirs of jehanum, etc., and much more to the same purpose, no less obscene than malicious.

On inquiry from the old men about the Court who had been longest on that coast, and who best understood the Moplah modes of reasoning and feeling, it appeared that the rage of Saul Jan was excited by the knowledge that Lutchmon Sing had married, but had kept his wife beyond Moplah bounds, and had, moreover, so secured her that no one could gain access to her dwelling ; and therefore Saul Jan considered that he had been defrauded of his rights in being denied access to the wife of Lutchmon Sing, after that Kafir (as Saul Jan expressed it) had made his (Saul Jan's) wife his servant.

In vain it was pointed out that as Lutchmon Sing's wife had come from beyond sea, she could not be a Moplah, and would not, therefore, be willing to submit to Moplah customs ; this, and other such arguments intended to bring the savage to a more reasonable state of mind, only served to elicit fresh bursts of rage and envy, till it was deemed needful to remove him, and to place fetters on his limbs.

These exhibitions of fury and desire for revenge on account of a supposed injury not only showed that there was a sufficient cause to account for such a deed of violence, but pointed to the man who had committed or instigated it, and strongly confirmed the suspicions generally entertained. Still, there was nothing that could be regarded as legal proof. To confine the man, and look for further evidence, was all that could be done.

Evidence came somewhat unexpectedly to disprove part of Kulmuck's statement, but nothing positive to connect either him or his master with the murder. The evidence alluded to was my brother's report of his examination of cloth, knife, and blood washed off his hand. Each of these had been carefully examined chemically. Albumen, fibrin, and iron were shown to be present. Thus the chemical tests agreed with and confirmed the evidence afforded by the sensible tests—*i.e.*, the sight, the odour, and the taste. These were decisive as to the presence of blood. But what blood? This was the question. Fortunately my brother possessed a good Smith and Beck microscope, and by means of the micrometer he adjusted precisely the magnifying power he employed. Then placing on a thin slide a minute portion of the matter stated to be *shark's* blood, the rolls of circular discs like those of *human* blood were evident; their diameter was also like that of human blood. Still, as the blood discs of some other animals resemble those of human blood very closely, it was scarcely safe to pronounce absolutely that the stains and clots were those of human blood. My brother simply stated their close resemblance to those of human blood, while at the same time he pronounced absolutely that they were not those of shark's blood. When this report had been read, the native Sheristadar, an intelligent and respectable Brahmin, asked permission of the Judge to inquire publicly of my brother how he was able to pronounce so decisively that the blood-stains were not those of the shark. In reply, my brother asked permission of the Judge to go home and fetch his microscope. This was at once granted. He also requested that during his absence a little shark's blood might be procured, if possible. As this might not be procurable until the next morning, it was arranged that my brother should be at the Court on the morrow at 10 a.m., and that the Sheristadar with the shark's tail, or any part from which a few drops of blood could be obtained, should be there at that time. Mr. H. also promised to be present shortly after the hour named. Next day, my brother with his microscope, and the Sheristadar with two fishermen and a whole shovel-nosed shark, were present in Court; and before my brother had set up or arranged the instrument, Mr. H. appeared.

The breathless anxiety and curiosity of the natives—I may say of everyone in Court—to see the microscopic experiment, can scarcely be described. The great majority of the natives looked on the whole thing as a kind of jadoo, or performance of magic; still, their curiosity was extreme. As soon as my brother had found the right focus of the instrument, he pulled out one of the hairs of his head, and placed it on a slide in the feet of the instrument, and then made the Sheristadar and one or two other natives in the Court observe it. Having thus convinced them of the power of the apparatus, and excited their wonder, he placed with the point of a needle on another slide a very minute portion of shark's blood. This, when sufficiently attenuated, showed the form and shape of the blood globules distinctly. My brother then requested the Judge to look at them. He did so, and was much gratified at being able to distinguish their form so clearly. After the Judge, the Sheristadar, the head writer (Mr. Pereira), and two or three others, looked at the shark's blood and saw the globules. All agreed that they were oval in shape, and not round. Then a little human blood, shown in the same way, was examined by the same persons, and all agreed that the globules were round, and not oval; and all were extremely pleased and gratified. Then a minute portion of the blood on the toddy knife was examined, and everyone perceived that the discs were round, and in rolls, just like the human blood that had been examined just before The same opinion was given of blood taken from the cloth, and from the hand. Thus it was proved, beyond the possibility of doubt, that the statement of Kulmuck was false; and that the blood on the knife, and on the cloth, and also that from his hand, was not the blood of a shark. Mr. H. was delighted, and, after some compliments to my brother, said, 'You have rendered us an essential service.' The Sheristadar and all in Court were in a state of excitement and exaltation that cannot well be described. They seemed almost inclined to make a little deity of my brother, and their words were those of extravagant praise.

Before my brother left the Court, while talking with Mr. H., he asked him if he had examined the lady who, after all, seemed to be the cause of this crime. He said he had not done so for several reasons. It was, in the first place, unusual, and repugnant to the feelings of the natives, to bring native ladies into a court of justice; and, secondly, her dwelling was out of his district. 'Nevertheless,' returned my brother, 'in a case of such importance, I would over-rule the native prejudices.' 'I will think it over,' said the Judge; and then they parted. The next day the Zillah Judge drove over to the Circuit Judge's house, and asked his opinion regarding the best course to be adopted towards the widow of the murdered man, who, it was said, was a Persian lady of good family, and who was, moreover, highly educated and accomplished, understood several Oriental languages, spoke English tolerably well, knew even something of French, and could read and write the Persian, Arabic, and Hindustani. She was also said to excel in music. 'If,' said Mr. V., 'this account be true, she must be a wonder ; and if her personal charms correspond to her mental attainments, she must be a most bewitching creature, and quite equal to the far-famed Nour Jehan.' 'I hear,' said Mr. H., 'from my Sheristadar, who knows one of her female attendants, that she is surpassingly lovely, with a faultless figure, and silken tresses that she can sit on : she has the most beautiful eyes in the world.'

'Upon my word,' observed Mr. V., 'your informant has painted a most enchanting picture. I feel quite envious and grieved that I'm not the Zillah Judge. You cannot surely drag such a superlative creature into Court ; you will have to take your Court to her. Pray don't do it personally, or perhaps Mrs. H. might not be pleased ; but under any circumstances you must write officially to have our permission in this case of difficulty, and I am sure A. and H. will concur with me in the precept for you to proceed to her house or castle, and to take down her deposition, if she has anything to state.'

Mr. H. accordingly sent in the official letter asking the opinion of the Circuit Judges, which was unanimous, and found expression in a precept directing Mr. H. to proceed to the lady's house with as little delay as possible. On receipt of the precept Mr. H. sent a mounted peon with a letter to the widow of Lutchmon Sing, asking politely if it would be convenient for her to make such statements as the ends of justice demanded, or, if she had no statement to make, to answer such questions as it might be needful to put to her in reference to her present unhappy position, Mr. H. adding that, to save her feelings as much as possible, he would not ask her to attend at the Court, but would himself, with his writers and needful subordinates, attend at her house, and there take down her deposition. In reply to this letter, Mr. H. received a beautifully written note in Persian to the effect that Aminè, the wife of the late Lutchmon Sing, would be ready to see the Zillah Judge whenever he might think proper to pay her a visit, and would answer any questions he might put to her. She moreover begged the Judge to receive her grateful thanks for sparing her appearance in Court.

The next forenoon, about 10 a.m., Mr. H. and his subordinates, who had left Tollicherry by 7 p.m. the evening previous, reached the lady's house. They found a sumptuous breakfast prepared for them, both in the European and native fashion, while the lady's butler attended to wait on them with a dozen servants. Before the Judge sat down to table, a female servant presented him with another note, begging him to excuse her absence until the business of the Court called for it, her sorrow and the Eastern customs being, she hoped, sufficient to extenuate any apparent want of hospitality. She added that she had given strict orders to her butler, and to all her people, to supply anything and everything that might be called for. When the Judge had finished breakfast, and his subordinates had done ample honour to an excellent collation of curries, pillaus, etc., etc., Mr. H. was shown into a large apartment or hall, with a paved courtyard and fountain which fell into a small tank or basin. The whole space was well covered in, so that the sunbeams could not directly penetrate, while open verandas all round gave abundance of light. In this courtyard Mr. H. established his Court, and here, shortly after he had announced that he was prepared, the lovely widow of poor Lutchmon Sing made her appearance. An elegant cushion or settee had already been placed opposite to that of the Judge for her accommodation. As soon as she entered the hall she made a profound obeisance to the Judge, crossing her arms on her bosom. The whole Court, including the Judge, rose up on the lady's entrance, and he, returning her obeisance, requested her to occupy the cushion prepared for her. She did so, at the same time so arranging her veil that she only showed her face partially, yet sufficiently to enable her to converse or reply to questions without difficulty. Enough of the breathing picture was, however, disclosed to excite profound admiration, and to charm everyone present. The administration of the Mussulman oath, usual inquiries as to name, station, dwelling-place, etc., having been answered in a sad though sweet voice, Mr. H. asked if the witness knew of any circumstance that could help him to fix the crime on any particular individual. The same sad, sweet voice replied that a thick-set, powerfully made man, whom she would recognise if she saw again, had on two occasions, when her husband was absent, endeavoured to force an entrance into her house. This man was at the head of a score or more armed men, and he would on both occasions have obtained an entrance had not the noise and scuffle at the outer gate given her servants time to secure the main entrance, every other means of entering being always barred. On both attempts some shots and sword-cuts were exchanged, but no lives were lost, though some men on both sides were wounded. The leader, after the last attempt had failed, had used the most horrid language, had threatened to have the life blood of every man in the place, and particularly that of Lutchmon Sing. She and several of her servants had heard these threats; she had, though at some risk, seen the man who used these words, having observed him through an iron grating, while her head and face were enveloped in a dark cambly, so that she could not be known or scarcely seen by those outside.

A day or two after these men had departed, her husband had returned, and she had informed him of all that had happened in his absence. 'He knew at once who it was that had attacked his house; he also told me the object of it, and of the vile and singular customs obtaining amongst his countrymen. I became dreadfully alarmed, and entreated him not to go about alone. I foresaw what would be likely to happen, and told him that such a desperate and determined ruffian as this man, whom he called Saul Jan, would have him murdered, if he were not himself the murderer.' The lady's statements were carefully taken down, and signed by herself and the Judge; then several of the servants of the house were examined, and their testimony confirmed that of the lady. They also said that they should know the leader of the band—the man who had used the threats and the bad language—if they saw him again. This evidence was also taken down and signed and countersigned. Mr. H. prepared to then take his departure. After many compliments, thanking the bereaved wife not merely for her kindness and hospitality to himself and whole Court, but for the clear and collected manner in which she had given her testimony, he declared that under such painful conditions her conduct was truly admirable. As he made his bow before getting into his palankeen he said: 'It is a pity that your husband did not take your advice.'

Aminè, now that the examination was over, had for a time yielded to her sorrow: her head was bowed upon her bosom, her tears were falling fast, and her women were doing what they could to soothe and console her; but when she heard Mr. H.'s remark, she stood up at once, and said, 'Sir, my husband was a brave man, and despised the threats of such a villain as this Saul Jan. As he said himself, he would not be prevented from going about for any man's threats; he was as brave and noble as the other was cowardly and base. But,' clasping her hands and looking up to heaven with her beautiful eyes streaming with tears, she said, 'Allah is great, and what He ordains, we, His creatures, must endure.' She then, with a queenly inclination of her head, retired to her own apartments. Mr. H. thought he had never seen such a beautiful creature —so quiet, so sensible, and so self-controlled while she had to give her evidence; so sensitive, so full of grief, and yet so full of fire for him she had loved and lost.

The reader may perhaps wish to know what eventually became of this beautiful and unhappy lady. Her husband on his marriage had made her heir, in case of his death, of all he possessed. As soon as she could obtain purchasers for her lands and tenements, and various kinds of property, she returned to Persia. From the time of her husband's murder, up to the time of her departure for her own country, she never either saw or spoke to any one of the numerous suitors who endeavoured in every possible way to pay court and worship to her.

After her return to Persia, she so arranged her worldly possessions as to leave herself but a third part of her income; the larger she expended in charities to the sick and poor, whom she visited daily. A certain portion of her means she expended in building a handsome tomb, standing in an extensive garden of roses and other sweet-smelling flowers. By means of reservoirs and basins, fountains were always throwing water; and by means of marble conduits for irrigation, and a score of gardeners, everything was preserved in the most perfect order.

Before she quitted Tollicherry, she had obtained possession of the mangled remains of her husband, and had them embalmed, all but the heart; this she had so burnt, under the guidance of an able chemist, that the form of the organ only remained in the substance of a thin kind of charcoal. The embalmed body she placed in a marble coffin or sarcophagus, on which she placed, in an exquisitely carved marble vase or urn, the representative atoms of her lover's heart. On the top of the block of black marble that supported her husband's remains, and close beside it, she placed an empty coffin and an empty vase. In this tomb Aminè spent a large portion of her time, not only in prayer, nor even in indulging her incurable sorrow, but in communing with her own soul, and in striving, by reading and study, to school herself to suffer with uncomplaining fortitude. Her garden and her flowers, when the heat would permit, afforded her, morning and evening, some resource. Her large charities, her embroidery with her maidens, and sometimes her lute, enabled her to bear existence for some few years; but the shock she had experienced had been more than she could long bear. She pined away daily, and at last sunk down, without any special disease, to die. She evidently rejoiced at her release from sorrow, and the last words she breathed were, ' I shall now go to fill the vacant space beside my lord.' She had, long before, repeatedly enjoined her people that, after burning her heart without access of air, the charcoal left should be placed with that of her husband, which injunction was held sacred, and was carried out to the letter. She died equally beloved and lamented by all around her, rich and poor, and was long remembered as the broken flower of Persia. Around the tomb where lie the relics of this unhappy pair innumerable small lamps are ever burning, and every day at sunrise young Persian maidens deck the double urns with flowers.

We now return to Tollicherry, where Saul Jan and Kulmuck lie under sentence of death. After the identification of Saul Jan as the leader of the attacks on the distant house of Lutchmon Sing, the circumstantial evidence was so strong, and so completely confirmatory of the previous suspicions, that it may be said no one entertained the slightest moral doubt as to the guilt of these two men.

Still, the one link in the evidence was wanting; the perpetration of the murder was not actually brought home to these ruffians. This evidence was obtained in rather a singular and unlooked-for way. One day, about 3 p.m., just after my brother had dined, he was called into his veranda to attend to a low-caste Moplah man, who, in consequence of drinking, had fallen from a toddy-tree, and had smashed the upper arm close up to the joint. The destruction of the soft parts, and the splintering of the bone, were so terrible that there could be no chance of saving the man's life unless the limb was removed at the shoulder-joint. This was clear; but how was it to be done? The practised operators at our hospitals in England have trained and skilful assistants to control a large vessel or take up a smaller one, or render aid in any way that can be wanted. My brother had no one to assist him except a poor half-caste Portuguese, who had never seen an operation in his life. He was willing, but could do no more than steady or support the crushed arm or hand as occasion required. This being so, and the man having in a great measure been sobered by the fright and the fall, and his nervous system not having suffered as much as might have been expected, my brother determined to operate at once. In order to secure the main artery (the brachial), my brother first passed a curved needle, armed with strong silk thread, from the anterior part of the wound close to that portion of the splintered bone near to the socket, and carried the needle and the ligature between the bone and the vessels and great nerves, and brought out the point through the integument so as to include about three-quarters of an inch in breadth. Over this, by means of the handle and the point of the needle, the ligature was turned back-ward and forwards, in the shape of a figure of eight, with sufficient firmness to restrain hæmorrhage completely. This having been effected, my brother rapidly removed the limb, having only to tie two vessels—the anterior and posterior circumflex; but still he was in considerable difficulty as to where he should get his covering—or, as it is termed pro-fessionally, his *flap*—from. He had tied the main vessel *secundem artem* before he removed the temporary control, and had then completed the removal of the limb. Then he cut from the severed limb a portion of the uninjured muscular tissue and integument sufficient, with part of the deltoid muscle and integument, to form the required covering. The case did well; union by the first intention took place between the portions of the deltoid and the piece cut from the inner and back part of the upper arm.

My brother kept the man in his own house for about a fortnight, and was very kind to him. The rude creature felt this, and knew that my brother had saved his life; so, before he was discharged, he asked to speak with him privately. My brother turned the servants out of the room, and then told him to speak freely.

'Nay, Saib; master has kept my life for me this time; but if I tell master, will master save me again?'

At first my brother thought the man wanted to beg some-thing, and it was some time before he found out that his patient was really afraid to say what he desired, unless pro-tection could be assured to him. He repeatedly said: 'Master no take care, those people kill me.'

'Nonsense,' said my brother, 'what are you afraid of? Those people, who are those people?'

'My people, the Moplah people.'

A ray of light at once shot across my brother's mind. 'Then,' said he, 'you have something to tell me about Lutchmon Sing's murder?' The man nodded his head, but did not speak.

'What, Timbuckjee, you don't mean, I hope, that you had anything to do with that!'

'No, Saib, nothing at all; but I see something.'

'You see something! what do you mean? let me hear.'

'No, Saib, master never tell keep my life, how can I tell master?'

'I can't keep your life, but the Judge can if you give evidence that will enable him to punish these bad men.'

'Nay, Saib, master promise, then I tell Master Judge. I not know him; he perhaps no remember.'

'Well, Timbuckjee, I will see the Judge and get his promise, or I will try to get it.'

'Master Judge give promise in writing, then he no forget. He give word promise he perhaps no remember.'

My brother could not help smiling at the caution and cunning of Mr. Timbuckjee; but as the matter was of such importance he wrote a note at once to Mr. H., stating that he had reason to believe that the man who had fallen from the toddy-tree, and had so crushed his arm, could say something that would enable him to convict the murderers of Lutchmon Sing; but that the man was in such fear of the Moplah people that he refused to speak unless he, the Judge, would grant him a written promise to protect him.

After some delay Mr. H. went to my brother's house and saw Timbuckjee. But he seemed little inclined to make any statement of any value, till a native vakeel was sent for, who, after a great deal of trouble, at last made him understand that if he gave evidence to enable the law to act the law would protect him.

At last Mr. H. said: 'If I give you a belt, and make you one of the Zillah Court peons, will that content you?'

'Yes, Saib, that will keep my life. You give me belt, and make me peon of your Court; they never kill me. Yes, I will tell.' He then went on to say, that on the very day Lutchmon Sing was killed, he, Timbuckjee, was following his business tapping palms, for which purpose he had climbed up a lofty tree, and was engaged fastening an empty chatty to the part which he had incised. When he had finished his work he was about to descend, but he did not do so, having observed two men at some little distance off, standing at the foot of another lofty palm, engaged in earnest conversation. He soon recognised the men in question to be Saul Jan and Kulmuck. Concealed as he was by the leaves and branches, and remaining perfectly still, he himself remained wholly unobserved, while he had a full opportunity of watching all that passed between the men named. He was not near enough to hear anything, but judging from their behaviour it seemed to him that Saul Jan was urging Kulmuck to accede to some proposition that had previously been made to him, but to which he steadily refused to consent. At last he seemed to yield, and then he held out his hand, into which Saul Jan counted 20 Rs.; these Kulmuck tied up, after again counting them, in a corner of his cloth, and then parted from Saul Jan, who took the way to his own house, while Kulmuck also went to his hut, where he remained about half an hour; then he left it and returned to the jungle. Timbuckjee did not dare to follow Kulmuck too nearly lest he should be discovered, but he kept him in sight till he entered the path that led to Lutchmon Sing's dwelling. There he lost sight of him. In about an hour he again saw Kulmuck, running in the direction of the hut where he remained to drink, and where he was found with his bloody cloth and knife. While he was running Timbuckjee observed that his cloth was stained.

This statement, having been sworn to after the Moplah fashion, was taken down, and Timbuckjee made to vouch for its truth by affixing his mark to it. The Judge then countersigned it. Now as no money had been found on Kulmuck's person when he was captured, it was clear that he must have deposited it somewhere else, and if Timbuckjee's story was true, he had been nowhere, after having received the blood-money from Saul Jan, but to his own hut; consequently, then, the rupees should be found there.

To Kulmuck's hut therefore at once went the Judge, my brother, several subordinates of the Court, a *posse* of peons, and some coolies with mattocks and picks. The whole floor of the hut was examined without discovering any sign of earth having been recently turned up; nevertheless it was dug up all over without avail. The whole of the compound was then treated in the same way, still without finding anything: doubt was beginning to attach to Timbuckjee's statement, when someone said: 'Try the roof.' In less than two minutes afterwards there was a shout, and one of the peons drew forth from the thatch a piece of rag evidently containing rupees. The little parcel was immediately handed to the Judge, who opened it before all present, and counted out the number of rupees which Timbuckjee had seen Saul Jan count out to Kulmuck.

This discovery proved the truth of all that Timbuckjee had said, and at the same time proved the guilt of Saul Jan and Kulmuck. I am glad to say that both these ruffians were sentenced to be hanged. Great efforts to save Saul Jan were made by the Moplahs, who declared that he had been defrauded of his *undoubted* rights, and that Lutchmon

Sing deserved his fate. And nothing would convince these brutal and savage disciples of a brutal and sensual creed that the murder deserved capital punishment. They threatened resistance, used very violent language, and seemed altogether so highly irritated and incensed that three companies of the European regiment stationed at Canamore were marched from thence to Tollicherry in order to overawe them, and along with the three companies half a battery of Horse Artillery. These decisive and judicious measures had the effect desired; the would-be rebels thought ball cartridges, grape-shot, and fixed bayonets unpleasant things to face, and that under the circumstances discretion was the better part of valour. The execution, therefore, took place without either disturbance or bloodshed.

AN HOUR LOST AT MR. G.'S DINNER.

AFTER the execution of the two Moplahs for the murder of poor Lutchmon Sing, nothing worth recording took place at Tollicherry during some months. People got up in the morning, went to bed at night, and ate their dinners in a very routine, humdrum sort of way, and nothing occurred to vary the monotony of existence except a new number of Lever's ' Charles O'Malley,' or the issue of cards for a dinner or evening party at the First Judge's house, which was a regular monthly institution with that most hospitable and generous man.

Things had been going on in this way for about three months when, so far as concerned my brother, there was a change, which entailed on him considerable anxiety, and a good deal of extra work. An officer of the Bombay army was sent to Tollicherry on sick certificate. He had landed, and had, by means of his servant, taken a small house in the town before my brother heard anything of him. He had, indeed, been three days so located when Lieutenant Mitchel, who was in command of the detachment usually stationed at the place, met my brother in his morning walk, and told him of the advent of Mr. M. of the —— Infantry, Bombay. 'Hasn't he sent you his case, and the private statement of the regimental medical officer?' asked Mitchel.

'He has not,' said my brother; 'indeed, until you informed me of it, I was as ignorant of the arrival here of Mr. M. as I was of his existence. But now, as he is here on sick certificate, I shall go and see him, though it was his duty in the first place to have sent me his papers.'

'Then,' returned Mitchel, 'we'll go and see him together; we may as well walk that way as any other.' So said, so done. On their way they met Captain B., who, after good-morning, inquired if they had got 'a purwoke to Waughan's, because if you haven't you will have. I saw the cards.' 'Well,' said Mitchel, 'V. deserves to be called the punir of Tollicherry; the place would be nothing without him. And then he gives such champagne and claret; it's really worth something to get a "purwoke," as our friend says, to his house.' 'You should be tender in making your quotations,' whispered my brother. 'I'll tender an apologue,' said Mitchel quietly, 'if you wish.' Here Captain B. parted from his companions, his road lying in a different direction.

When he was gone, my brother remarked to Mitchel: 'I think if you did "tender an apologue," as you put it, you would only make bad worse. Poor B. does not know that he made any mistake, nor does he perceive that you were laughing at him; but if you make any apology, however "tender" you may be in your mode of expression, he cannot fail to perceive it.' 'Well, *magister meus*, I am schooled. I will hold my peace, though he breaks the Queen's English into many a piece; but I must keep the peace as well as hold my peace, or you will be jealous, and say I have stolen your trade, and set up an opposition shop, etc., etc.; and I should be sorry to run counter to your wishes, as the peaceful disposition evinced this morning clearly proves.' 'If you would weigh your words over your counter a little more carefully there would be some hope of your succeeding in business. As it is, your stock-in-trade is rather of a meagre description ; it is neither bonded stock, nor consolidated stock, nor foreign stock, nor even rolling stock. It can only, I think, be described as a stock of assurance, though I'll be sworn you possess no life policy, and——' 'Oh, stop!' said Mitchel ; 'you have the devil's own faculty of "iteration," as the fat knight says, and, moreover, here we are at M.'s bungalow.'

But at first it was in vain that the two visitors sought an entrance. After knocking repeatedly at the door of the house, which was closed, no response could be obtained. 'This is queer,' said Mitchel. 'Are the people all dead? What is the reason that no servant or maty boy makes his appearance? It's clearly a case of enchanted castle, inhabited by an ogre who never comes out till night-time.' 'I think' said my brother, 'I can find a key to the ogre's castle door.' And accordingly he walked over to the godown attached to the house. He had observed that the door belonging to one of these outdoor offices had been cautiously opened so far as to permit those inside to see who they were who were so bent on getting into the house, without being seen themselves. The door in question, it is true, had been again cautiously closed, but the opening and shutting of it having been noticed further defence was vain. My brother threatened all kinds of pains and penalties, and Mitchel struck the door so violently with his foot that the whole place shook again. He was about to repeat his efforts when the garrison surrendered, only entreating that the Saiblogue would have a moment's patience. 'Suspension of arms' having been thus agreed to, the door was, after about a minute's delay, unbarred and opened. 'You d——d rascal,' said Mitchel, 'what do you mean by keeping us waiting here without answering our summons?' 'Nay, Saib : what for master angry? My master sick ; he

tell he not see anybody.' 'Aye, but he must see us. I am
the medical officer to whose charge he is consigned while
sick, and if he should want help in any way he is bound to
put himself in communication with this gentleman, who is
in command of the detachment stationed here. Now, open
the door of the house and let us see your master.' 'But,
Saib, my master no give order; he tell no see.' 'You are
an impudent scoundrel,' said Mitchel, 'and I have a good
mind to give you a taste of my riding-whip for refusing to
do what you are ordered to do, knowing who we are.'
'Pray be quiet, Mitchel,' said my brother, 'and let me deal
with this fellow, whom, to tell you the truth, I rather like
for his sturdy fidelity to his master. Now you, sir, listen
to what I say. If you do not open the door of the house
I shall have to complain of you to the Zillah Judge, who
will be in Court shortly after ten o'clock, and you will get
punished, and peons will be sent to force open the door, so
that you see all you can gain by resistance is a few hours, for
which you will bring trouble on yourself and your master.'
'By Jove,' said Mitchel, 'you have given him better terms
than I would have done. But take your own way; I shall
leave you to settle it.'

The maty was evidently undecided, but the calm determination shown by my brother convinced him that it would
be best to submit to what he felt he could not successfully
oppose or prevent, so after a little hesitation he said:
'Master too strong; I do as master order, but my master
very angry.' 'That's a sensible fellow,' said my brother.
'I will tell your master that you held out to the utmost to
obey his orders.' Then the man, making a low salaam,
said: 'Master good master, but not know all; when master
go in then master see, and then master know.'

Surely no words could express the impression made on
the minds of the visitors, or explain the situation more

clearly, than the maty's words, however poor the English. They found Mr. M. in his shirt and trousers lying on a cot, round which were strewed beer and brandy bottles, some empty, some untouched; the smell of these liquids was very strong, and the man himself was really an object equally of compassion and disgust. His face was so swelled and bloated that his eyes were partly closed, and its hue was fiery red; he either would not or could not speak. Hiccoughs, alternating with a sort of stertorous breathing, were the only sounds he emitted; his skin was dry and hot, and his pulse bounding. The unfortunate man did not seem able to rise and scarcely to move. After sending in the sweeper to remove all nuisances, and to cleanse the room in every possible way, doors and windows not admitting sun being kept wide open, the whole of the bottles were removed, and placed in a godown under lock and key, only a very small allowance for the day being left out in charge of the servant. Finally, the official papers, which the boy knew where to put his hands on, were given to my brother. Before his departure he ordered the patient's body, head, neck, and arms to be sponged, constantly or frequently, with weak vinegar and water. He then left word that he should see Mr. M. again after breakfast.

On reaching home he took up a letter that was addressed to him by Mr. M., senior, in which he spoke of his son and his son's evil habits in a very fond and parental way, making all sorts of excuses for a low and disgusting indulgence that admits of no excuse, except that the person exhibiting it had lost all self-control, which might with equal propriety be put forth to defend any other crime. The writer entreated that my brother would use representation, persuasion, and every moral means in aid of his medical treatment, in order to reform as well as cure his unfortunate son. He then explained his son's position in the army. He said that, by means of family interest, he had got his son gazetted for a staff appointment, but that it had not been taken up, in consequence of his son's sickness, which, through the kindness of the medical officer, my brother would find put down in the case as *fever*. 'In his private letter to you,' continued the old gentleman, 'I cannot tell what he has said, but whatever this may be, I should esteem it a lasting obligation if you would kindly put down in your official report the same disease, *fever;*' and that if my brother would be so kind as to do this, his son could be sent home on sick certificate for three years without losing his claim to a staff appointment, and that not only he, but the whole family would be for ever grateful.

Long before my brother got to the end of this precious epistle, he felt so indignant and disgusted with the doting and unprincipled old writer, that he more than once determined to return the letter in a blank envelope. He did not, however, act on his first thought; he remembered old Mr. M.'s gray hairs, and that he was a father who was wrapped up in his only son. My brother contented himself with acknowledging the old gentleman's letter as briefly as possible, adding that he would do all that was in his power for his son.

He then glanced over the official case, which was so drawn up as to afford little information as to the state of the patient. This was of no consequence; what my brother had seen was quite enough. The private letter was a degree more truthful; but the facts were so softened, and so many suppositions were introduced in order to account for the symptoms, that it was, or appeared to be, more calculated to conceal the real condition of the patient than to make it evident. My brother thought of Talleyrand's *mot* regarding language, smiled, and then sat down to breakfast with his wife.

This narrative not being either a medical treatise or report, my brother omits all details of the treatment of the case. It must suffice to say that he did his best, and at first with such success that hope of reform began to be entertained. It was, however, a delusive hope. The patient broke all his promises, secretly obtained from the Parsee shopkeeper a fresh supply of beer and brandy, and again reduced himself to much the same state as that in which he was first found. The intoxicating liquids were again taken from him, placed under lock and key, and then two Sepoys were placed on guard night and day at Mr. M.'s bungalow to prevent the entrance of anything whatever not ordered by my brother. Mr. M., on finding himself thus forcibly controlled, was at first so furious and violent that it became necessary to employ peons to restrain him and prevent him from making his escape.

When he found that neither threats, nor force, nor bribes would avail either to procure him liquor or favour his escape from control, he became sullen and morose, and refused even to speak in answer to questions. Lieutenant Mitchel had all along felt a great interest in the case, and had furnished the guard in the frankest and readiest manner.

Very early one morning he met my brother en route to visit Mr. M. 'I'll go with you,' said Mitchel, 'if you have no objection.' 'None in the world,' returned my brother. 'You have seen the patient several times ; you saw him when I first took charge of him, and you know how persistently he has destroyed his chances of getting better.' 'Yes,' replied Mitchel, 'he has done all you say ; the madness for drink has got hold of him, and until this rage or madness moderates or passes away for the time, I fear you will get no good of him ; but still, I pity the poor devil !' 'Oh, pity him as much as you please,' returned my brother, 'so long as you don't give him anything to drink.' This brought the speakers to M.'s house. They went upstairs almost together, and as they entered his room they perceived that he was lying on his cot in his shirt and long drawers.

As my brother approached him to feel his pulse and skin, his features assumed a very ugly scowl, and at the same time he put his right hand under his pillow. This action my brother did not notice at the instant, but Mitchel did, and as quick as light pinned M.'s hand with both his. A struggle ensued; my brother held down M.'s left hand while Mitchel drew out the right, grasping a large carving-knife, which he had secreted under his pillow. It was quickly taken from him by the superior force present, and although he made desperate efforts to disengage his right hand, Mitchel's double grip was too firm for him. He kept his hand on the bed while the others unclasped the fingers, thus no one was wounded.

It was clear that Mitchel's quick eye and movement had saved my brother's life. Speaking of the affair afterwards, Mitchel said: 'I did not like the look he gave at you, and when, in reply to your request to let you feel his pulse, he put his hand under the pillow, I suspected something, and luckily, on the impulse of the moment, pinned his hand.'

'Luckily indeed for me,' said my brother; 'six inches of cold steel under one's ribs is not a pleasant experience at any time of day; yet I should certainly have had to make it this fine morning but for you. I cannot well thank you; your own manly heart will do it for me better than my poor words can.'

'Halt, dress!' said Mitchel; 'none of your heroics. I'm right glad, though, that none of us got hurt; that's a very ugly sort of weapon, that long pointed knife, at close quarters especially.'

All this passed in less than two minutes; then the maniac, for such the man was at the time, was carefully secured by

soft bandages, his head was shaved, and cold lotion constantly applied to it. Every knife and fork in the house
was kept out of the room, he was allowed no food but what
he could take with a spoon, and a constant guard was kept
in the room as well as at the door.

As Mitchel and my brother were leaving the poor victim
of alcoholic stimulation, G. came up to them to inquire how
M. was going on. Poor G. turned quite pale on learning
how near murder had been to them that morning, and
specially near to my brother. However, he soon rallied,
and, after a few words of congratulation, he said : 'This
day week I hold you both engaged to dine with me ; I
mean to give a dinner in honour of Mitchel for this morning's work.'

' All right,' said Mitchel, ' I'll be most happy to go and
punish your champagne ; but don't make mountains of
molehills ; don't exhibit me as a sort of wild animal of a
new species just caught : don't do that, pray. The Doctor
was going to launch out into something, but I managed to
stop him, as I must try and stop you.'

' Very well,' said G., ' as you are to be the king of the
feast, you must have your own way, and we won't say one
word as to why it is given. We won't even ask if a knife
has a sharp point or a keen edge.'

' For fear of its wounding or cutting me,' said Mitchel.
' That's capital ; I always thought you a comical blade.'

' What, Mitchel, at it again ? You are, I see, determined
to try the temper of the blade,' observed my brother.

' Oh, stop that fellow with his heroics and his *ribaldry*.
When he begins, there's no chance for me.'

' Why so cranky, Mitchel ? But for you, I should not
this morning have a *rib all dry*.'

' That shows you all the more ungrateful. You won't
let a fellow have a chance.'

'Quite the contrary,' said my brother; 'it is you that won't let a fellow have a chance. M. tried hard to get one at me this morning, but you wouldn't let him have it.'

'Good-morning, good-morning,' said Mitchel; 'that fellow's got tongue enough for a dozen. I'm off.'

'No, no,' said G.; 'come and breakfast with me. I can't ask the Doctor; he has to go to his wife. How I pity him! But, poor fellow! he can't help it now.'

'Well, don't be envious of your neighbours, G.,' returned my brother; 'it looks strongly as if you were determined to follow my good example.' And so the trio, with jest and raillery, and in high good humour with all the world and themselves, parted.

Great was the stir, and much was the commotion, in the little community of Tollicherry, when it was known that my brother had been in such imminent peril, and that his life had been saved by the gallantry and promptitude of Lieutenant Mitchel. The story had to be told over again and again, and the questions to be answered respecting the occurrence could not be enumerated. At last, like every other nine days' wonder, people began to get tired of it, and the dinner to the hero of the tale came in its turn to occupy public attention.

On the morning before that named for the dinner, G. and my brother encountered each other near M.'s bungalow, where my brother had just been. The conversation that ensued referred almost entirely to G.'s coming party. 'I've asked everyone,' said G., 'except V., who is on circuit, and A., who is on leave, and old B., who is sick of the gout.'

'*Sick of the gout!*' returned my brother. 'I should think so. Who wouldn't be that ever had a taste of it?'

'Come, come, Doctor; it's too early in the morning. A man should be scrupulous about taking drams in the morning.'

'Oh, G., G., how can you?—stale, flat, and unprofitable, and hypocritical besides, while pretending to give your friends advice. But tell me who you have got.'

' H. will come,' replied G. ; 'but from the distance at which he resides, he stipulates that he is to go as soon as he has had coffee. The Zillah Judge will come too, though I suspect he obtained leave with great difficulty, as he adds, " You will not press me to stay later than half-past nine, as we always retire to rest at 10 p.m." Then Mitchel, our two selves, young B. and old B. (the Captain, I mean), will make up the party.'

' Won't you have the missionary, Mr. G. ?'

' No, that I won't ; he'd only be a wet blanket,' said G., 'and I don't want any wet blankets—in fact, I never liked them.'

' Poor fellow !' replied my brother. ' How I feel for him ! How his bowels will yearn when he hears of a feed that he's not to have a share of !'

' Well,' returned G., 'his bowels may yearn, then ; for he won't get a share of mine.'

' He'll be very indignant, if not spiteful,' said my brother. ' You'd better have him ; he'll talk about the tithe-offering, and quote Leviticus to no end.'

' Well, he certainly will quote Leviticus to no end on this occasion, for I certainly won't have him,' said G.

Young B. and Mitchel then came up, and the whole four then sauntered on to G.'s to take early tea or coffee. While thus engaged, the conversation again turned on guests expected. ' But do you really mean to say,' said young Henry B., 'that H. has got leave to come ? I can scarcely credit it. My worthy cousin Harriet would scarcely permit such a breach of discipline.' The conditions under which Mr. H. had accepted the invitation were then made known to him ; he burst into a fit of laughter. ' " Retire to rest," is it ? I wonder how people can tell such open and apparent *terra dilles !'* Then he indulged in another outbreak. 'Faix, as Paddy says, they won't break their hearts with resting, I'll engage !' 'Come, come, Master B., you must behave yourself !' 'Behave herself, did you say ? No doubt she does—like an angel under trying circumstances.' 'Challenge him, Mitchel, to a game at billiards—do anything to arrest his wicked conversation,' said G. 'Remember my respectability is at stake.' 'Oh,' said B., 'it's three to one against you ; what's it in—ponies ?' 'Worse and worse !' replied G. 'First he throws away his loose words, and now he wants to throw away his loose cash.' 'Oh, you cave in, do you ?' said B. 'Well, so be it ; but now I'm going to be serious.' His eyes were dancing with laughter, and the internal chuckling was so overpowering that he could scarcely speak. 'I've got a little plan in my head——' 'A maggar, or anything else that's lively,' interposed Mitchel. 'No,' replied B., 'I wouldn't deprive you for the world ; but it's this : If we all set to work carefully, set all our watches an hour slow, and you, G., set all your clocks to the same time, it will be our own fault if we can't persuade H. that his watch is an hour fast.'

'Oh, that will never do !' replied G. 'Mrs. H. always sends his palankeen for him at the time appointed, and he always goes by that, and with that, or in that, if you prefer it.' 'That's capital,' said Henry B. ; 'that will make all sure. I will go out when the man I shall set to watch tells me that the palkee is coming, and direct the bearers to take it to the back of the godowns, and to wait there till Mr. H. sends for them ; and then if your butler provides them a good curry and rice, and the wherewithal to wash it down, I'll be bound they won't disturb their master.' 'On my word,' said G., 'it looks promising ! I've really half a mind to try it. But will you, all of you, loyally support me and back me up?' 'Of course they will,' said young B.; 'only you resolve to have a whole mind, and not a half one, every man will be steadfast and true.' 'You may count upon one man, at least,' said Mitchel. My brother, led away by the spirit of fun and frolic, confesses that he also promised to be one of the conspirators, and to aid and abet as far as in him lay. 'Oh, but there's still old Captain B.!' said Mitchel. 'Never mind him,' said G. 'I will undertake to seduce him, though I'm not a blooming young maiden of bashful fifteen.' 'Who's wicked now. I wonder?' said Henry B.

'Now's the day and now's the hour,' said Mitchel, as he entered G.'s dining-room. 'And "see the conquering hero comes,"' said my brother. 'That's the text on the present occasion.' 'No, no, Doctor, it's agreed we're to have none of that.' 'Well,' returned my brother, 'it reminds me very much of Scott's story in "Guy Mannering," which records how a number of the porters, criers, and others of like degree attached to a High Court of Judicature were, for the nonce, appointed to determine the difficult and intricate questions arising from a long dormant claim of inheritance, the essential conditions required being that those who were to determine the case should be men of *no knowledge*. So we are met to do honour to a certain valiant knight, but are not to describe or specify his achievements. On my word it's delightful: nothing can so present the "Lucus a non lucendo" principle more luminously.' 'But *I* say,' said Mitchel, 'we are here assembled to punish G.'s good things, and not to carry out any visionary ideas of vain glorification and self-laudation, simply to rejoice in the conviction that "all's well that ends well."' 'So be it,' said G.; 'and here comes Hooper,' who was greeted cordially by all present. How could it be otherwise? I never knew the man who did not like and respect him. He was greatly amused at hearing of the conditions of the feast. 'Truly, you ought to be called the club of Odd Fellows; but *chacun à son goût*. It's a relief to me, as, otherwise, I should, I suppose, have been called upon for a speech.' 'Oh,' said G., 'you will certainly have to make a speech, and it must be in honour of Mitchel. The only peculiarity is that you are not to say what he is to be honoured for.' 'That's the regulation, is it?' said H., laughing. 'Again I say you certainly have earned the title of Odd Fellows; besides, I don't see how such a whimsical regulation can be complied with.' 'You'll see your way out of it, never fear,' said Mitchel, 'when you have had a few glasses of côte d'or.' 'I hope I shall, but I don't now,' replied H.

Mr. Henry B., Mr. H., and Captain Brennan now made their appearance. The newcomers were warmly welcomed, and almost immediately afterwards dinner was announced. Dinners are so much alike that it would be almost an impertinence to enter into details; it is enough to assure those interested in such matters that the champagne and claret, the soda-water, etc., were all properly refrigerated, and the punkah-pullers did their duty. The table was a round one, and the party seven, so that the conversation was general.

After the feeding was over, and the wine had circulated two or three times, the gathering became a very merry one. By-and-by Mr. Hooper was called on by the host to give the toast of the evening, but requested to bear in mind the conditions imposed. Mr. H. rose and spoke thus : 'Gentlemen, I have been requested by our worthy host, under certain conditions, to propose a toast. I can truly say that no gentleman rising in a certain honourable House to deliver his maiden speech ever felt himself in a position of greater difficulty than I do at this moment. Were I a new Demosthenes, or a Cicero, or both rolled into one, it would still be difficult to speak of a noble action without referring to it, without describing it, and without stating what it averted.

This being so, I must leave you, who feel on this subject, I am sure, as much as I do myself, to interpret my feelings for me, and to imagine all that I would have said, had not your special regulation, by which you have fairly earned the designation of Odd Fellows, prevented me. Neither do I forget the old saying regarding brevity : therefore, in proposing Lieutenant Mitchel's health, which I trust will be drunk with all the honours, I beg leave to say that in my heart I believe I am proposing the health of as brave and generous and noble-hearted an officer as there is in the service, and if I knew of anything stronger than this to say in his praise I would say it. Gentlemen and friends, I beg to propose the health of Lieutenant Mitchel, of the —— Regiment, M. N. I.' As Mr. H. sat down there was most vociferous cheering, clapping, etc., and Mitchel's health was drunk in the most approved fashion.

Lieutenant Mitchel now stood up and said : 'Gentlemen, speechifying isn't my line ; therefore I feel sure that you will not insist on my attempting what I know I can't do. But, gentlemen, pray believe me when I say that I feel your kindness most deeply, though I have not the gift of words to express it. I beg to drink all your healths, and thank you heartily for the manner in which you have drunk mine. I also beg to thank Mr. H. especially for the kind and handsome way he has spoken of me.'

'Bravo, Mitchel ! A very good speech indeed !' said Mr. G, as soon as the shouting and hip-hipping allowed him to be heard. ' Now, Doctor, we must call upon you, who, after all, are the most interested in this affair.' ' Truly, as you have said, most noble President,' replied my brother, as he rose to respond to the call made on him, ' I am the person most interested, because I am the person most benefited, and were I without a wife or family I should say solely benefited. At any rate, I have received that described

17

elsewhere in these words, " What will not a man give for his life ?"   Sure, to a brave man, the stab of a poniard or knife, the stroke of a sabre, or the blow from a ball, are, as respects himself, little heeded, and are faced without a moment's hesitation on very slight grounds.   But, gentlemen, there are pangs that strike deeper, and pangs that are felt more keenly by the bravest than any that can affect him personally.   Can a husband, think you, feel no deeper pang at parting for ever from a beloved wife ?   Can a father, think you, leave helpless orphans behind him and feel no deeper pang than lead or steel can inflict ?   Your own kindly hearts, silently yet eloquently, answer my questions. Can I, then, measure the extent of my obligations to a friend who has saved me from sorrows such as these ?   Life-long gratitude is insufficient to mark that measure.   Well may I repeat his simple but genuine expression of feeling when I say, " I have not the gift of words to express it." Gentlemen, I am forbidden by the regulation which has been established, not because we are " Odd Fellows," as suggested by our excellent friend Mr. H., but on account of the extreme modesty of that matchless friend to whom I owe so much, but may not name.   The king of our party for this evening has enjoined us to go into no details, and to avoid all particulars.   I am thus forbidden to speak as I would wish of that lightning-flash of intellect, which, guided by his rapid eye, revealed to him instantaneously a danger that no one but himself perceived.   In like manner I am debarred from enlarging on that decision—that wonderful decision that guided his action.   A single second's delay would have enabled the poor maniac to strike, and so close and with such a weapon, death would have been inevitable. Neither am I permitted to describe that instantaneous and robust action which converted the internal electric message and order into practice.   Intelligence like intuition, decision without an instant's hesitation, with courage, strength, and skill, as well as reckless self-devotion, are all manifested here in the highest degree : qualities which, when united, win the love, respect, and admiration of all who witness them, and which, in addition, so far as concerns myself, have con. verted a casual acquaintance into a grateful and attached friend for life.

'Gentlemen, I should infringe our regulation if I stated the name of the man to whom these remarks refer ; but it needs not, there is a *vox non audita*, as well as a *lex non scripta*, and this inaudible voice will teach you to whom my words apply : and also those words I have not spoken, those words which would in part convey by sounds the thoughts and feelings that must remain unspoken, ineffable, the thoughts and feelings of a grateful heart. Gentlemen, before I sit down, I beg leave to drink all your healths.'

During the whole time that my brother was speaking there was a profound silence ; when he sat down there was a hum and a subdued thumping on the table, but not the uproarious applause that had greeted the two previous speakers. During almost the whole time occupied by my brother's speech, Mitchel had remained with his head bowed over the table ; when my brother sat down he stretched his hand over to him, and there was a long pressure of hands, while both were perfectly silent.

Mr. G. now got up and said : 'The deep feeling and the good sense of the Doctor's admirable speech seem to have subdued us all, but at the same time to have decreased our mirth. This must not be ; we are met here to illustrate the value and the wisdom of our dear Shakespeare's words, "All's well that ends well," so let us have a hip ! hip ! hurray for the Doctor's speech, and then we'll call on one of our friends to sing or do something to enliven us ; or we'll order coffee, and get up a match at billiards.' So the hurraying was duly gone through, and then, as no one seemed inclined for more wine, coffee was ordered; and shortly after Mr. H. took his departure.

Henry B. then said aloud to one of the peons: 'Will you go and call my boy, Ramasawmy. I've forgotten my cigar-case.' Ramasawmy appeared almost before G. could say: 'Never mind your cheroots. I've got a lot of good ones here, so help yourself.' 'Thank you,' said B., 'I'll take one to amuse me till my own are forthcoming; but I don't wish to lose my case. I dare say it's in the palkee.' Ramasawmy departed, but having been carefully instructed shortly came back to say he couldn't find it. 'Oh, you're a stupid fellow!' said B., 'I'll be bound I find it in a minute. Just excuse me for a moment or two, and I'll be back almost before you can look round.' So B. and his boy, Ramasawmy, went to the palankeen, and of course found no cigar-case.

'Now, boy,' said B., 'you know where you're to watch. Here's the cigar-case; you are, as soon as you see the palkee coming, to run back and give the case to me publicly. I shall then ask you where you found it, and you must reply: "Come with me, sir, and I will show"—you understand.' 'Yes, sar, understand.' After this little private dialogue, B. returned, saying as he rejoined his friends: 'It's odd I can't find the case in the palkee, so I have ordered the boy to go home for it.' 'What a fuss you make about the case, B.; you can get cigars and plenty here, so make yourself easy, man, and take up a cue,' said G. 'There will be four of you without me; I'll look on.' 'I'll be hanged if you do!' returned Mitchel, 'we'll draw lots; lowest figure sits out.' 'I'm afraid,' said Mr. H., 'that you must not count on me; you must make up your match without me; you know that I bargained with you, G., that I was to leave about half-past nine.' 'All right,' said G., 'it's a long way off that now; there's oceans of time for a match.' 'Well,' said H., 'if I do play, the match must be a short one, say fifty.' 'Don't be alarmed, man,' said G., 'there's plenty of time for a hundred.' 'No, no,' said H., 'I can't play if it's more than a fifty.' 'Come,' said G., 'split the difference, we'll make it seventy.' 'So be it then,' said H.; 'let us make our sides at once. Mitchel is the best amongst us, therefore whoever has him must give ten points.' 'Agreed,' said G., 'but who sits out? There's the Doctor, Captain B., and Henry B.' 'I really can't play till I hear about my cigar-case,' said H. B. 'Upon my word, B., you make more bother about the confounded case than it's worth,' said Mitchel. 'I shouldn't wonder,' said G., 'that he has got some notes on pink paper richly perfumed in that same case, instead of cigars.' 'Oh, that's it, is it!' said H.; 'I really began to think he was getting off his head. I never knew him to care two straws about a cigar-case before.' 'It's very hard,' said B., with a pretended mock-modest air, 'that a man can't look for his cigar-case without having all his little peccadillos inquired into, and without, as it were, being hauled up for summary judgment. I say "live and let live;" you go on with your game, and I'll go on with mine.'

All this was really so well acted that poor Mr. H. was entirely thrown off his guard. Captain B. could not see very well by candle-light, so he declined playing; thus the sides were G. and my brother against H. and Mitchel. The game was begun with great spirit by Mitchel, who scored a dozen before G. had made a point. By-and-by Mitchel was put out, and H. and G. played very evenly; then G. was put out, and it was my brother against H., both cautious, the score thirty-five to twenty-eight. 'If we don't get on faster than this,' said H., 'I shall have to throw up; my palkee will be here shortly, and as Mrs. H. sits up for me, I never keep her waiting.' 'Of course you could not do that,' said G. 'Of course not,' said my brother. At this moment Ramasawmy entered panting and holding up the cigar-case, and exclaiming : ' I've found it, sir !' 'Where did you find it ?' said B. 'Was it at home, or was it, after all, in the palkee?' 'Come and see, sir ! I show place in the palkee.' 'Before you go,' said G., 'let us see what kind are the cigars you've got in it.' 'Not for the world,' said B., possessing himself of the case, and buttoning it up in a breast-pocket ; 'not for the world.' 'That's too bad,' said Mitchel, 'after all this palaver, not to let us see what the tobacco's like ; very shabby, upon my life.' 'I see,' said G., laughing ; 'I say, B., tell us her Christian name.' But H. B. was off to his palkee to see where the case could have been hidden ; but instead of stopping at his palkee, he walked on rapidly in the direction indicated by his boy. He soon met Mr. H.'s palkee and bearers ; he stopped them at once (and being master's cousin they had not the slightest suspicion that the Saib was cozening them), and said to them : 'Mr. H. does not want to go home just yet, so you come with me, and I'll show you where to put the palkee ; and while you wait I'll tell the butler to send you a good curry, and a bottle of brandy.' Bearers are very good fellows as a rule, yet they are but men, after all ; therefore, after a little show of resistance, they followed Mr. B., who took them to the back of the godowns in perfect silence, then qualms of conscience, or more properly fear of consequences, overcame their resolution, and the head boy said : 'But, sar, missis very angry, not bring master home soon.' 'Yes,' said Henry B., 'missis a little angry, but master much like to stay.'

While the boys were hesitating, the curry and rice and the bottle of brandy made their appearance. This almost decided the matter, but fear again interfered in this shape.

'But, sar, what can tell when come too late—what can tell?' 'You can say that Mr. G. so good; give curry and rice while master play. Then when curry and rice done eat you lay down to sleep, and you make a little mistake and sleep a little too long.' The rascals grinned, evidently relishing the joke and the prospect. Still they might have refused had not B. judiciously vanquished their scruples by placing 10 Rs. in the hand of the head bearer. They looked at one another, their eyes gleamed, and then they severally pressed Mr. B.'s hand against their foreheads, which he perfectly understood as a sign of fealty and allegiance for the time; then he left them to enjoy their feast, and went back to his friends.

On his return he said: 'It was no great wonder that I couldn't find it; it had somehow slipped from the pocket between the panel and the lining. Even when we got to the palkee the boy himself was some time before he could again find the place.' 'Very good,' said G.; 'the mysterious disappearance of the case is at last accounted for. But won't you, now that you've got it safe, let us look at the tobacco? What can your objection be?' 'Really, G.,' said H. B., 'you wouldn't ask me to do such a thing! I appeal to you, would it be honourable, or gentleman-like, or generous, or—or proper in any point of view? Now would it?' 'Good heavens!' returned G.; 'you quite overwhelm me. Is there anything dishonourable, or un-gentleman-like, or improper in showing a little tobacco? You must be dreaming.' 'No, G.; but you know what I mean. Now don't, like a good fellow, press me. Of course there could be nothing wrong in showing a little tobacco; but you know (don't press me too hard)—suppose, I say—suppose it were possible that the case did or might contain—— I say, suppose it were possible that it did contain——' 'Well,' said G., laughing heartily and in good

earnest at the admirable way in which B. acted his part—
'well, if there should be, what?' 'Upon my life, it's not
fair.   You know very well, every gentleman knows, that
there are some things which honour forbids him to speak
of, and some things which honour doubly forbids him to
show.' 'Game,' said G., as he made a winning hazard and
a canon at the same stroke. 'I bow,' said Mr. H.; 'and
now it's time for me to go.' 'Nonsense!' said G.; 'it
isn't near your time yet. We ran this game off so quickly
that there will be time—plenty of time—for another short
game.' 'It is not so, I assure you,' said H.; 'in fact, I
ought to be off now. But I can't think what detains my
palkee.' 'Why, it's not much beyond half-past eight yet,'
said G. 'What's the hurry? You're due to us till half-
past nine at least.' 'But,' said H., 'it's half-past nine now.
See for yourself' (pulling out his watch); 'it's just half-past
nine.' 'Half-past nine! It's impossible! We haven't
been playing half an hour, and I'm sure it wasn't more than
eight when we began.' 'Facts are stubborn things, friend
G. If you won't believe my watch, look at your own.'
'I never was so deceived if it is so,' said G.; 'that's all I
can say. Chasra, on my dressing-table you'll find my
watch; bring it me.'

While G.'s watch was being sent for the other conspirators
consulted their watches. Mitchel said: 'I can't look at
mine, for it's at—for it's at—I'm ashamed to mention where,
lest my uncle should reproach me.' All laughed at this
sally till H. said: 'Why, what's that in your waistcoat
pocket? And is that handsome chain attached to nothing?'
'Oh, this,' said Mitchel—'this is only for show, and as for
the other, it's only a dummy. The real Simon pure is gone
on a ticket of leave; in short, it's a case of tick, tick.'
'Well, you're a humourist, Master Mitchel, as well as the
king of the evening; but this does not prove that it's not

half-past nine.' 'Half-past nine !' said Henry B. ; 'it's quite
out of the question. I've been waiting to hear what the
others said, but here's my ticker—not gone on a ticket of
leave as my friend's has—and it says no such thing ; but
as I'm not very precise in setting and winding up, I wait to
hear what others say.' Captain B. now produced an old-
fashioned watch of amazing dimensions, which he showed
to my brother, begging him to say what time it pointed to.
'Half-past eight p.m.,' said my brother. '.\h,' said the old
Captain, 'it never varies a minute in the twenty-four hours.
It's a chronometer, though rather an old one ; set it at
6 a.m. in the morning, and at 6 a.m. the next morning
there won't be the difference of a half minute.' 'What does
your watch say, Doctor?' inquired H. ; 'it's very extraordinary that there should be such a difference.' 'My
watch,' said my brother, 'points to half-past eight precisely.'
Here G.'s Chasra came in with G.'s watch in his hand. G.
opened it, and held it out triumphantly to H. 'I can't
make it out,' said that gentleman ; 'the watch was all right
this morning, and I can see it hasn't stopped. I can't think
what has happened ; all the watches agree except mine.'
'It is very remarkable,' said G. 'I really can't quite understand, nor explain it either, unless you by some accident
set your watch an hour too fast.' 'That's just it,' said
Henry B. ; 'that's what he has done that he might get
away the sooner. He says it was an accident.' 'I never
said anything of the kind,' said H. ; 'it was G. who
suggested it, as a possible explanation. But what do your
clocks say, G.? You have one very good hall clock by
Frodsham, and a Samuel Slick ; if they agree and say
8.30 p.m., I shall think that, by some mental preoccupation,
I must have made the mistake you suggest. But truly it's
a singular accident that never happened before.' 'He says,'
said B., 'that he thinks it must have been an accident. I

have my own opinion as to that; he's an artful dodger, is this worthy cousin of mine. An accident done for the purpose might perhaps explain the matter. Here he comes with G., after examining the clocks.'

'Well, what say you now?' said H. B. 'I suppose,' replied H., 'I must have made the mistake of setting my watch an hour too fast, though how I can have done so, and not have observed it all day, is past my comprehension.' 'What's the use of talking?' said H. B. 'The thing is clear enough. All our watches agree, and so you find do the clocks. But there's another proof—if your palkee were here, you would be sure that you were right, and that we were wrong; but you see it isn't here, and you can't suppose that Mrs. H. has made any mistake, can you?' 'Why, no,' said H.; 'she's very accurate as to time.' 'Well,' returned H. B., 'that must be a great comfort to you,' though he could scarcely restrain his laughter. 'Now let us have another game,' said G., 'for a hundred, and that will give you and Mitchel a chance of recovering your lost laurels.' 'Aye, come along H.; we'll beat them this time,' said Mitchel. 'And as you've got ample time for play, there need be no hurried strokes.' 'Ah!' returned H.; 'I intend to play this time.' 'Bravo!' said G., though he could scarcely speak from his desire to laugh. My brother kept silent from the same cause, and Captain B. was openly on the broad grin. But all this passed off. H. was fairly talked down, persuaded by the cumulative evidence brought to bear against him that his senses had on this occasion deceived him; to use the popular expression, he was fairly persuaded out of his senses, to which result the non-arrival of the palankeen mainly contributed. He knew very well that Mrs. H. was not likely to make any mistake relative to her personal comforts; so, his mind being set at ease, he bent his whole energies to the play, and right well he did play. When the game was over, Mitchel confessed that it was H., and not himself, who had won it; and when G. and my brother acknowledged their defeat, H., in high feather, said, 'I must say it serves you right; you've done nothing but laugh and joke, and have paid attention to everything but your game. If fellows, when they have any kind of opponents, will do that, they deserve to lose.' 'Spoken like a judge, indeed,' observed G.; still, for some unaccountable reason, he continued to chuckle and laugh. '"Spoken like a judge!"' I say, "Spoken like an oracle,"' said Mitchel. 'Judges are sometimes wrong; oracles never.' 'Ah, there it is!' said H.; 'it's this kind of chaff that's been the ruin of your game. You keep on provoking each other to laugh, till none of you can hold a cue steadily. The Doctor twice missed the simplest canon, merely from laughing.' Here H.'s harangue was cut short by H. B., who came in from outside to announce the arrival of Mr. H.'s palkee and bearers, to whom he had in a moment given the welcome intelligence that they need make no apology for being late, as Mr. H. had not required them. In a few seconds after, Mr. H. B. did so in his own peculiar manner—*i.e.*, by calling out 'Mr. H.'s carriage stops the way,' which was scarcely pronounced when the bearers announced themselves by their 'hum, hum; ha, ha,' etc. H. at once descended from the judgment-seat into the obedient husband. He lost no time in bidding good-bye and shaking hands with everyone. 'Can't stay any longer, thank you, G. You know I bargained to go at half-past nine, and it's fully that now.' 'Yes,' said H. B., 'I think it's full that now; therefore it's time for you to go. I know Mrs. H. won't go to bed till you go home. Well, if ever I take a wife, I hope I shall get such a blessing. Good-bye.' 'Good-bye,' said H. As he got into his palankeen, he said, 'I thank you, G., for a very pleasant evening.' 'Good-bye,' was returned

by all. As Mr. H. moved off, he said, 'Let me recommend
you all to follow my example.' 'We would if we could,'
returned H. B., 'but we haven't got the opportunity.' 'Oh
yes, you have ; you can all retire early if you will.'

Mr. H. was no sooner gone than the whole party gave
way freely to the laughter they had been so long contending
against ; it was hearty and long continued. The first who
recovered himself was G. 'I did not know,' said he to
H. B., 'that you were such an accomplished actor, B.
Your acting about the cigar-case and the supposed *billet-
doux* was really inimitable.' 'Yes,' said Mitchel ; 'he did
it so well that he really deceived me, and made me think
that he actually had got something of that kind in his case.'
'There it is,' said H. B. ; 'if you can find any *billet-doux*
therein, you may keep them for your trouble.' 'There,'
replied Mitchel ; 'I agree with G. that you are a first-rate
actor, or dissembler, whichever term you like best.' 'Oh,
they're both so highly complimentary that all I can do is to
bow and say, " Pray spare my blushes," ' which he uttered
with such an affected and coquettish air and manner that
again he set the whole party in a roar. 'H. says,' resumed
H. B., 'that he thanks G. for a very pleasant evening. I
hope he will find it equally so when he gets home ; but, as
our friends on the north of the Tweed say, " I ha'e my
doots." ' 'I also " ha'e my doots," ' said G. 'I don't
think,' said my brother, 'that I " ha'e any doots " ; on the
contrary, I strongly suspect (if what I hear be not altogether
libellous) that he will find the atmosphere at home uncommonly hot just now.' 'I shouldn't wonder, from his
haste to be gone as soon as the palkee came here, that he
has a fear of what's coming,' said old Captain B. 'Well,'
said B., 'I agree with you, and shouldn't wonder if before
he reaches the petticoat he has an attack of cold shivers.
Some ladies, for the offence of keeping them waiting, would

content themselves with making the atmosphere cool, or cold, according to the gravity of the crime, and the length of time it had been persisted in ; but dear Mrs. H. is of such a temperament that I am sure poor H. will find neither coolness nor coldness in his domestic atmosphere—it will be hot, very hot, you may rely on it.' 'If,' said the old Captain, 'he does not get his wig combed by a three-legged stool, he may think himself lucky.' 'Well said again, B.,' said G. 'You've been silent all the evening, and now you're beginning to come out in good style.' 'The truth is, I was afeard to say anythink, lest I should laugh outright ; and I never likes to spile sport,' said the old man. 'No,' said G., 'I'm sure you don't ; you're too good a sample of an old salt to do that.' 'Sailors ain't commonly fond of doing that, I do think,' replied the old boy, highly pleased at the compliment. 'Only think,' said H. B., 'how H. is catching it now ! I should pity him, if I could for laughing.' 'I confess,' said G., 'the fun overcomes the pity, in my mind. If a man *likes* to have dirty water emptied on his head *à la* Mrs. Xantippe, he deserves what he gets. We have, after all, only detained him an hour, so that there isn't anything really to complain of; and he is perfectly innocent of any pre-meditated crime. We can all bear witness that it was only by a ruse that we got him to stay at all. Knowing this as he must do, he shows himself to be neither manly nor wise,' remarked G., 'to suffer himself to be so used ; but if he likes it, let him have it.' 'So I say,' said Mitchel ; 'let him have it.' 'But,' said my brother, 'what was the object, Mitchel, of your pretty little tale about your watch and your uncle, and all that, when, not more than ten minutes before, I saw you put a handsome gold hunter into your waistcoat pocket?' 'Why, you see,' replied Mitchel, 'I don't like telling any more lies than are needful, and therefore I evaded the question.' 'Commend me to your nice and delicate conscience !' replied my brother. 'You tell half a dozen unnecessary lies to avoid one.' 'Come, Doctor, that won't do. Is there no difference in fabricating terradiddles such as these, and answering a direct question by a designedly untruthful reply?' 'Now,' replied my brother, 'you are turning jest into earnest ; you forget the whole thing was a joke.' 'No joke to H., you may rely on that, as he has found out before now,' said H. B. 'Oh, let us hope,' said G., 'that the fire has burnt itself out, and that they have made it up, and set things right by this time.' 'Amen,' said Mitchel ; 'let them fight, or love—it's all the same to me.' It was now near 12 p.m. My brother had taken his departure some time before ; Captain B. had done the same ; Mitchel and H. B. only were left, and they now wished G. good-night, both declaring that they had spent a very jolly evening. Just before H. B. got into his palkee, he said, 'I think I shall call on Mrs. H. to-morrow.' 'No,' returned G. ; 'you haven't impudence enough for that.' 'Haven't I? We shall see,' said H. B. 'Yes, we shall see,' said G. 'Good-night.' 'Good-night,' returned B., and off he went.

The next day, as my brother was returning from his hospital, at which he had had an extra and emergent case, he saw B.'s palkee at G.'s door, and though he was anxious to get home to his dinner (he always dined at 3 p.m.), curiosity prompted him to look in at G.'s for a few minutes. G. said, as he shook hands with him : 'You've come just in time to hear B.'s report of his visit to Mrs. H.' 'To Mrs. H.? Surely he has not had the audacity to go there ! I should have thought that after the little performances of last night that was the last place he would have ventured near.' 'So did I,' replied G., 'and though he said last night before he left that he thought he should call on Mrs. H. this morning, I didn't believe he meant to do it.' 'But

he has done it,' said H. B., 'and if you like I'll tell you
what passed between us.' 'Of course we should like to
hear the report beyond everything.' 'Well,' said B., his
eyes dancing with the sense of fun, 'as soon as I stepped
out of the palkee the maty came running to say Mrs. not
very well; couldn't see me. I expected this, and was
prepared for it. I had written on one of my cards in pencil
"Very particular." I gave it to him, and told him to give
it to his mistress, and that I would wait for the answer.
By-and-by he came to say that if I would step into the
drawing-room and sit down for a few minutes Mrs. H. would
see me. So I sat down, and in about ten minutes the fair
lady made her appearance, and without saying good-morning, or shaking hands with me, or any of the usual pro-
prieties, she said at once: "Very pretty doings at Mr.
Goodwin's last night — doings that I don't think at all
respectable — keeping my husband out half the night."
"Oh, not so bad as that, Harriet" (we are cousins, you
know), interrupted I. "As to the exact time I can't say,"
said Mrs. H., "but I know he was much later than he
ought to have been, and much later than he promised me
he would be, and I don't thank you for helping to detain
him—in fact, from his account you were quite as bad as
Mr. G. himself." "If you knew all," said I, "you wouldn't
say that." "If I knew all," said Mrs. H. "What do you
mean"—opening her eyes wide—"if I knew all? Pray
explain yourself." "It is for that reason that I am here,"
said I. "Well, what is it?" said the lady, becoming im-
patient. "But I know "—making her eyes small again—
"you have nothing to tell me; you only want to excuse
and smooth down that very pretty, gentleman-like trick of
deceiving my husband as to the hour. I wonder you were
not all of you ashamed to combine together to tell a falsehood in order to deceive a poor——" Here she stopped.

"Weak silly fellow" I thought was coming, but she recollected herself in time and stopped, and then said : " But I'll take care how he goes to Mr. G.'s again, that you may rely on. And pray, sir " (I saw she was getting warm), "what may this explanation or excuse be that you say on your card is so *very particular ?*"   "Why, really, Mrs. H., though I have come here for this very purpose, I hesitate to tell you." " But I insist upon knowing, sir, though you have not acted in this instance as a relative.   I consider you are bound in honour and as a gentleman to tell me what you have called me from a sick-bed to hear.   Pray go on, sir. But tell me, before you do so, how it was that my bearers were decoyed to eat and drink with Mr. G.'s servants before they announced themselves.   Was that another of his pretty little devices to induce a husband to break his promises, and spend his evening away from his wife?   A very pretty and respectable leader for all the young men of the place ; but it's quite consistent with his disreputable mode of life.   But for you, a relative, to league yourself with such a man, and to aid and abet him in his vile arts and practices, it's too bad—really disgraceful !   And then there's that disreputable Doctor, leaving his wife to spend what he calls a jolly evening.   As he doesn't seem to know it, it's a pity his wife doesn't teach him his duty better, and she would if she were the right stamp of woman ; but she isn't, poor benighted creature, with her papistry and superstition !   If it wasn't for this she'd teach that good-for-nothing, disreputable husband of hers not to go on in such a disgraceful way."   Here she really couldn't go on for want of breath, so I said : " But what does the Doctor do that's disgraceful?"   " Does he not leave his wife to spend the night by herself in order that he may consort with bachelors and boys?   He, a married man, and a medical man too !   Isn't that disgraceful?   But I suppose not in your estimation." "On my honour, Mrs. H., I can't see any harm in the Doctor's spending an evening with a friend, though he has the misfortune to be a bachelor." "Oh, there are always two ways of putting things, Mr. B., and if the company in themselves were not highly un-becoming for a married man and a medical man and a senior to keep, was it not unbecoming and disgraceful to help in telling a lie? You may not consider such conduct disgraceful, but I do, sir, especially when I know the object. Then, to make your party the more select, you could find no one, besides the vulgar old sea-captain, or whatever he may be, and that roistering, drinking, smoking, gambling, irreligious young fellow, Lieutenant Mitchel, making good the old saying, 'Tell me your company and I'll tell you what you are.'" She had nearly run herself out, but I was patient, and only said: "Truly, Mrs. H., you have given the whole party all round a sharp dressing." "Sharp dress-ing! I only wish I had the power to do so; you'd see I wouldn't spare them!" ("I'm sure you wouldn't," said I to myself; but I spoke no word.) "Sharp dressing indeed! Not half as much as they deserve who invent and tell lies with intent to do mischief and breed disturbance in families! Faugh! I haven't patience with such doings or such people! And then your magnanimous, generous, and hospitable friend, Mr. G., could extend his hospitality to everyone in the station but poor Mr. Gundert, who is too poor himself to drink a glass of champagne, though the good man enjoys it, when he does get it, perhaps a little more than he, as a clergyman, ought to do. Him Mr. G. couldn't include in his invite. No; a good and pious, really religious man would be out of place at Mr. G.'s table, and wouldn't be acceptable, I suppose, either to himself or the rest of the set he has there." Having now gone all round the ring, and thoroughly run herself down, she returned to the question which, in her anger and indignation against Mr. G. and all his friends, she had allowed to remain dormant for a time, and once more she said: "What is this explanation that is so 'very particular,' and which nevertheless you, in your great delicacy and diffidence, hesitate to communicate? Will you now condescend to mention it, or will you leave it unspoken? Only as I am not well I request you to come to a decision without more delay." She then allowed her hands to fall into her lap, and looked me, with her eyes wide open, full in the face. It was well for me that she hadn't the strength or claws or fangs of a tigress, or undoubtedly it would have been bad for me. As it was, I bore her stare without flinching, and said: "If you will permit me to make the remark, I have been waiting with some little patience for you to give me the opportunity of making this explanation. I could not do so sooner without interrupting you." "Well, sir, I am waiting your pleasure."

' "Then, Mrs. H., I can truly say that all we did last night was done with the best intentions, and I am sorry to see that our little harmless joke has been taken up by you so very seriously."

' " Harmless joke!" ejaculated Mrs. H.; "a nice sample of a harmless joke indeed, to deceive an unsuspecting man and make him break his word to his wife and thereby cause dissensions; a nice harmless joke indeed! But pray, sir, what do you mean by your 'good intentions'? No doubt they were as good as your acts. But what do you wish me to understand by the expression? Pray be brief, and, if you can, candid."

' "Why, then, Mrs. H., we did it solely to please your husband."

' " Stop, sir; don't add to your other ill-deeds by insulting Mr. H. as well as myself. A statement like that is too gross to tolerate."

'"There it is," said I. "You won't hear me, but keep on pitching into me, and say that I am insulting H. and yourself."

'"Yes, sir, I do say so, when you have the assurance to tell me that in deceiving my husband you did it to please him."

'"Well, Mrs. H., why won't you let me explain to you my meaning?"

'"Your meaning is insulting, sir."

'"Don't be angry, Harriet, without cause."

'"I have cause; and don't Harriet me. I don't wish to acknowledge relationship with one who acts so unlike a relation."

'"Pardon me; I do not act unlike a relative. It is you who imagine that I act so. Now tell me, is it insulting to imagine that your husband likes a game at billiards, and that he would like to play the return game, only that he couldn't in consequence of his promise to you; is that insulting?"

'"That is not insulting," returned Mrs. H.; "but I don't see what you are aiming at, and I know there is something behind."

"'Well, then, so far, you admit, we were not to blame. Now, to afford him the opportunity of playing, while all the while he was perfectly innocent of any intention either to deceive you or to break his promise, is, after all, not a very serious offence, is it?"

'"You have certainly honourably exonerated my husband from lending himself to your practices; but, in doing so, you have taken on yourselves the whole odium of the proceeding." And, getting angry again, she said: "Pray, sir, how do you know that my husband really wanted to play and have this return match, as you say? It is, in spite of all your ingenuity, a very poor compliment to me as well as to my husband to say or to insinuate that he preferred your sweet company to mine, for that's what it comes to."

'"Oh no; nothing of the sort, Mrs. H. Consider Mr. H. has you always, and has seldom the chance of a match at billiards."

'" Thank you, sir; your candour is equalled by your politeness; but I don't put the slightest faith in your story; I don't believe that my husband showed, by word or deed, that he would rather stay away from me. It's a vile insinuation and a libel. If I thought so I'd—— But no, there isn't a particle of truth in the idea. What proof can you bring forward; what foundation have you for so scandalous a supposition?"

'"I see you turn everything against me," said I, "and that whatever I say I only come in for more blame; therefore I'll say no more, though as to the proofs for our opinion they were palpable enough. People, all as one man, can't mistake joyous looks, and lively manner, and sparkling eyes for displeasure or for anything but signs of satisfaction; but I see you don't believe me, and that I am offending you still more."

'"You are, sir, both displeasing and offending me. I wonder how you dare to traduce my husband behind his back in such a way, and to my very face, too; but, as I said before, it's a vile calumny, and I don't believe there's a shadow of ground for such an impertinent assumption; but the moment my husband comes home I shall ascertain if there is, and if—— But I know it's all your evil disposition and imagination. I wish you good-morning, sir."

'"Good-morning, Mrs. H.; I'm sorry to see that, instead of mending matters, as I hoped to do, I have——"

'"There, sir, that will do," as she swept out of the room, waving me away from her with her hand. I restrained myself till I got into my palkee; since then I've done nothing but laugh—shook the palkee so much, that the boys looked in to see what was the matter; and then I heard them laughing among themselves, and I have hardly recovered yet.'

'Upon my word,' said G., 'you possess an amount of cheek that I didn't give you credit for, nor did I think that little spitfire would let out so furiously.'

'But poor H.,' said my brother, 'he got bastinadoed last night, it appears; and now you have let him in for a second castigation.'

'Pooh, pooh!' said G.; 'if a man is such an ape as to allow himself to be so used by that little virago of a wife of his, he deserves all he gets for staying out an hour later than the time promised—to have all the dirty water in the house emptied on his head; he well deserves the libation for submitting to it so tamely; it is a very perfect illustration of the "palmam qui meruit, ferat."'

So each of the parties was left to his own mood; G. contemptuous, though amused; my brother thoughtful, though inclined to laugh; and H. B. revelling in the fun and perfectly indifferent to everything beside.

For two months after this date, Mr. and Mrs. H. passed each and every member of the party at G.'s with averted heads whenever they met them. Mr. G. and all his friends saluted them on every occasion just as usual, till at last this dreadful feud was healed, outwardly at least, by Mr. V.'s good offices; but H. never went again to any of G.'s parties.

THE END.

Elliot Stock, Paternoster Row, London.

www.ingramcontent.com/pod-product-compliance
Lightning Source LLC
Chambersburg PA
CBHW060607030726
47498CB00005B/1582